JUSTICE FOR #997543

JUSTICE FOR #997543

A Novel
By
Patricia Cage

A Tigress Publishing Book

ISBN: 978-1-59404-052-8
Library of Congress Control Number: 2012933843
Printed in the United States of America

10 9 8 7 6 5 4 3 2 1

Dedication

For Jayme....I will always be saddened you couldn't be saved from the pure evil that resides in what is otherwise a fairly decent world.

Chapter 1

God, she loved her job! Elaine Bennett smiled as she pondered this thought while jogging up the steps of the maximum-security prison, briefcase and lunch bumping against her hip as she moved.

She waited impatiently for the outside control doors to slide open after pushing the button on her side. Finally—when the guards had stopped their conversations about football and women long enough to check her out on their camera and push the button—the heavy security door opened, admitting her further into the bowels of the beast.

Another metal door opened with a bang and Elaine stepped into an enclosure where she waited until the control officer got a good look at her Department of Corrections' badge. Only then did he push another button, allowing her to step out of the stationary elevator into one last small room that faced the command center of the entire prison. The fortress she now faced was where armed guards issued orders and directed protocol. Elaine could see the racks of rifles, the boxes of protective gear, and the wall where the identity chits and prison keys hung. These, supposedly, kept the bad guys in and the good people safe.

"Come on, Clark," Elaine said. "I need my keys. I'm going to be late for class!" She passed a hot espresso through the metal slot for him, along with her numbered brass chit. "You want a riot on your hands when my students have to stand outside without their beloved teacher?"

"Keep your skirt on, Elaine," he said. "We're busy in here. You get my coffee right this morning? Last time it was pretty cold."

"Yeah. Like I'm really worried about that, considering this prison wasn't built the last time you paid me for acting like your personal Barista."

"Yeah, yeah," Sergeant Clark said. "Here's your keys. Don't lose them for a change, okay? We really don't want these animals loose."

"They're not animals! Also, I've never lost my keys and you know it," Elaine said. "You have a nice day now, you hear?"

Clark turned to ignore her, but pushed the last button that allowed her out of the control area and into a long empty hall, past two more manned guard stations and the final gauntlet which entailed walking on the sidewalk past the football field of the 'big yard.' She looked straight ahead and tried to ignore the inmates who ran the track or walked in groups behind the cyclone fence. Elaine barely tolerated this part of her trip to the classroom as sometimes uncouth inmates yelled out unsavory comments about parts of her anatomy.

Finally she breathed a sigh of relief as she moved up steps that landed her in the middle of another large group of inmates. These men too would give her grief while she unlocked an outside door and another inside door so they could finally take their coats off and get down to the business of learning. Elaine always smiled through these taunts because these came from her students and although the comments were still barbed, they were playful and respectful.

Being a part of something important, being a sister to all the officers, and the rest of the staff, made her feel valuable and strong. She joked professionally with some of the inmates she had known for years. She juggled keys in order to open doors. She could have asked an inmate to hold some of her stuff, but she knew the cameras on the razor wire were recording her every move and handing personal items to a prisoner would get her a nice little written reprimand or possibly suspension. She'd never

2

do it anyway. She was a Department of Corrections' employee when she was behind the walls and she never forgot it. Her first love was teaching, but Elaine knew *where* she was teaching. Her students were hardened criminals, whose first love was manipulation, not learning.

She took great pleasure in how her students entered the room quietly, got their books and went right to work. It was a sign of respect for her. She felt good as she sat at her desk, taking roll and catching up on paper work. She looked at her students. Some were small, others huge. Old and young, dark and light, but all working like little kids, instead of posturing like the broad shouldered, tattooed, loud mouthed cons she passed on her walk past the big yard. Those fools didn't understand how empowered their own lives could be. They did their time by lifting weights, playing sports, writing letters to naïve females, fighting with one another and managing to exit the prison meaner and more dysfunctional than they had been upon entering.

Not her students. They wouldn't be coming back—at least not all of them. They were getting educated. Elaine rose to go sit by each of the student who had tried to leave an empty chair next to him at each of the six man tables. She knew they did this so she could come sit by them and give them individualized help. Some worked on basic math, some on primary reading books. She loved these guys because no one laughed at anyone else. This was a sanctuary. You never brought attitude in here or you got thrown out or beaten up by fellow inmates in the big yard. That wasn't a D.O.C. rule. It was Elaine's rule, enforced by Elaine's Teaching Assistants who were life sentence inmates who helped run the prison. Everyone knew they ran the prison, even though the lifers themselves always acted as if the guards were in charge.

As Elaine moved from student to student, she realized most had left their coats on. No one had turned the heat on. She could call over to the offices, but doubted the director or secretary

3

had come in to work yet. Oh well. She'd do it herself later. She stepped away from her desk and settled in a chair next to a young man who seemed to be having trouble with multiplication.

Leaning her arm over his paper to point out his mistake, he took the opportunity to bend his side into her and brush his arm over her breast. Bad mistake! She rose without finishing her correction and moved to the next student. He knew never to touch staff. And she knew he'd pay for that aggressive move after class ended.

There were no guards in the classrooms, but Elaine's clerks and teaching assistants had been with her for years and they saw every movement. She never said a word to this recalcitrant inmate. This stupid young man would come back to class tomorrow bruised, but serious about his studies, or he would not return at all. It was a shame, but Elaine had learned long ago she couldn't save them all. She needed their respect or she couldn't teach any of them. She didn't like it much, but that was the reality.

At 11:00 am, when the students filed back to their cells for midday count, Elaine sat down at her desk to eat her lunch. She felt content. She enjoyed looking around the cement classroom made attractive with motivational posters and thick foliage plants. Glancing up at the high barred windows, her only way of gauging the weather, Elaine sipped the last of her V8 and carefully placed every little bit of foil and utensil in her carrier to take out. She threw nothing away inside. Aluminum foil would be used for tattooing, spoons would be sharpened for shanks, and sandwich sacks become containers for hiding drugs. Elaine always shuddered when she remembered where they hid the bags.

Satiated after a meal and a productive morning with her students, Elaine wandered around watering plants with water from an old sink in the room. She was mildly curious about when she would hear her colleagues return from lunch. They'd asked if she wanted to join them, but by the time you locked up, went back out through security, got car keys, drove down town, ordered, ate and then did the entire process in reverse, you were always late for the afternoon classes. Elaine found it exhausting and more often chose to eat at her desk. Once in awhile, she joined them. But not normally. It was just too much trouble.

That wasn't the only reason. Elaine had never told anyone, but she was afraid of the main hallway the staff used to get to and from the control room. Hundreds of inmates, from all four tiers, spilled at one time down stairways into that hallway before entering the chow hall. Once, Elaine found herself caught in that mass of angry humanity and a fight had broken out. She hadn't known it until then, but when an altercation occurs in that hallway, big garage size security doors slam down hard from both ends. Anyone unlucky enough to be walking that gauntlet is locked inside until D.O.C. can contain the problem. She'd been pushed and shoved, and her fear level had gone off the charts. Custody pulled the steel garage doors up after only a few minutes and she'd walked out unscathed but unsteady. Since that incident she scurried through that passage way as quickly as she could— and never during 'movement' time. She might love her work, but she had no interest in dying for it.

After locking her classroom door, going across the hall, unlocking the office door, locking it behind her, unlocking the bathroom door, locking it behind her, unlocking it after freshening up, locking it after exiting, checking her mail, unlocking the office door, locking the office door behind her, and unlocking her class room door again, she reflected once more on why she didn't go out to lunch much. Elaine sat down, still cold because she had forgotten to turn the heat up while in the office, and patiently waited for her students to meander in for the afternoon session.

Once count cleared she heard other staff members talking in the hall. Students began filing into the room behind her teaching assistant and her clerk. Elaine greeted each man as he quietly got his work and sat down to study. Her clerk and T.A. went to their desks in the back of the room and began to type lessons. Elaine sat down and took roll from a seating chart. She noted the young man who had touched her breast was absent. After reading the mail she'd picked up at lunch, she rose to assist each man with work he should have mastered before junior high. Most of her students had no confidence in their own decision-making and needed constant reinforcement an attempted answer was correct, no matter how elementary. Having assured, complimented and corrected enough for the time being, Elaine went back to her desk to respond to correspondence from colleagues she kept in touch with all over the world. When she looked up a little later to see if anyone needed her help, she noticed two young cons staring at her. Hard.

It wasn't too unusual for prisoners—particularly young ones—to initially come to school with hostile, sullen demeanors. They usually got over their posturing quickly when they saw the atmosphere was safe and friendly. These two criminals, though, ignored the message. Their look upon her reeked of open hatred and sexual assertiveness. Two more young cons leaned on the backs of their chairs to stare at her with malice.

"Turn around and go back to work," Elaine said as she placed her small hand on the phone. This was a direct order and she was well within her right to make it. To ignore it would trigger a call for officers to come and take these intimidating men out. A few times in the past years she had made that call. She didn't like doing it, but she would.

"Turn around and go back to work now!" The second command, issued in her sternest 'corrections' voice', got the attention of everyone in the room. The other students wrote faster, ducking their heads lower over their studies. The T.A and the clerk were alerted, but they were also at the far end of the room.

The four young criminals turned slowly in unison, obeying her—or at least pretending to. Elaine sat for a moment; hand on the phone, waiting for her heart rate to go back to normal.

Her T.A. and clerk resumed work. Finally she took her stiff hand off the receiver, sat back, and realized she was perspiring in the coat she'd never removed. Attempting to convey calm, Elaine rose, took off the coat, walked to the hook behind the door and reached out to hang it up.

She sensed the movement before hearing it, and was struck on the head before she could turn around.

Chapter 2

Elaine woke to the sounds of pounding. She huddled in a tight, tense ball, her long, army-green, Dr. Zhivago coat tucked tightly around her. Slowly she realized a correctional educator's worst nightmare had come true: the prisoners were rioting. She was being held hostage and everything around her burned.

The once-clean, neat, cheerful developmental classroom, with the lush green plants, books on shelves, motivational posters on the walls and donated computers on desks now lay in disarray. Computers were shattered into fragments, scattered and broken, unburned only because the metal, glass and plastic would not ignite. Dirt and pieces of pottery spilled over bookshelves, metal chair frames, along with plants and containers, had been thrown at the start of the standoff between twelve hundred very angry inmates and those who would or could not meet their demands. Everything reminding Elaine of the sane, organized world in which she had taught for eight hours a day, five days a week, for over twenty years, was destroyed.

She crouched on the cold, dank cement, watching two of her former students stoke the bonfire in the middle of the room. They were throwing in the last of her wooden desk, breaking it up with their steel-toed boots without bothering to clean it out first. Pictures from France, England, and Japan, where Elaine had attended international correctional educational conferences; important folders, grades and lesson plans, were all being burnt along with the shattered wood. Memories and hard work literally going up in smoke as she sat cold, terrified and helpless to do anything but watch.

Never in her wildest dream did she expect a riot.

In some ways she should have seen it coming: tension had been growing in the prison for months. The practice of "double-celling" had taken the six-hundred-bed prison up to twelve hundred men and mandated putting two full-size human beings in a cage measuring six feet by eight feet.

The heavy pounding on the classroom door awakened her then ceased, as an inmate unlocked the door and allowed another back inside the room. Elaine's heart pounded hard as he approached her; Damien, a multiple killer and one of the crueler leaders in the institution, apparently ran this riot. The public might believe staff and guards control the inmates in a prison, but the inmates run any institution and they do it from a hierarchical base. Each inmate's crime determines his or her power or lack thereof. And Damien wielded a great deal of power.

Thus far, she hadn't been additionally harmed, probably because after twenty years she was well-respected by some of the more powerful men. They'd kept the more animalistic predators at bay; but she feared it was a factor of time before her dubious protectors were overpowered, either mentally or physically, and she'd be turned over for a version of pleasure one inmate told her she would greatly enjoy, but through which she knew she'd not want to live. A fighter all her life, she vowed to not change now.

As Damien leaned above her, feet apart, hands on hips, Elaine inched further back into the corner and drew her now filthy coat tightly around her. While her petite body recoiled, her mind clicked back to the D.O.C. training that had so far kept her alive and functioning, and on which she knew she must depend now if she hoped to escape further danger.

Elaine knew it was true, you could smell fear. She tried hard not to show the terror she felt. Elaine made herself rise to her feet—fighting the cramping pain creeping into her bones and joints after hours of sitting on the floor. She hoped her movement would force Damien to either back up a little, or risk her touching

10

him as she rose.

Relief and strength crept back into her soul as he did indeed back up a step to allow her to stand and face him. She gave a small "yes" to herself. All those hours of hostage training coming back. She'd been taught three things to do if taken hostage. One: never allow the captors to see her as demanding and threatening. If and when they decided to kill someone, they would kill her first just to shut her up. Second: don't become submissive, because they would view her as an object without worth. Third: appear composed, a real person they could relate to and feel concerned about harming.

This calm manner of functioning was almost impossible to maintain, but Elaine knew it was imperative she fake it if she wanted to come out of this alive. Damien's act of backing up was an important sign she was still managing to conduct herself correctly. It meant Damien still saw her as a person·with value, someone to respect, if only for the moment.

Elaine looked across the room, past Damien's massive shoulders, to where Richard Adler, a colleague and friend, sat on the floor against the wall, watching her intently. She saw his fleeting, encouraging smile. He too had seen her little victory in getting Damien to step back.

Richard taught in this prison for over thirty years, and Elaine thought of him as a friend and mentor. Not many females were successful working in adult male prisons. The turnover of female staff was extremely high. Hard as Elaine found it to believe, the women would not only quit because of the stress, but some would also get fired when they fell in love with an inmate. It was always an extremely dangerous predicament for them, and a serious breach of security endangering everyone else.

One of those few, fortunate people who actually grew older gracefully, Elaine, although small in stature, was striking in appearance. She had dark eyes and hair and high cheekbones inherited from Cherokee ancestors. Few females were successful in this world. Elaine was an exception, and she partially credited Richard for her success. At this moment, nothing could have given her more strength and courage than his brief, quiet smile of encouragement. Richard had been roughed-up, but because of his longtime reputation as a stand-up guy with the inmates, he hadn't seriously been harmed—yet.

Damien, realizing his power and control had slipped, if only minutely, in allowing Elaine to stand and stare past him, pushed her back—thus regaining his version of respect in front of the others. "Listen, bitch," he said his voice loud and dangerous. "Pay attention to me, or I'll teach you how. We want you to talk on the phone to the Captain. Get your ass moving, now!"

Pulling her coat around her—more for protection and a feeling of privacy than any need of physical warmth—Elaine followed Damien to the locked classroom door. George, a young Native American inmate opened the door. His eyes seemed to fluctuate from a glazed expression to wild animated surging, signs of the crank he'd undoubtedly been snorting off and on since the riot began. Prior to the takeover Elaine knew George as a sensible, shy young man who worked hard in class. Now she could see substance abuse was a serious problem for him. It was most likely the reason he was engaged in criminal activities.

Elaine took one last look at Richard for moral support, and then walked through the door with her shoulders back and head held high. Damien led the way down to the registration office for the school. Now it was the command headquarters for the rioting inmates.

Behind her desk, disheveled and in obvious pain, huddled Raylyn, secretary to the education director. The change in her appearance was devastating. While Elaine was being escorted by Damien to the office, she had heard the inmate leaders brag about having raped Raylyn repeatedly. They were keeping her in the director's office for their pleasure. Elaine felt mixed emotions as she drew closer to Raylyn. She tried to suppress them, but couldn't. She knew from the inmates' banter that Raylyn had been having an affair with Damien prior to the riot and had unknowingly assisted the inmates in the takeover due to her misplaced loyalty and indiscretions.

The rioters had guns and knives apparently mailed to the Education Department, evidently through Raylyn, in her position as secretary to the Director. She'd been giving Damien the packages unopened, blindly believing his story they contained text books the D.O.C. wouldn't authorize. He'd told her he really needed the books to finish his correspondence college degree.

Officers who should have been suspicious looked the other way. And this was the payment for Raylyn's blind loyalty to her lover: he had turned her over to his partners as a reward for helping him plan and execute the takeover.

Raylyn, who always wore too much makeup and perfume, her clothes too tight for a prison setting, now looked like a broken clown. Mascara and eye shadow ran down her cheeks, and her long brown hair flew every which way. Elaine's resentment at Raylyn's part in causing the riot was still strong but was mixed with sympathy for the woman's condition and a sense of guilt that it was Raylyn who had been violated, while she remained untouched. Elaine wasn't necessarily proud of her emotions, but they were real.

The emotions churned in Elaine's stomach as she took the phone from Raylyn, whose eyes told of the shock she'd endured— shock being the best and only escape she could hope for, from the mental and physical abuse that was likely to continue.

"Hello," Elaine stuttered into the mouthpiece, not sure what to expect at the other end.

"Elaine?" The voice sounded vaguely familiar. "Elaine, this is Captain Ivy Pepper. How are you?"

"I'm okay. Just tired and dirty."

The voice on the other end of the phone chuckled softly; everyone who worked with Elaine knew how fastidious she was about her appearance. She liked to look well-groomed. She felt it set the right tone for the inmates, whose typical female role models, according to research, were whores or Madonna figures, neither of whom they respected. They usually saw women and girls only as property or commodities. Elaine worked hard to teach them differently.

"They tell me they've not harmed you," Captain Pepper continued. "Is this true?"

"Yes and no. I don't like being held prisoner, and they burned my desk with all my classroom materials."

"Elaine! That's not what I'm worried about," she said sharply. "Have they touched you?"

"No, but they talk about it a lot."

"Well, that's a relief. We are trying to negotiate a deal as quickly as possible. So be brave a while longer. Whatever you are doing must be working. Keep it up. How is Richard? Have they hurt him?"

"No."

"Good. Look, there's something I need for you and Richard to do. Okay?"

"I'll try."

"I know the men are listening to your end of the conversation, but I need to get some information from you that will help us without their knowing. Are you and Richard both in your adjoining classrooms?"

"Yes."

"Is anyone else there from staff?"

"No."

"Elaine, try to get everyone in your classroom by 2:00 p.m. Okay?"

Just then, Damien grabbed the phone and yelled at the captain. "Look, you bitch. I know you're trying to get information so you're done talking. Like I told you, she's fine. For now. Just get us the food you promised if I let you talk to her."

14

"Okay, okay," the Captain said. "Calm down. You'll have your food, but I need to know what you really want."

"We'll get back with you," Damien spewed back at her.

Click.

Damien yanked Elaine out of the chair in a fit of anger. Captain Pepper sounded calm and interested instead of panicked. Damien didn't like that at all. Elaine was sure Ivy's ability to remain composed was one of the reasons Ivy Pepper had made it to the position of Captain. She was in fact, one of literally 5 or 6 female Captains in the entire United States.

Damien dragged Elaine down the hall and back into the classroom. Once inside, he hurled her across the room where she slammed against the wall in an undignified manner and slid onto the floor. That was too much for Richard. He jumped up, was immediately smacked down by George and could do nothing other than swear at Damien to take the focus off Elaine. Damien stared at her in a truly sinister way. The ploy worked, as Damien rushed at Richard and pummeled him. With his hands tied behind his back, Richard could do nothing until Damien decided to quit.

The smell of smoke wafted through the high barred windows, and all faces turned toward them. Inmates climbed up on broken chairs to see where the fire was coming from. The classroom—in fact the entire educational building—was located at the far end of the big yard. At the other end, prison cell blocks were filled with tiers of men. The fire came from that direction.

Up until now Elaine thought the takeover was confined to the educational and vocational buildings, the Program Activities Building, the laundry and chapel. Elaine knew in a riot situation, men who did not want to be involved would voluntarily go back to their cells and lock themselves in until it was over. Custody would then know who was involved and who wasn't. Complying inmates, now locked in their cells, were in terrible danger; one inmate standing on a chair reported fire in all four cell blocks.

Elaine envisioned the fear engulfing submissive inmates complying with direction. They'd be returned to their cells and now faced the terror of fire coming at them, with no possible means of escape. She wondered what her husband, Daniel, was doing as he waited for either her release or demise.

☾

Daniel Bennett wasn't as far away as Elaine thought. He stood on the sloping grassy area that terraced the front of the prison, his dark gray eyes watching the most bizarre scene he'd ever witnessed in twenty-five years as a reporter. He'd been around the world many times, covering wars, coronations, and natural disasters, but this sight was surreal.

Every window of the four-story brick exterior of the gothic building had been blown or knocked out. Usually, when he visited the prison to cover an event or have lunch with Elaine, he couldn't see through the heavily barred windows; now he could see into the cells behind the bars and watch men leap, run, or stare ominously back. Some threw flaming torches down. Others tossed clothing or books. The firefighters below the windows ran forward and extinguished small blazes before retreating for cover.

Daniel couldn't imagine how the men inside were breathing as black smoke blew continuously from the now-naked windows. He was tired. He'd been there from the onset of the riot, when someone from command called and told him what was going down. His tired muscles complained and his usually responsive body ached with the need for rest and warmth, neither of which he would seek until Elaine's release proved real. He knew he should go to the media tents set up down the hill and file a story, but he wasn't about to leave the closest vantage point they would let him have until she was out.

He felt terrified for his wife. The only muscle in his body truly hurting was his heart—it actually ached for the strong yet fragile woman whom he knew to be in perilous danger. He beat himself up mentally because he'd acted abominably that morning to his wife, friend, and lover of thirty years. What an ass he was! Lately he was failing to make Elaine happy but instead of spending time, as she'd asked, to work out the problems, he'd been doing his usual 'start a fight and flee' routine. And that was how he'd left her this morning.

He loved Elaine to distraction and would gladly trade places with her right now, despite his self-centered, work-consumed, insensitive, piggish nature. No hugs, no kiss, no terms of endearment would help Elaine through the difficult hours; only the same nagging concerns she'd tried to talk to him about when they'd been together. He knew she would be playing out the insecurities she felt, instead of the safety, love, and protectiveness he wanted to give her. These were the gifts he'd left her with to fight off dangerous, violent, out of control bastards. For the millionth time Daniel prayed to God he'd be given the chance to make it up to her.

Almost telepathically, Elaine felt Daniel's presence. She knew he must be outside the walls and concentrating seriously on her this very moment. They'd always had that kind of connection. Many times they had compared notes on thoughts that occurred at the same moment when they were apart. Such moments, when shared later, brought them together spiritually, made them closer physically and emotionally. Or at least that's how it used to be.

What had happened? When did the purity and perfection of their love take on sharp edges digging into them both, damaging trust and confidence? A front desk officer named Tessa Grubbs, one of Elaine's favorite people, observing Elaine and Daniel at a party remarked that the unspoken communication between them was the loudest she'd ever heard. Tessa made the comment in jest, but after reflecting on it, Elaine wondered if maybe that was part of their attraction to each other. They were old friends, the kind that finish each other's sentences and hear statements made when no words are spoken. They'd always looked out for each other, been there for each other, defended each other when the world attacked them, even if the criticism leveled was justified. Their values and beliefs were similar.

Most binding of all were the memories, the history. Those and the children who used to jump on their bed in the mornings and who even now, as adults, gave them great joy.

Elaine stirred from her reverie, shaking her head at the sentimental thoughts doing nothing to change the present. She was no longer the shy, poor college girl she'd been all those years ago, when a sullen-looking football player stopped her in the student union. Oh the excitement of that first date, the homecoming games, and the commencement they went through after two years of married life on campus.

She was now a multidimensional, attractive, well-educated woman who had become bored with her marriage, frustrated over the state of the prison system, and disillusioned with the world and her place in it. Her adventures had become riskier and the pleasures she derived from them less rewarding. But that was before she had become a victim of the system she'd been trying to change, a hostage of men she'd been trying to help, and a captive of only one emotion: fear.

The fear grew when the door flew open and a body was disrespectfully tossed into the room; that of a part-time instructor named Pamela. For a moment, time froze as the door closed and everyone stared silently at this mound of hair and feet and hands, at the face that did not move—that didn't seem real at all.

18

Chapter 3

"Shit," said Damien, breaking the silence that had fallen upon the group. He walked over to the limp form and slowly turned it face up with his boot. Pamela had a bullet hole in the right side of her temple. The absence of panties and the bared breasts clearly indicated death hadn't been the only injustice done to her. Pamela had been another maladjusted, insecure female, who was only given a job because of her personal affiliations with the director. She was hated with a passion by the inmates because of her belittling, nasty tongue. Now she'd never say anything mean again. That tongue would never make the men feel less confident than they already did for not being able to read to her satisfaction, or do a simple math problem quickly enough. Pamela's tongue had been cut out of her mouth.

Oddly, Elaine felt nothing as she stared at the lifeless body. Pamela had never been anything but sarcastic and rude to her, and Elaine had been growing increasingly disillusioned by the director's choices in hiring either people who owed him, could help him achieve political favor, or in some way assist his ambitious nature.

People like Pamela made Elaine's job harder. They were not sound educators and they didn't like working with the inmates. Pamela hadn't been a healthy addition to the staff, but Elaine was surprised at how cold she felt looking at the dead woman's corpse. To be fair, she, more than likely, faced a similar fate and could only concentrate on one thing at a time.

Then all reflection ceased, as the room was plunged into darkness. The electricity was either turned off by whichever group was presently in power, or the fire burning more and more brightly through the windows, had reached the main. Elaine couldn't believe a back-up generator wouldn't soon alleviate the situation, but as her eyes adjusted to the semi-darkness, and she saw the Dante-like figures reflected in the smoldering fire from the classroom and the eerie jumping shadows through the window, she didn't feel confident.

Every year she signed a five hundred page Emergency Response Plan, attesting to the written belief the Department of Corrections had an effective plan for just such emergency. But she'd been told, when she started, that in case of trouble all she had to do was knock the receiver off of her phone and an officer would be there in less than three minutes.

One day she had accidentally knocked the receiver off. An hour later it finally dawned on her—it wasn't hooked up to anything!

No one had come then. Would they come now? The harsh reality was in this prison, as in most, the hostage policy was very simple: There was no policy because there were no hostages. Everyone entering the institution signed an understanding to that effect. Elaine was no exception, and she knew it.

Elaine lay down in the corner, drawing her body into as tight a ball as she could. After a long while, sleep came again. No dreams, thank God, just a state that must be similar to death. Upon awakening, Elaine was in a dull haze. The smell around her she imagined was similar to a bat cave. The musty odor of unwashed bodies permeated the entire area. The fires had burned out or maybe there was simply nothing left to burn.

As she opened her eyes fully, she saw that mercifully, Pamela's body no longer remained. The only disgusting sights left belonged to inmates, sleeping in various positions around the room. Elaine almost felt tranquil as she peered beneath hooded eyelids, her attention coming to rest on her good friend Richard, who'd fallen asleep propped against the far wall.

Elaine's heart warmed as she remembered the good times spent with Richard, riding horses in the high country and discussing life, as only those with the hearts of cowboys and cowgirls could. She was still reflecting on those more pleasant times in her life when a sudden movement alarmed her.

She turned her head—and her eyes locked on Damien, whose piercing black eyes bored through her clothes. She knew the time had come again when she'd have to fight or flee, and the latter was not an option.

Damn! Where was Custody? Why hadn't they come? She remembered her promise to get everyone into one room at a certain time. Now in the clear light of reality, Elaine wondered how to accomplish that feat. The inmates wouldn't let her talk to Richard across the room, much less ask about those held in other buildings. Fear froze her thoughts as Damien stood up, stretched his well-muscled body, and spoke quietly to one of his friends.

Elaine mentally added up all of the staff back in the Education wing of the prison. Several buildings actually housed Education. There were shops, dry-cleaning, automotive, sewing. She must try and think clearly! Jerry, the auto shop teacher, was probably dead by now. He'd never willingly submit to a takeover by the inmates.

An old friend of Richard's, Jerry had been a guard before becoming a vocational instructor. Once before in a riot, he'd been shot in the hand wresting a gun from an inmate. He loved to tell the story and brag that "the bastards could never take him!" A lovable old guy, with one year left to retirement, Elaine hoped, rather than believed, he was still okay.

Two other men she thought might be in the back area were part-time drafting instructors. Both brand new. They hadn't yet had D.O.C. emergency response training. From the few times Elaine talked to them, she saw they feared this predominately male environment and only took the jobs for the money.

Over the years Elaine noted new men acted as though every inmate was going to cut their throats. Women on the other hand

21

seemed overly confident. Neither position worked well for this job. Julie, the cute twenty-five-year-old computer teacher, was typical. Department of Corrections said they sent all new staff for training before they began working "behind the walls," so that staff would know how to handle themselves before they got in trouble. Julie told Elaine she thought it was "stupid" to take a day away from her teaching in order to attend the safety training so she hadn't gone. Since that training consisted of how to handle yourself during a riot, Elaine wondered what Julie was thinking now.

Elaine wondered how she could get Rob out of the barbershop and Harry over here from the welding shop. There were the two secretaries in registration, and Raylyn behind her desk. God—how to get them all into one room? It didn't seem possible, especially while Damien swaggered toward her, yawning loudly, scratching his hair with one hand and his groin with the other.

He seemed to be in a good mood as he bent close to her face, and with the breath fouled by his meth-ruined teeth, said, "Sleep good? Ready to help yourself and your friends get out of here alive? Good. We're going to call the captain again and get that food we ordered."

One of the inmates yelled, "Make 'em give us good shit, Damien. Not that kitchen crap."

"Yeah. Hear that, Elaine? We're waiting to hear how good you really are at this. We want good stuff to eat and drink. So move your ass."

As he said this, he looked Elaine up and down and licked his lips. Elaine's heart sank as she looked around the room—as much to avoid his ugly, smelly face as to desperately seek a miracle in one of the faces watching them.

Richard would be able to do nothing. The inmates had him tied up securely and would love an excuse to kill him; as they now saw him as one of their prisoners, not a teacher. The others in the room, all hardened criminals looking for action, satisfaction, and revenge against the perceived or actual injustices life dealt them—all except one man who hadn't been in the room when Elaine had looked around earlier.

His name was Billy Robinson. Elaine assumed he came in while she slept. He stood out because of his flaming red shoulder-length hair and his stature. At thirty-something he stood well over 6'4" and always worked out with the weights D.O.C. kept threatening to take away, but never had in the sixteen years Billy had spent in this institution. He was a lifer, a sentence earned for participation in the cold-blooded beating and killing of an old woman who in exchange for drugs used to let him and other street kids sleep in her home. They'd beaten her for a few dollars and the respect of the older street kids they were trying to impress. Billy would not have a chance to see the outside of a prison until he was well over forty years old.

Billy was Elaine's teaching assistant and a tutor in her literacy program where educated men were trained to teach the illiterate ones to read one-to-one. She knew much about him because she read all the jackets, or files, of all the men she placed in responsible positions.

She stopped her visual scanning and locked eyes with his; here was her best and probably only hope, and a possible rescuer of the others. Billy stared back with a look of such concern she turned away from the intensity of it. This man was definitely ready to kill someone, but it wasn't her.

For over ten years Elaine had watched, nurtured and advised Billy in the roles of superb computer whiz and teaching assistant. Though lacking in confidence and self-esteem, quiet around inmates and shy around her, he'd nonetheless become an excellent employee. He never misused his status or took advantage of the freedoms she gave him. From the gangly boy she hired he'd grown into a remarkable man; one she knew full-well liked her.

Normally she'd never take advantage, but in this dire situation she might have to use his loyalty in order to get everyone out alive. But how? How could she get him involved in something that might well get him killed? She would have to ask him to break the one law all smart inmates followed, the Inmate Code. Simply put, the Code went like this: if it ever comes down to them (people from the outside) or us (people on the inside) you have to choose us. Choosing "them" would get Billy either dead or living in protective custody for the rest of his sentence, maybe his life. Best case scenario? He would always be alone. Worst case scenario? No matter which prison he was sent to, inmates would spread the word and he would be shanked.

Elaine's plot was short-lived. Damien grabbed her shoulder, hauled her to her feet, and propelled her to the door; en route she saw Billy and Richard's eyes follow them, each seeming to beg her not to lose her infamous temper, which she was close to doing. She took several deep breaths, straightened her coat, and headed out the door and down the corridor with Damien close behind.

Chapter 4

As Elaine entered the registration office she saw Raylyn was no longer there. Once again she was shoved unkindly into a chair, handed the phone and ordered to instruct Captain Pepper about where and when to bring the food. Elaine's courage soared just from hearing her friend's calming tone of voice.

"Elaine. Ivy here. How are you?"

"Stiff," she admitted.

"Have you located anyone else?"

"No."

"Can you?"

Right then Elaine knew exactly what she'd do, that she would likely have only one chance to get everyone together. So she took it. "Deliver all the food and drinks to my classroom. Everyone is to be in that room, or no deal. Are those the terms, Captain?"

"Is that what you want me to agree to?" Captain Pepper asked Elaine.

She repeated the urgent tone. "If all the hostages are not in that room, then you will not deliver. Is that right, Captain?"

"If that's what you want."

"That's what Damien wants," Elaine lied, as she looked up at him with what she hoped was a sincere and innocent expression. "You'll only deliver at 2:00 p.m. and you want Billy Robinson, my clerk, to pick up the food himself or no deal?"

"If that's what you want." Captain Pepper said. She sounded mystified but willing to accept whatever Elaine was proposing.

Damien too looked puzzled, then pleased with what appeared to be a fair delivery plan; true to character, he still acted like an ass. "Tell her me and my men ain't going to settle for the kitchen garbage. We want pizza, all kinds, and it damn well better be hot, and the soft drinks cold, or the little teacher will be our lunch instead."

Elaine repeated the threat as he and his men laughed in the background. She heard Captain Pepper take a deep breath, and ask if any staff were dead. Elaine bit back exhausted tears. "Yes."

Captain Pepper gasped and then asked Elaine how many pizzas Damien wanted. Elaine knew this wasn't because she cared if one of these monsters went hungry, but was rather trying to assess how many inmates were still loose and hostile. Damien told her to say they needed food and drink for two hundred, which didn't help much and he knew it. At most he had twenty men on their feet with weapons, but Elaine couldn't figure out a way to tell Ivy.

By this time Custody had regained some control, started a head count and locked cooperative inmates in those cells not gutted. They had some idea of who and how many were still loose. From the high windows everyone could see the diminishing fire in the cellblocks, although smoke continued to circle the razor-wires.

In the corridor Elaine just walked, three bodies lay. Inmates whose crimes were against children, taken care of by fellow prisoners exacting their own law. When the institution normalized, and she knew it would with or without her, these men would not be missed or mourned by anyone. She thought about how Daniel would write about the riot for the newspaper and magazine he worked with, and how he would deal with it personally.

Reflection was once again short-lived. Damien dragged her to her feet, ignoring her protest that she'd move if he'd simply ask. He shoved her down the hall and back into the classroom. Though he probably didn't mean to, his strength forced her off balance; as a result, her heel caught in the hem of her coat and she stumbled headfirst into the heavy door frame.

Elaine didn't remember anything after that, until she awoke looking straight into the eyes of Billy. He had placed wet paper towels on her forehead and was holding them there as he knelt over her. Looking around she saw herself back in the burned-out classroom, lying on the cement floor, rolled-up coat tucked under her head for a pillow. She felt grateful to be alive, but could have lived another lifetime without seeing the look in this young man's eyes.

Killing is a strange thing. Those who'd never done it, or been around those who killed didn't understand. But Elaine did. She had seen what it had done to childhood friends who'd gone to fight in Vietnam. She'd worked with hundreds of murderers as students, clerks, and TA's in the prison. Only twice in ten years, but two times too often, she'd also seen the curtain lift from a murderer's eyes.

Or maybe it was more like a membrane, she thought; the lid behind a lizard's eye pulling back when it blinks. For a moment in time, she'd seen the real face behind the mask and those few moments changed her forever. The mask only fell away for a split second. A look into the dark side of a soul only lasted a fragment of time, but for people unlucky enough to witness its evil presence, it made them realize they too were capable of killing. The emotions made a person face her own mortality. And it made one believe there could be true evil in all of us.

The moment had passed and she collected herself, questioning whether she'd actually seen it at all. The only thing Elaine could compare it to in her own life was childbirth. The pain of the birth receded; otherwise no woman could face having a second child or condone it for her daughters. Elaine never spoke of what she'd seen to anyone. She didn't know how.

But now she'd seen that look in Billy's face, and it terrified her, though he recovered quickly and it hadn't been directed at her but on her behalf. Still, the knowledge did not lessen her terror. She tried to sit up, but a wave of nausea and a throbbing on her left temple made her acquiesce to the gentle pressure on her shoulder from Billy's large hand. In prison, no inmate was ever allowed to touch staff in any way; for one second Elaine wondered whether Billy would get in trouble for touching her. She must have smiled at the silliness of the thought because Billy smiled back and sat facing her on the floor.

When she woke again, the throbbing in her head was mostly gone and so was the nausea, but she felt acutely embarrassed when she realized Billy repositioned her body so she lay curled against him, her coat laid over her. She glanced up to see him smiling sheepishly.

Elaine hurriedly turned out of his embrace and sat next to him. The sudden movement triggered the pain in her head and the churning in her stomach, but she didn't care. Neither felt as bad as the blush she sensed rising up to her cheeks from their closeness.

She looked around and saw Richard glaring at Billy, helpless to assist except through ferocious eye contact that warned of real danger when and if he were freed.

Elaine surveyed her surroundings. There were ten inmates in the room; no Damien or hostages other than Richard and herself. She glanced at her watch and almost panicked: it was 1:30 p.m. The hostages had to be delivered to this room before the lunch arrived at two. That was the only hope. If the situation wasn't resolved soon, Elaine knew the inmates would lose patience and more people would die.

Elaine, knocked unconscious before Damien got the Captain's feedback, knew he was anxious to talk when a messenger reported she was awake. He must have dumped her unceremoniously on Billy when he'd heard her mention his name to the Captain. Though he didn't know the connection, Damien must have figured there was one, and he would make it work for him. Elaine, on the other hand, knew she must get Billy to help her any way she could. She'd no choices or time left before Damien ordered Billy to go get the food. As Damien argued with another inmate, Elaine turned to Billy and filled him in on her plan. He'd go get the food and drinks and be slipped a weapon. She'd get Damien to gather all the hostages in the room before Billy came back. Billy would then overpower Damien and convince the other inmates to end this pointless takeover.

Billy stared at her open-mouthed, as though she had asked him to rush out to the big yard with a gun and open fire on the well-armed officers in the towers. She couldn't blame him. He'd absolutely no reason to help her.

Use her, yes. Help her, no.

Elaine believed she meant little to him. These men, on the other hand, were his whole world. His life with them was the only one he knew, or would know for the rest of his adult life. To betray them would leave him nothing. He'd *be alone*. It was suicide. It was unthinkable. She could read it in his eyes.

She stood up, brushed past Billy and walked toward Damien. Time was up.

Elaine told Damien to bring all the hostages into the room; otherwise, the promised food wouldn't be delivered. Captain Pepper would know since Elaine had to write a note for Billy to deliver, when he went to pick up the food. Elaine was not going to write the note if it weren't so.

Damien searched her face and said nothing. He then left to confer with his officers, as he called them. Elaine turned back to Billy, who still wore the same horrified look on his face. His huge body shielded her as she smiled up at him, but he just shook his head and turned away. Knowing full-well the danger she was putting him in, she moved around to face him again and spoke as softly as she could, about paybacks and new beginnings. He looked past her, as though she didn't exist, which was easy to do given his greater height. He said nothing.

Elaine was known in the prison as the "lady who cared."

Asked about the nomenclature, Elaine always said it just meant she hated losing. She hated seeing a young inmate quit school, so she talked and argued and pushed and bothered the kid until it was easier to do what she said than listen to her. She'd used the same technique on her own children, and they had turned out pretty well. She really cared. Perhaps too much. She genuinely wanted these "throwaway human beings" to succeed, and they knew it.

She pushed now with Billy. She used every nice and not-so-nice tactic in her bag of tricks to persuade him. She told him they might reduce his sentence for having helped (she had no idea if this was so). She told him he owed it to the staff who had always helped and been kind to him. She got down and dirty, and told him he owed it to the old lady he'd helped kill. He would at last be paying his dues for her murder.

Elaine felt badly as she said it, but desperation drove her. A lot of innocent people needed her to get them out of this dangerous situation alive. She didn't want her own life ended either.

Finally, just as Damien started back across the room, Billy looked down at her with the most intense expression she'd ever seen and said, "I'm going to do this, but for only one reason. I love you."

Now it was Elaine's turn to stare open-mouthed, neither comprehending nor wanting to comprehend what he offered. When it sunk in, she immediately realized it was the one reason she couldn't allow him to risk his life. Thus, she couldn't let him carry out the plan. For him to die to make up for killing someone else, or to take a chance he might get out of prison earlier, was one thing. But to die because he loved her, the person who asked the favor, was unconscionable. She couldn't allow it. She'd think of another way to save them all. This plan would no longer do.

Damien, luckily, became distracted again. It gave Elaine the reprieve she needed.

"I can't let you go through with this," she told Billy. "You're misguided. You only think you care for me because I've become like a friend or mother to you. You don't know many women. I'm sorry. I can't involve you in this. It's crazy. It won't work."

"It *will* work, Elaine." He'd never called her that before. She looked away. "And you won't owe me. If this riot hadn't taken place, I wouldn't have told you my true feelings. I wouldn't have because then you'd feel uncomfortable around me and wouldn't have let me stay and work with you day after day, month after month, and year after year. That was my life. I was content to help you, just see you, hear you and in some respects shield you from some of the ugliness of this place. That was enough. But everything has changed, and so does the way I show you how I love you. That's all I have that's worth anything. I want to do it right. If I had been out on the streets, I would have met you and loved you. You need to believe that, and you need to trust me. Everything will be all right."

Damien was walking over, his gaze on Billy, not Elaine. "You gonna do it?"

"Do what?" Billy answered.

"You gonna get the food for the lady, smartass!"

"What's in it for me?" Billy questioned.

"How about I let you live? That good enough?" Damien answered, laughing and looking at his gang.

"I don't think that's your decision, Damien," Billy casually responded. "Those twenty lifers still loose outside the education building aren't there for you. They're there for me. I think you realize that. If not, you're a bigger fool than even I thought you were."

Damien's dark eyes began to twitch, but he smiled and said, "Hey, man, we're working together. What do you really want?"

"I want you to bring all the hostages in here before I come back with lunch, and I mean all of them!"

"Okay, okay. Give me five minutes. Then we'll talk." Damien left, and Billy and Elaine sat down with their backs to the wall. For the first time since knowing Billy, she actually felt his presence,

31

not as an inmate or assistant, but as a man. She was afraid, not for her wellbeing, but her feelings. Though they didn't speak or touch, the tension and intensity of the other's presence and nearness were palpable.

She tried to tell herself how ridiculous her emotions were. She was scared. He was lonely. But she knew in her heart there was more to it than that. She was older. He was younger. She was a teacher. He was an inmate. Somehow just now none of that seemed to matter.

Billy didn't stir. He didn't seem to blink. He just sat there with his knees drawn up to his chin, looking straight ahead. Elaine wondered how often he must sit like this in his part of the cell. He sat in a trance, a catlike pose he could spring from at any second if need be.

She, on the other hand, fidgeted and squirmed and struggled to think how to stop this insane plan she had put into motion. The door opened, and the hostages came stumbling in. Damien followed. Elaine felt a pang as she realized she'd forgotten about one teacher, Mr. Garcia, when she tried to remember who was in the prison. Then again, Pete Garcia was an easy person to skip. T.S. Eliot's "Love Song of J. Alfred Prufrock" always came to mind when she looked at him. A small man, he conveyed no confidence, energy, passion or opinion except about his paycheck. In the ten years Elaine knew him, he stayed hidden behind a newspaper. He did as little work as possible, never learned his students' names and always agreed with the boss.

He's in hostage hell now, Elaine thought. The abject terror she saw on his face confirmed this impression. Hardly able to walk he was shaking so badly, his silly toupee askew on his balding head, his eyes darting back and forth as he wrung his hands together.

"Elaine, thank God you're here," he said as he rushed over to her. "What are we going to do?"

All the years they had worked together, Pete constantly suggested that women didn't belong working in a man's prison.

He never let up. Year after year, the same things: "Women can't handle it." "Women are a liability." And now he asked her to help him?

Instead of venting, she hugged Pete while he shook, and reassured him everything was going to be all right, trying desperately to convince herself at the same time.

As Elaine looked at the terrified people she spent most of her waking hours with, she tried to figure out why she had been designated their leader. She saw the expectation in their petrified eyes, hopeful expressions on their dirty, haggard faces. She exemplified their last hope?

She looked at Richard, hoping for guidance and possible assistance, but after his attempt to help her, Damien had gagged him. Only his eyes spoke to her and that couldn't assist her. She looked to the others who were still conscious and untied for support.

Jerry, the old timer who taught in the auto shop and had been a custody officer at one time, was unconscious. If she hadn't seen his chest rise and fall, she'd have thought him dead. His head was cradled in Julie's lap. Julie herself seemed to be in shock. Neither emotion nor recognition registered in her body or face; she just stared vacantly.

Bob and Joe, the drafting instructors, stood together almost defiantly. This posture, Elaine noted, would either help her or get them killed, whichever came first. Rob, the barber, seemed calm and aware enough. He might actually be of some help. The men liked him. Over the years he'd worked to develop a beauty school that prepared inmates for jobs in society. His students always tried to get Elaine to let them take care of her hair.

But Harry, the welding instructor, was by far her best choice of ally. A friend, but more than that, he was smart and strong and aware of how to function in this environment. She watched as his eyes darted alertly from one inmate to another, assessing the situation and their chances. There were only a few minutes before

33

the food arrived. Elaine had to do something, not only to stop Billy from sacrificing himself, but to save them all if possible. Damien was busy with his inmate friends as she walked slowly toward Harry. He was leaning up against a wall away from the others, which made it easier to speak with him privately. He saw her approach and inched his way in her direction.

It seemed like forever, but after a minute or two they sidled near enough to whisper without drawing attention. In a gesture that almost made her cry, Harry took her hand and squeezed it tightly. They stood side by side, backs to the wall so as not to draw suspicion.

"Harry," Elaine said, "in just a few minutes food will be delivered along with a weapon I've talked Billy #997543 into sneaking in for us."

Harry said nothing, just stared straight ahead holding Elaine's hand.

"I don't want Billy to do it. It's too dangerous, but he won't listen."

"He has to do it," Harry replied finally. "It's our best and only chance."

"No!" Elaine exclaimed under her breath.

"Yes! But when he gets here, I'll help him. You need to tell him that, Elaine."

She looked over, but where Billy should have been, there was empty space. She scoured the room with her eyes, but he was nowhere to be seen. Her heart fell. Had he left and taken up against them with the other inmates? Where *was* he?

Her heart raced as she looked at her watch. Almost two p.m., and she had heard nothing. She looked back at Harry and shrugged her shoulders in frustration. Harry knew who Billy was and didn't see him in the room. Nothing left to say or do, Elaine grasped Harry's hand more tightly and prayed. However, thinking holy prayers as hunger, thirst and more basic physical necessities kept interfering with any thoughts of an ethereal nature interrupted her. She concentrated on God or family, but there it was, she needed to pee!

Ten minutes, twenty minutes, thirty minutes passed. What was the Captain thinking? Elaine wanted to believe the Department of Corrections would get there on time. Elaine forgave herself the error in judgment; she had thought this situation might be so important they wouldn't screw it up. Hah! Who was she kidding?

Damien entered furious. He'd come in the room, then leave. Then return. Then leave, slamming and stomping. By two, still nothing had happened. And now he came at Elaine.

Elaine didn't realize she still clutched Harry's hand until Damien approached. Harry turned to her and said, "Stay calm. It's okay, stay calm."

Damien grabbed her and began pushing her ahead of him toward the door. Her legs buckled. If she hadn't been holding Harry's hand she would have fallen. Harry grabbed her elbow and braced her until she regained her balance. He didn't utter a word, just stood there, holding Elaine up.

At that moment she feared she was going to wet herself. The potential shame turned to anger. She just didn't care anymore. She straightened and said to Damien, "Get me to a bathroom—now!"

Silence in the room up to that moment was now total absence of sound building the tension to a new level. She didn't wait for permission. She didn't wait for an escort. She just started walking toward the door; stepping over bodies, down the hall to the registration Office, where she stopped at the staff bathroom door, with Damien right behind her.

"You have my keys to the bathroom. I need you to open the door," she spat out.

He did. She walked in and closed the door in his face. Almost not making it in time, she relieved herself, washed her face and hands slowly looking around for something that might be a weapon.

She thought better of it when she heard a noise right outside the door, and knew she'd be searched upon exiting. Damien was exactly where she had left him, facing the door. He unbuttoned her coat and roughly checked every possible place she could conceal something. Elaine quietly submitted to the humiliation.

Eventually, he acted satisfied. They walked back to the main office where he handed her the phone. Captain Pepper answered on the first ring.

Damien covered the mouthpiece and ordered Elaine to ask where the food and drinks were. Elaine did as he demanded.

"Elaine, can Damien hear everything?"

"Yes."

"We've stalled as long as we dared to allow time to get the staff in your room. Were they successful?"

"Yes."

"Tell Damien we're on our way, but we want one inmate to meet the officers with the cart. Billy Robinson. Number 997543."

"I can't find Billy." Elaine admitted.

"That's okay. We will," Captain Pepper replied.

"I don't want anyone hurt—"

"Neither do we," Pepper responded.

"Well, then, I guess lunch is served."

"Yep. Hang in there. You're doing great."

"I don't feel like I am," Elaine answered softly.

"You're alive, aren't you?"

"Okay, I get the message."

"Bye for now, Elaine."

"Bye, Ivy," Elaine almost whispered.

She transferred the information to Damien and he ordered his lieutenant, as he called him, to go find Billy. At that very moment, Billy entered the room, glanced quickly at Elaine, and then gave his whole attention to Damien.

"Get out there and get the food, Billy," Damien ordered.

"Get it yourself!" Billy replied.

"Look, punk. You with us or against us?"

"You call me punk again, and you won't have to worry about a side."

"All I want is for you to go get the stuff. What's the big deal?" Damien sneered.

"I don't like the way you asked me. You need to talk nice if you expect me to do anything for you," Billy replied.

"Okay, okay. Calm down. Please go get the fuckin' food. That better?"

She was not two feet from the altercation between the two very large, strong, agitated prisoners. They were nose to nose the entire time. As far as she could tell, one or the other was going to go off. If a physical fight ensued, she was sitting in the way.

"Much," Billy replied, and left without another glance in Elaine's direction.

Billy, now on his way out the door, maybe to his death, because of her didn't look back. She rose to stop him. Damien, having no part of it, said, "Where do you think you're going, bitch? Did I say you could move?"

"Look," Elaine said desperately, "I did what you wanted. Now let me get back to the others—"

"I don't think so. I want to keep you here with me for a while."

Elaine sat down with a heavy heart as she realized the new predicament she was in. The food would be delivered to her classroom. The S.W.A.T. team would come and rescue everyone in the room but she would not be among those rescued. She would not be taken out with the others. She knew the S.W.A.T. team had specific orders: "Get in and get out." That's it. And she'd just told Captain Pepper everyone was in her classroom. She slumped back in the chair, a real sense of doom descending over her.

Chapter 5

How sweet it had been in the beginning. Hands in the back pockets of each other's corduroy jeans as they walked from class to class together. Their eyes searching for the other across the cafeteria. Quiet hours spent studying, with the heightened anticipation of the lovemaking that would take place before he walked her back to her dorm. It seemed funny now, but in those days there were women's dorms and men's dorms, and the women had a curfew. Elaine had liked it better the old way. Now there was no mystery between the sexes. Therefore, there was little romance.

Then the children came along. She loved her son and daughter to distraction and felt blessed to have them in her life. But to be brutally honest, which she might as well be in her current predicament, they had taken a toll on her marriage. She and Daniel were alone. They'd had no help and looking back, they'd had no confidence in their parenting skills because of their own skewed childhoods, and as a result had tried extra hard.

They'd worked hard at parenting and at their jobs. There wasn't time left over for much else, so their once intimate relationship suffered. Daniel took assignments all over the world. She taught and did activities with the kids until they took the wings she'd helped them grow and flew away. That was the correct order of life, but what an immense void their leaving had in her! She'd so much time on her hands and no idea how to fill it.

That was when she started taking her profession seriously, made new friends, rode on horseback over the high cliffs of the

Cascades and created a new life to take the place of the one she'd had with her children.

Sometimes Elaine regretted not trying harder to meet Daniel's needs instead of her own; but she never felt he'd tried to meet her halfway. She still loved Daniel. They shared so much history, and the same values, which was important. But now she liked being independent.

And what about these ridiculous feelings for Billy? Must just be stress, she reasoned. They would disappear just like he had. She felt so frightened, so discouraged. So very, very tired.

Her reverie broke with the sound of a cart being pushed down the hall. Voices caught her attention next, as the men started applauding for the pizzas, even before she could smell them. Elaine realized she was hungry and wondered if she'd be allocated a portion. Having attended many inmate banquets and celebrations over the years, she didn't think so. After having seen these men eat, she doubted anyone would remember her until after all the food was devoured.

Then she heard popping sounds, and a different kind of shouting took over. The bangs were gunshots, the shouts turned to screams as those inmates who didn't relinquish their weapons fast enough for the S.W.A.T. team died.

Three inmates stayed with Elaine in the registration office. One was Damien. When they rushed out to the hall as they thought pizza was being delivered, Elaine was left alone momentarily. She thought of using the phone to call Pepper and tell her she was stranded in the office but changed her mind when Damien and another inmate rushed back into the room, firing into the hallway and locking the door behind them.

When Elaine heard the firing, she'd ducked under a desk. Now Damien and the other inmate slid it in front of the door, with her under it.

It was five minutes before the men dared get up from behind the cabinets. Damien made the other inmate look through a hall window and determine all was quiet. Then he began shouting, "Shit, shit, shit!" He randomly threw papers and books and anything he could reach across the room. The other inmate and Elaine hovered quietly, waiting for his rage to subside. Finally, before he could slide her along with the desk away from the door, she crawled out.

He stared at her, as though he'd never seen her before. A slow sinister smile started from one corner of his mouth and spread until it lit up his entire face, except his eyes. They were as cold and dead as ever. Elaine wondered if she should have tried to escape during the shooting, but she knew she'd never had much of a chance.

And now she had no chance at all.

"Well, well. How could I have forgotten about you, my ticket?" Damien mused, stepping forward and brushing tangled hair away from her perspiring forehead. "It seems old Damien isn't done for yet. Let's go see if there's any pizza left, shall we?"

There was a lot of pizza left, if you didn't mind eating it off the floor, walls and broken windows, where it landed as the S.W.A.T. team entered the room. Drinks spilled everywhere; but missing were Elaine's friends and colleagues. Several bodies lay on the floor, but they belonged to inmates. Elaine's first emotion was elation for the others, but more quickly than she liked to admit, she felt envy and anger. Here she was, the one who had orchestrated their rescue, and they had left her! What in the holy name of Mary was she supposed to do now?

At least before she'd been comforted knowing she and the others were in the same situation. She hadn't been alone. She had nobody now and for the first time she felt she'd die.

◌◐◌

Daniel hadn't been sitting on his hands, waiting for his wife to be killed. He enjoyed contacts, and although as a reporter he wasn't really supposed to be near the command post, he'd called in markers and been given free rein of the area, so long

41

as he didn't get in the way or report anything. Daniel knew senators, the governor, the chief of police' and the deputy commissioner in charge of all the prisons in the state; and he had been communicating with them as the time passed. He knew the line staff in this particular prison and they'd kept him up to date about the S.W.A.T. team's maneuvers. His hopes soared when he found out the S.W.A.T. team had rescued everyone and would bring them out of the prison compound momentarily. These hopes fell just as quickly when he saw the line of bedraggled staff brought in for debriefing or loaded onto ambulances, Elaine not among them.

When he came to Harry, he heard the gruesome story, but Harry could only say Elaine was taken off to the registration area right before the rescue occurred. Harry, sick about having to leave her, told Daniel he had begged the S.W.A.T. team to go back and get her. They would not vary from their orders, which were to get everyone out of the classroom and then get out themselves, no detours.

Daniel threw down his cold coffee and stomped down the steps to the steel control door separating the administration building from the main prison. He began pounding and yelling at the guards to let him in. There was no possibility this would happen. However, Daniel was led upstairs by two gentle guards, who knew his situation and felt extremely sorry for him.

Captain Pepper became furious when she realized Elaine was not among the rescued hostages. She was particularly angry when Harry told her he'd tried to get the S.W.A.T. team to not leave her. But she felt her officers did the right thing, so she could only be angry with herself that she hadn't foreseen this snag. To digest that Elaine was now alone with Damien, who must be furious, particularly worried her.

She'd been trying to call the education office, hoping Elaine would pick up; but if they were there, no one was answering, which also disturbed her.

Captain Pepper was standing in the hall where everyone—S.W.A.T. team, medics, hostages and other staff involved in the crisis—was deciding who needed to be debriefed or needed medical care. Officers mingled and replayed their success while adrenaline and testosterone returned to near normal levels. Pepper stood watching this and talking quietly with Tessa Grubb, the front desk officer, when Daniel bolted through the door, screaming he wanted his wife out of there, now!

The Captain took one look, waved away officers who were moving in to grab him, and walked to her office with Daniel at her heels. "Calm down," she told him as she went around the massive oak desk and sat, leaning forward on the desk, her fingers locked together.

Instead of sitting, Daniel towered above her, his face close to hers. "I'm not going to calm down until you get Elaine out!"

"And I'm not going to talk to you until you calm down and sit down," Pepper barked back

After trying to sustain eye contact, Daniel slumped in the chair in front of the desk and waited.

Pepper began, "No one is more sorry than I that Elaine didn't get out with the others, but damn it, we're doing our best, and I don't appreciate your going off like some ignorant fool in front of my officers. You know better. All you did was made the situation more volatile and I don't need that."

By this time Daniel had straightened up and was listening so intently that Pepper felt she could talk logically with his full attention. "We will get her out," she emphasized. "We're going to call right now. Do you think you can stay calm? If so, I'll let you stay. If not, get your ass out of here and let me do my job."

"I'll be quiet," Daniel replied.

The Captain motioned the other men in the room who were setting up electrical hook-ups in one corner to make the connection again. All of them waited, as the phone rang and rang and rang.

Meanwhile Elaine, Damien, and the second inmate had been visited by Billy and several other lifers. Elaine found his timing perfect. The presence of Billy and the other men required Damien to once again give her a reprieve. "Thank God," Elaine thought, so happy and relieved Billy was alive and seemingly unharmed, all concern for her own safety and the precarious position she was in faded. She nearly went to him to hug him, but wisely desisted when she looked in his eyes. They were warning her to stay away. Instead, Billy fixed his attention on Damien.

"Well, Damien, you screwed this whole thing up royally. How many men do you think you have left?"

"We're it," Damien said, looking at the faces of the men behind Billy.

"Well, that's it, then. Give me your gun."

"Hell no! Why should I give you my gun? I don't trust you!" Damien yelled.

"I could give a fuck if you trust me or not. You're no longer in charge—I am. You know it, I know it. So just give me the piece and maybe I'll let you and your punk live."

Damien saw several men behind Billy actually pushing past to get at him. Elaine saw he understood that if he got a few shots off, they would pull him down and rip him apart like the rabid dog he was. Elaine slowly moved up behind Billy, too far away now for Damien to grab her. The game was almost over.

Damien couldn't figure out what the game was these inmates were still playing. Moreover, he was already serving a life sentence without possibility of parole, what else could D.O.C. do to him? Then again, the death penalty is legal in this state.

While Damien was mulling this over, Billy calmly walked up to him, took the gun from his slack hand; using the gun, he hit him across the face hard enough to drop the inmate to his knees. Just then, the phone rang again and Billy picked it up.

"Yeah, yeah. It's all over. Elaine's fine. But someone come get this piece of shit off the floor." He hung up, and Elaine stared in bewilderment at these lifers—tutors she'd worked with for years, men who had just saved her life—and she started to cry. Billy came over and put his arms around her. He held her tightly until the sobbing subsided. Once that occurred both pulled away, almost simultaneously. Then one of the other inmates came up and helped Elaine into a chair, another got her water to drink.

She looked at them with eyes bright: Christmas Eyes, her dad used to call her, because she would never go to sleep on Christmas Eve so they could deliver presents from Santa. And these hardened souls, human beings who would probably never get out of prisons, waited on her, cared for her, comforted her until the S.W.A.T. team came to take her out. She watched as the men lay face-down on the filthy floor. They were being cuffed when a S.W.A.T. officer led Elaine out of the room. Billy and the others faced months of segregation, until Intelligence could investigate and sort out the mess.

Officers escorted Elaine outside, past the big yard, through the turnstiles, into the dreaded hallway that separated the different blocks of cells, past the Control Booth, up the steps and into the administration building. As she walked with the officers, she couldn't help noticing the carnage that had once been an orderly, clean, sane prison environment. Fences torn down, fires smoldered, bodies lay defenseless over a wide area.

She wondered if she could ever come back to such a violent place. As she continued to walk past the horror toward the friends and family she loved, she remembered the kind ministrations of the lifers. Cruel criminals. Men who murdered. Men who saved her life! She again felt the embrace of Billy, and knew she would be back, if only to thank him.

Chapter 6

Elaine was embarrassed. She'd crashed and burned, a weakness she hated in other people. "Weakness of Will," she called it. "Being lazy." "Acting like someone from that trashy old book *Valley of the Dolls*." But now, just a few short months after the riot, she'd fled. Here she sat, on some stupid veranda in some country she'd never even wanted to go to, drinking wine and popping prescription pills as though she didn't have a care in the world.

It had been so easy. After her rescue from the riot, the prison doctor gave her a few Prozac to calm her during the debriefing. Then he gave Daniel a prescription to fill before he took her home that night. She kept taking the Prozac regularly because it turned off her disquieting thoughts.

However, she still wasn't sleeping, even when Daniel decided to take her on a trip; so again from the General Practitioner came the Ambien. "Float away like a butterfly," she thought the ad on TV said—or was that another kind? At first, the medicine worked. She didn't actually remember any butterflies, but she zoned out at night. Then in the a.m. she would pop another Prozac.

When she complained after a few months that she was starting to feel depressed whenever she remembered the riot, the same doctor, who felt so sad because of what she had been through, generously upped the dosage on both drugs and sent them to her in the mail.

And so she had sat, drank, and focused on nothing and no one in particular. She wasn't really happy, she finally decided one bright morning. Well, Elaine, she thought, get off your lazy butt and improve your life. No one is going to do it for you. To think, you thought maybe they would.

Four months since the riot left over fifty dead. The dead included officers, staff and inmates. Elaine accepted a leave of absence and spent most of that time with Daniel on a Caribbean island. Her children visited and friends joined them for a week now and then. Elaine was tan and toned. But much of the time she spent alone. Daniel, once he made sure she was physically okay, reverted to his old ways, where assignments took him off for much of the time.

Not that she minded, really. Elaine changed, and though she appreciated the attention of family and friends, she felt oddly disconnected from their efforts to distract her from her pensive moods, and reflections of that most horrific day.

They just couldn't understand. She was desperate to get back to Corrections, to Educational and Custody people. Maybe they would give her back some sense of balance and a measure of perspective.

Nothing seemed terribly real anymore. She knew she shouldn't feel sad. The amazing blue water, pristine skies, sand like spun sugar, all blended together to make her days smooth and comfortable. One of Daniel's wealthy friends leased them his villa after learning of Elaine's ordeal. There were cooks, chefs really, and maids to provide the slightest creature comfort. There was nothing to break into one's reveries. Still the sounds of gunshots, screaming and the smell of fear punctured Elaine's sleep causing her to awake in the middle of the night drenched in perspiration and shaking. The pills, she decided, didn't work.

At first Daniel argued he shouldn't leave her in such a vulnerable state, but as the months passed, his wanderlust got the best of him. Elaine assured him she felt wonderful and he need not worry.

And maybe she did. Now she didn't try to sleep, at least not until she ran on the beach for miles and drank at least three cognacs. These she chased with a sleeping pill or two. Then she lay down on the enormous bed and watched the waves brush gently across the beach until she passed into a light sleep from which she didn't care if she awoke.

No one knew she was escaping from her nightmares in this fashion, and she'd have been greatly ashamed if they had. Around others she was vivacious and energetic and could discuss the events of that day in the prison with detachment and humor. She'd retell each part of the situation, making people laugh with her parody of Mr. Garcia and how she'd slammed the bathroom door in Damien's face. No one cared that she left out her vivid memory of Raylyn and Pamela's faces.

Still, she couldn't go on this way for much longer; her speech was starting to slur just a bit and her memory failed her. She'd witnessed enough drug abuse to recognize the signs.

Was she ready to reassume her duties inside a prison as a correctional educator? No one knew, but Elaine had to try. She missed the edginess of the work, the constant stimulation the job provided.

Who was she kidding? She also missed Billy and wanted to see him again.

Luckily, or perhaps unluckily, Daniel explained Department of Corrections had allowed Billy to stay at the institution since he'd helped Custody stem the outbreak. The lifers who'd assisted him had also been allowed back into population. Damien and those who caused the mayhem were shipped separately to harsher prisons out of state in an exchange for other incorrigibles. This was a common practice used to keep rebellious inmates from gaining power from one another over a long period of 24/7 living.

There would always be Damiens and Raylyns. Elaine knew she could count on that if she worked inside a prison long enough. But wasn't there just a little bit of Raylyn in all women who worked in such a place? Just as there was some of Damien in all the inmates?

Elaine pondered this premise while dumping all the pills she could find down the toilet. Determined to quit self medicating and take back her life, she told herself she was strong enough to do it.

⁂

Two months later and completely detoxed, she flew back to her home, her family, and her work. As the huge jet skidded to a landing, Elaine braced herself for the upbeat persona necessary to convince the welcoming committee. She didn't want everyone to worry and she'd come to realize she had to help herself regain her life, maybe make it better than it was before. She still had to deal with some emotional issues and intended to contact a therapist to help her adjust to going back to work. The therapist could also help provide her with tools to reduce the risk of Elaine once again resorting to pills to cope. Elaine knew, in her heart, she was strong enough to work. However, first and foremost was to see Billy rewarded for his valor.

Once on the tarmac, her grandchildren threw themselves at her as she bent to hug them. How big they were getting! Elaine pondered that for a second as the others moved forward with flowers and embraces. Both her daughter, mother of the little ones, and her son-in-law, who seemed a second son, were there. He'd actually taken time off work, which was rare for him, and it touched her deeply. Daniel hung back, but her son grabbed her, yanking her off her feet.

To her great surprise, she saw some of her colleagues who had been inside the prison that fateful day were also at the airport. At first she thought it was just a coincidence, but as they broke into grins and came forward to embrace her, she started to cry.

First to reach her was Richard. He grabbed her in a bear hug, fitting for his cowboy manners, and swung her around as though she weighed less than nothing. She heard him saying something about "the backside of a horse is good for the inside of a person" so she made a mental note to include horseback riding with

Richard as part of her get well plan.

Next to him, pressing to get closer to Elaine, was Jerry, the auto shop teacher who'd been badly injured. He patted Elaine cautiously, and said, "About time you quit faking and came back to work," sounding almost embarrassed at his own emotions. When he let go, Harry (whom they always called Handsome Harry, the man who had held her hand that day) approached and they hugged. He said simply, "Welcome home, Elaine" in a kind voice.

Looking around at all the people she loved and missed, Elaine spotted a familiar uniform and grinned at Captain Pepper who was leaning against a wall and smoking in a nonsmoking airport. Elaine thought Pepper looked as if she wished she were somewhere else. Elaine walked over and they both started talking at once. Elaine motioned the captain to go first.

"Good to see you could finally end your vacation and join the working stiffs again," she said.

"Captain. Sorry, I'm not coming back just yet. I know you miss me terribly, but I'll come in and tell you about my plans on Monday. Okay?"

"Take your time. The prison will still be here if and when you decide to join us," Captain Pepper smiled.

"I'm coming back! I just have some issues I want to address first," Elaine said quietly.

A dark shadow crossed Captain Pepper's face. "Wait a minute! I was told you hadn't been hurt physically. Elaine, I'm so sorry. Why didn't anyone inform me?"

"It's okay, Cap. I'm fine physically. Probably in the best shape of my life. Let's just talk next week. Okay?" Elaine touched the Captain's shoulder.

"Sure. You take as much time as you want. I'm so glad you are back, Elaine," Captain Pepper said and then marched off, looking like she wanted to kill someone for not keeping her updated.

But this was not the time or place to explain her concerns

with her drug use. She wasn't just another sorry, middle-aged pill abuser. Elaine turned back to her family and friends. Daniel hoisted her carryon luggage. Her colleagues said goodbye, and she and the family headed toward the baggage claim to retrieve luggage and gifts she'd brought back from her time out.

She found the house quiet and neat when she and Daniel returned. Elaine was quite sure her considerate daughter had taken care of things, as there were cut flowers in all the rooms and no clothes or newspapers strewn around, as was Daniel's habit. She walked immediately to the bar and poured herself a large glass of wine. As she turned to offer Daniel something, she saw him standing in the doorway, staring at her intently.

"Care to join me?" Elaine offered as she raised her glass to him in a mock salute.

"No thanks," he said and started up the stairs to take her luggage to their bedroom.

Elaine thought she heard a note of criticism in his tone, but chose to ignore it in lieu of taking her drink to the big bay window and stare out at the view. She was proud she wasn't desperate to take a pill.

She was still there when Daniel called down a few minutes later. "Hey, didn't you hear the phone? It's for you," he yelled with what she now knew as a decidedly irritated tone.

"Oh, sorry," Elaine responded, rushing to the phone she'd heard but chosen to ignore. "Hello?" she queried.

"Hello, Elaine, I know you just got home," Richard said, "but some of us are riding up on the Pilchuck Mountain tomorrow and I thought you might want to join us."

"Oh, Richard, that sounds so good, but I think I should stay home with my husband, don't you?" Elaine responded.

"Well, I suppose if you must, but we will miss you. Me most of all," Richard said.

"I really appreciate that," Elaine responded teasingly.

"Remember, you are my number one partner and I have a

horse ready for you anytime you are available." Richard sounded disappointed.

"I'll let you know, and thanks for thinking of me. That meant a lot to me, you guys all at the airport," Elaine responded, choking back tears she couldn't explain. "Good night," she added.

"Good night," Richard answered, sounding concerned at her small voice and quiet tone. "You okay?" he asked before she could hang up.

"Sure, just tired, I suppose. Jet lag. I'll call you soon," she promised.

"All right, but remember what I've always told you." Richard said.

"What's that?" she asked, knowing what he would say, but wanting to hear it for the millionth time.

"Remember to smell the roses, Elaine. Okay?"

"I'll try."

"Nope, trying doesn't work," he said reprovingly. "You have to *do* it."

"Okay, okay. Leave me alone for now. I'll be tougher tomorrow, I promise."

"You don't need to be tougher—just stronger. I'll help you, okay?" Richard said lowering that rich baritone Elaine was so fond of hearing.

"Okay, have fun tomorrow. I'll be thinking of you," she said, laughing for the first time in what seemed like years.

"Good night." Richard responded and hung up.

Elaine wandered back to the bar and thought about refilling her glass. Instead, she resisted the urge and decided to go upstairs and unpack so she could visit with Daniel while they got ready for bed.

Walking into the spacious European-style master suite, with its dressing tables and walk-in closets, Elaine was dismayed to see Daniel packing his cowhide overnight case. She stood watching as her heart fell, realizing he was leaving. Again.

"Where are you going?" she asked, her voice betraying just a slight quaver of dismay.

"Oh, man, I thought I told you. I have to cover the hurricane in New Orleans. No one really knows how big it's going to get yet, but it's heading directly for the city. I was supposed to be there yesterday, but I wanted to make sure you got home and settled safely," Daniel explained, while continuing to pack.

"Oh. I thought we would have a few days together before our lives started getting hectic again," Elaine said, hoping she didn't sound petulant.

"We will, but you know this is my job. This is what pays the bills, Elaine," Daniel said without looking up. "I don't want you going back into that prison."

Elaine decided to go downstairs before she said anything she'd regret, remembering from the riot how fleeting life was and how one didn't have second chances to take back angry words. She poured another glass of wine and stood looking out at the darkness. She'd been down this road so many times with Daniel, she wasn't greatly upset, just sad that nothing between them changed, and so far as she could see, nothing was going to.

She did what she'd been doing more and more in the last few years. She picked up the phone and called Richard back, hoping he hadn't given her horse away.

"Elaine? What's going on? Is everything okay?" he asked anxiously when he heard her voice.

"Yes, everything's fine. I was just wondering if I could still tag along on the trail ride tomorrow. Daniel is leaving early to cover the storm, and I really don't want to spend the day alone. A ride sounds really good to me."

"Fantastic!" Richard exclaimed without hesitation. "You know I like to get to the trail early, but since you just had a long plane ride, I'll let you sleep in. So I will be there to pick you up at eight a.m. Okay?" he asked with a laugh.

"I suppose," Elaine groaned, "but I'd better go to bed now, or

I'll never make it. Good night again—and thanks."

"No problem. See you bright and early. You get some rest. Seriously, this will be fun and good for you, Elaine. I promise."

As she hung up the phone, Elaine wondered how she was ever going to get up so early. She slowly walked up the stairs again, trying to remember where she'd last seen her riding clothes. She decided unpacking could wait another day.

Daniel was sound asleep when she got to the bedroom. She didn't wake him. He was gone when her alarm rang at seven a.m. and she stumbled downstairs for coffee. Eight a.m. came too soon, but she was ready with her tack and a hot mug of coffee when Richard pulled up in his old rig. The sight of it warmed her heart and brought back ten years of fond memories she chastised herself for suppressing too long.

Elaine threw her tack bag in the side compartment of the horse trailer. She opened the top of the trailer to feed a bit of apple to Lulu, the horse Richard brought for her to ride. Then she threw her personal gear in and climbed up to the cab, pulling the heavy door closed in one swift movement. It seemed natural, just like old times. Elaine settled herself in the passenger seat as he maneuvered the truck and trailer down the steep hill and onto the road.

Once they were settled on a straightaway, it felt natural for him to reach over and squeeze her hand as they drove out to the trailhead. Elaine didn't have to ask which one. She knew it would be Lake Valhalla, right off Stevens Pass. Her heart soared as she realized by noon she would be eating her lunch at the lake, one of the most beautiful spots in the world.

As the miles passed and the sun rose higher in the sky, conversation turned to mundane things like the weather and the horses, settling finally on how sore Elaine would be after two years without her own horse and six months since riding at all. Then they pulled into the trailhead, got out and began the arduous task of getting two horses and riders ready for a full day of serious work.

"I'm going to sign us in," Richard said. He didn't have to explain; Elaine was aware you never stepped foot or horseback into the high country without notifying the forestry department, filing the "who, where and when" of your trip. This information was dropped into a box the rangers checked periodically in case any emergency arose. Elaine couldn't remember if it was the law or just good trail practice, but Richard always did it, whether they were going out for one day or ten. That kind of detail to safety was one of the reasons she loved the guy and would follow him anywhere—and sometimes had.

She wandered off to find the restroom facilities, her practice before they set off so she wouldn't have to use the bushes as often. She chuckled remembering the first time she'd ridden a ten-hour trek and Richard spoke critically because she'd refused to go to the bathroom in the woods. When back at the truck, he said she couldn't ride with him again if she was going to be so silly. She'd not eaten nor drunk all day so she wouldn't need to stop. She'd thought that quite clever but Richard didn't agree. "To be my trail partner, you'll have to smarten up and act like a survivor, because that's what you have to be, whether you go in the wilderness for an hour or a day. And the first thing you have to be able to do is go to the bathroom."

She felt embarrassed and nothing much was said on the trip home; but the next trail ride she told him to lead her horse and ride ahead, while she relieved herself in the brush just as millions of frontier ladies before her. After that first time it got easier until it became second nature; just like cleaning up after her horse in the stall or eating lunch sitting on a log or a big old boulder in some remote part of the Cascade Mountains.

When Elaine returned, Richard finished brushing down his big bay gelding, and she hurried to catch up with her tacking, since she knew waiting was not Richard's favorite pastime. He moved quickly with little patience for those who dawdled, as he called it. She quickly brushed Lulu's back, underbelly, and around her face. She picked out the horse's shoes and fly sprayed her face and flanks. The big horseflies were starting to congregate and Elaine knew from experience their bites would become fierce as the thousand-pound animals sweated up the five mile grade to the bowl of the lake. As usual, the other riders hadn't shown up. "All hat-no cattle."

She congratulated herself for having thought to bring a vial of repellent for both herself and her horse.

"How's it coming?" Richard asked from the back of the trailer, where he worked on his horse. Elaine couldn't see him, as both animals blocked her view, but she could see he was way ahead with Wilbur, his fine roping horse. He had the blanket, saddle, cinch and breast collar on, while Elaine was still doing her brushing.

"Good," she called without conviction. She heard him chuckle and hastened her pace, but she could tell Lulu didn't enjoy the quick movement. She slowed down again, and cursed Richard under her breath.

When he finished, he came around behind and stared as she fumbled the bit in Lulu's mouth. She'd tacked up this particular horse a dozen or so times, but now she couldn't get the horse's head low enough to fit the hard steel shank in her mouth. Elaine sighed in frustration and reluctantly handed the bridle to Richard.

"It's okay, Elaine," Richard said, no ire in his voice. "You haven't done this for a while. It'll all come back. Just give it time."

Elaine did not appreciate Richard's kindness. She hated anyone feeling sorry for her. For Richard to do so was unsettling. He hadn't helped her tack up a horse in years. *Wouldn't* help her, if she was being honest with herself. If she wanted to ride with him, she would learn to take care of herself, he'd always said. And she had.

Now here she was, acting like a greenhorn, detesting herself for it, especially in front of this man. Richard was one of the few people in her life Elaine liked to impress, to have the admiration and respect of, to make proud. In all the years she'd known him, she'd yet to figure out why that was the case. He was a younger version of her dad, whom she'd adored. He was a cowboy and she'd always had a fondness for them. He was educated, but not arrogant about his achievements. He was proud, ambitious and interesting, but not to the detriment of those he cared for. She surmised that he was actually a lot like her but in male form. They were a lot alike, it was true. This led to conflict working together in a volatile, high-risk situation, but it also forged a strong bond that spilled over into their personal lives, especially when it had to do with horses.

"You want a leg up?" Richard offered as she cleared her head and once again focused her attention on the task at hand.

"No, I'll use the fender," Elaine said with disdain. Richard smiled and handed her the reins. Instead of letting Richard support her foot while she swung her leg over the large back of the lovely Lulu, she struggled to reclaim a bit of her independence and maneuvered the animal over to the trailer, where she climbed up to reach Lulu's back. It was a petty bit of defiance, but it made her feel better all the same.

While she was juggling horse and rider, Richard calmly locked the truck, untied his horse, climbed aboard and started off down the trail, whistling. Elaine thought this was unnecessary and a sign of his own independent streak.

At that moment Lulu took off after the other horse before Elaine was seated. Now she was half out of the saddle, trying to pull herself on, while Lulu trotted to catch up to Wilbur "The little bitch," Elaine thought as she righted herself and pulled on the reins to slow her down.

Perhaps, she thought, all this independence is contagious!

Chapter 7

Ten a.m. on a pristine fall morning. The smell on the earth was of old leaves, dried moss, ageing bark. Somewhere far away, water careened down the mountains, left over from the rains higher up in the Cascades. Small animals scurried through the underbrush. Birds cawed and chirped as the beloved clip-clop of the horses' hooves and breath from their nostrils spoke of danger to God's small creatures as they took the incline at a steady, rhythmic pace.

Elaine could not believe how wonderful she felt. Joyful, giddy and at peace, all at the same time. How could that be? Alive was the word. Feelings were what she was experiencing and she liked them for a change. They didn't hurt. They didn't scare her. They were making her body tingle and her heart race. She loved it.

Just at that cathartic moment, Richard swung around in his saddle and caught her smiling. He didn't say a word, not wanting to break into a very special healing experience just beginning for Elaine. He simply went back to his whistling, setting a fast, steady pace for the horses so they would reach Valhalla in time for a nice picnic lunch.

Eventually Elaine caught her breath. She thought it only polite to speak in some conversational manner to her partner, who'd been able to break through a fog so deep and ugly the strongest tranquilizers had had no effect.

"This is fantastic, Richard. Thank you so much for bringing me. I'd forgotten how much I enjoy riding a horse!" Elaine said, with just a bit of shyness.

"Oh, it's just the horseback riding you're enjoying, is it?" Richard answered in the mock Irish brogue he used to lighten the mood.

"Well, I suppose if I put my mind to it, I must admit I've missed the birds and the animals we always find in the forest."

"Thanks a lot," Richard quipped.

As the path grew narrower and steeper, crossing over granite wet with runoff, Richard cautioned Elaine pay attention and cue her horse to the mountainside. He did the same. Although they'd ridden this trail many times, it only took one misstep of the horse, with or without the rider's assistance, for both to go tumbling over the edge. They tight roped, at this stage of the ride, on a thousand foot precipice. No room for error. They continued on in silence, aware of the danger, but experiencing the high of risk taking only those who dare identify with.

The miles burned by. Warm September sun crept along the cliffs, brushing the riders with welcome heat after the frosty morning. Elaine's spirits soared as they turned single file up a sharp corner to the right and came upon a meadow and, in the distance, the most magnificent lake in the world, Lake Valhalla. They were still some one hundred feet above the lake basin, and probably would not actually descend to the water's edge; that was an all-day trek better saved for the kind of overnight ride Elaine was beginning to hope they could take before the winter snows set in.

Valhalla set in a bowl almost perfectly round in shape, blessed with such depth there appeared to be three distinct waters within it. The shallow shore shone yellow from fallen leaves, algae, sticks and debris floating near its edges. Twenty feet out, in what appeared to be a perfect circle, the waters were as green as emerald and gently waved back and forth as though some great invisible child dropped pebbles to break the surface. The center of Valhalla was deep blue, so deep one could not see the bottom but only imagine Viking ships and treasure resting there from old. Trees dressing it on all sides were golden aspen, pinion pine and the majestic cedar, dropping its welcoming arms upon the banks from heights of two hundred feet or more. These were old growth trees; the difference between them and the replants was that of a young woman's beauty compared to one with wisdom and time upon her countenance.

Both horses reined to a halt as the riders drew in the unique beauty of the scene. Richard announced the end of the reverie by riding on to a grove of young aspen and dismounting. Elaine followed suit. Before anything else occurred, the horses' cinches were loosened, bits removed and the riders looped the lead ropes to trees. Since it was autumn, the horses had drank running water and grazed along the climb. Now all they required before the trek down was rest.

With the beasts of burden secured, the tired riders removed the packs off the horses and placed them on a favorite rock. Elaine decided early on when riding, she would take care of herself and her horse. Most people she rode with were men, so this gave her the sense of control and power her psyche needed.

Rarely bringing anything fancy to eat, she knew nourishment, like potty breaks, was a big part of this sport. Today she pulled out of her day pack six month old trail mix; nuts nicely blended with the M&Ms from the rocking of the horse. She also had two bottles of water. Having already eaten a banana on the ride up, she wasn't hungry, but she knew she would eat like a horse at dinner and love every bite.

Ah, first the restroom. Elaine made sure she had Kleenex before she wandered back down the trail to find a hidden spot.

She returned to a picnic lunch for two, complete with tablecloth, wine, cheese, soft French bread and a bottle of her favorite Chianti. Richard beamed at her surprise. The pastoral scene, her friend, the horses, her jet lag caused Elaine to cry.

Richard got up from the ground, walked over and held her until the tears subsided. He guided her to the picnic spread as she wiped her eyes with a tissue.

Quietly Richard said, "I had to thank you somehow for saving my life, didn't I? You can't possibly think I was going to let that go without some show of gratitude. If it weren't for you, I wouldn't be up here, enjoying this little piece of heaven. Come on. Sit down and eat."

Elaine did as she was told, and after two glasses of the excellent Italian table wine, she felt composed enough to eat, smile and enjoy the moment. "How did you bring all this without my knowing, Richard?" she asked.

"You never noticed my overnight pack on the horse. I organized it before picking you up. It wasn't such a big deal. You want to walk a bit to get the soreness out before we get back on the nags and start back down? It's already getting late and I don't want us going off these cliffs in the dark." He sounded as though he were trying to fill space and avoid the awkwardness between them in the last few minutes.

"No, I'll just gut it out, climb onboard and worry about how sore I'm going to be tomorrow. Right now I feel pretty darn good. The wine and all, I suppose."

"Okay, let's get this stuff put away. Don't forget to tighten your cinch. I loosened them when we stopped." Richard rose to gather their things.

Elaine rose, then stumbled. Richard was right there to catch her as she laughingly said, "My legs are rubber, but I'm fine, really." He released her and she helped pick up and put away everything that had helped make such a delightful day.

She tightened her horse's cinch, put the bridle bit gently in Lulu's mouth, tied her lead rope around the horse's neck and slowly walked her over to a rock to mount. By the time she was done, Richard had his horse turned down the mountain. Elaine picked up her reins and gently nudged Lulu along behind.

As they descended, the sun was setting and the moon and stars hung in the sky. Both being visible at the same time always amazed Elaine as she watched the red and blues surround her. Richard was very quiet; she assumed he was lost somewhere in his own thoughts. It was a comfortable quiet and a good tired, which was often the case after a ride with her friend.

All too soon they arrived at her home. She knew she'd slept a bit on the drive back, but was still shocked when Richard touched her hand, resting between them on the passenger side of the truck cab, in order to wake her. The jet lag had caught up with her. She didn't remember going in the house or lying down; but was still in her smelly clothes when she awoke later. She got up, had a light snack, showered and crawled back in bed to dream of riding bareback. She and the horse flew over green pasture, not even holding on, but laughing and waving joyfully to someone beckoning in the distance.

Monday found Elaine sitting in Captain Pepper's office, waiting for Ivy to finish with another appointment. Elaine used the time to scan her surroundings. Although the administrative offices of the prison weren't in the secured part of the prison, it was still definitely a government facility. The century old stone structure, once a boy's reform school, still carried the name 'Reformatory': a true oxymoron.

The four major prisons that now straddled this mountain held over 5,000 deviants. One prison held the criminally ill, one sexual predators, one was a minimum security, and Elaine's prison was gently named 'the big house'. It was a medium/maximum custody prison housing the worst of the worst, the baddest of the bad.

Elaine thought how sad the nomenclatures were for places that housed thousands of human beings: the poor, misguided, hopeless and disenfranchised from the American dream. Less than one percent were the incorrigibles, the monsters, She'd learned the day of the riot many of these 'incorrigibles' had compassionate sides. Some of these men saved her life. She looked

63

forward to seeing them again when she returned to work inside; and she was determined to thank them profusely.

Elaine looked around and thought, for the hundredth time, a few posters and a fresh coat of paint could do wonders for these walls. Maybe even a few hanging plants. She made a mental note to suggest this to the Captain some day.

Finally a man came out with Pepper. Gray suit, receding hair, and by the way he shook hands and said goodbye to the Captain, probably no sense of humor or personality. Well, in Olympia, those characteristics can get you the job. He was probably very good at his job. He ignored the Captain's secretary so he must be way up on the food chain.

Pepper came over, smiling and nodded to indicate Elaine should come into her office. She quietly gave instructions to Barbara, her secretary, regarding follow-up from the last appointment. Elaine stood and preceded Pepper into the office and sat across from the old wooden desk. Examining Pepper's space for the hundredth time, she decided she actually liked this particular room. It was huge, had vaulted ceilings, an enormous hundred-year-old bookcase and a massive conference table with a dozen old military chairs. Elaine remembered sitting around the desk during various meetings. The seats got awfully hard after an hour or so. Maybe that's why so many officers put on weight after a few years of service, she thought with a smile. The extra padding would certainly make these uncomfortable chairs more bearable.

Chapter 8

"Before Barbara rings and says your time is up," Elaine spoke with a smile, "catch me up so I can get out to my classroom and find out what is going on there."

"You know you're on your own," Pepper responded with a wide toothed grin. "We haven't been able to replace your director. After we did our investigation, he was fired and the college hasn't started looking for someone else yet. None of the secretaries came back, and Paul decided to retire, which shouldn't surprise you. At this point, it's just Richard in the academic part of the school. And he's anxiously awaiting your return. On the vocational side we still have welding, barber shop, printing, and automotive going. So those guys are back. Obviously you need to get yourself a new inmate Teaching Assistant and start doing your own advertising for students in GED."

Pepper stopped to see how Elaine was absorbing so much information

"What do you mean? I need to look for a new TA?" Elaine asked urgently. "Why can't Billy work for me? Did he take another job while I was gone? And I still have my inmate Lifer Literacy tutors, don't I?"

Pepper took a few seconds. "I thought someone would have told you by now," she said. "All the Lifers who were here during the riot have been shipped to other prisons. Billy is awaiting arraignment for the murders of Damien and Officer DeLory. You're telling me no one told you all this?" The Captain sounded incredulous.

Elaine turned pale while she tried to collect herself enough to respond. "Damien is dead? No one told me anything. I knew there were casualties, but I certainly never knew Billy was accused of anything except saving my life. Can you honestly think I would have sat on some stupid beach on some stupid island if I'd been aware of any of this?" She rose from her chair and there was fury in her voice.

"Well, I'm sorry you weren't informed, but you probably see why your friends and family didn't tell you. They didn't want you more upset than you are right now. Calm down!" Pepper ordered.

"Calm down? I will not! Billy didn't kill anyone. And the other Literacy Lifer tutors helped him save my life. How did you and your Intelligence Team decide otherwise? That's what I need to know!"

"Elaine, I'm going to tell you what I told your husband when he almost came after me when we hadn't rescued you with the other hostages: Sit your butt down and shut up or I will not talk to you at all. Do you understand me?"

Elaine sat down, knowing Pepper would hold true on her threat, and needing desperately to know what had happened while she escaped on sleeping pills and antidepressants for months.

"Elaine", Pepper began, "what we know now is preliminary, but there is a strong case against Billy and the other Lifers who were out of bounds that day. They were in an unauthorized area during a lockdown after being directly ordered to return to their cells or report to an officer for count and confinement. They disregarded those orders purposely. Right there was enough to ship them out! In the killings of Officer DeLory and Damien, the S.W.A.T. team says it went down like this:

"Officer DeLory went up to the classrooms without authorization and disappeared out of the sight of the officers in Control Station 7 about 2:27 p.m. We still do not know why he did this. When the S.W.A.T. team went in, they found him, his throat slit, at the west door; the same one Billy brought the food through, having been given it by the officers in Control Station 7.

Billy had to wheel the cart practically over the body to deliver it. "Damien's death is a bit more puzzling. His throat was also slit with the same homemade shank, but the timing for the crime is contested. The S.W.A.T. team says after two of the team members removed you from the danger zone, Billy got away when they were searching and cuffing the other lifers-- and slit Damien's throat before they could subdue him. That would have made it approximately 2:20 p.m. All of this is being investigated, of course, and more will be known before the cases come to trial."

"Has Billy admitted to these murders?" Elaine asked calmly.

"Of course not, and the other Lifers say Damien was alive when all were taken away, including Billy. I hope you aren't saying all twelve members of my top S.W.A.T. team lied."

"Well, someone is and I don't believe it's Billy and the other Lifers, so think what you want Captain," Elaine responded icily.

"You know, Elaine, I'm sorry you haven't had time to digest this information, but the facts are there, and the truth is you are biased; for whatever reason, your life was spared and I'm sure you believe you owe these murderers for sparing it. It may just have been luck my men got there in time, or we would not be having this conversation."

"That's absurd, and to tell you the truth, we aren't going to have more of this conversation. I can see you're going to take the old 'blue line', and to tell you the God's honest truth, it really disappoints me. Those murderers saved my life when no one else did a damn thing to help me, even after I helped you save others. The truth is if Billy hadn't put everything on the line for me, I wouldn't be here, and if you can't see that because he's an incarcerated felon, then you and your so-called Intelligence team aren't looking too hard. And I have to ask myself why? It scares me to think about an answer to that. I will tell you this: I'm not going back inside this prison until I find out who is perpetrating this cover-up and why—even if I'm the next person who dies.

"Something is terribly wrong and you're obviously too close

to see it. I'm going to do whatever I can to clear Billy of this injustice and to help the other Lifers get transferred back here where they're closer to loved ones and have the programs they were working on when you shipped them out, to shut them up."

Elaine got up and walked out. She was so angry, she knew if she kept talking, she would say things to an old friend she would regret. She knew she could get fired for what she'd done, but she didn't care.

She got in her car and sat, trying to absorb the information she'd just heard, trying to plan her next move.

She drove directly to the Everett jail and asked to see Billy. She knew a few people and she also kept her D.O.C. badge on so she was admitted to a lawyer conference room. Elaine knew she was digging a larger hole for herself, as she had no authorization to be doing any of this, but anger compelled her to do so.

After a few minutes, Billy was escorted in, handcuffed and shackled. Elaine hated seeing him like this, but she didn't think she should push her luck by asking the restraints be removed.

Billy didn't appear surprised. He kept a hooded, impassive look in difficult instances. A self defense mechanism, Elaine thought he had every right to, even with her, after this experience.

"I didn't know, Billy," Elaine began. "You believe me, don't you?"

"Sure. It doesn't matter, anyway. I told you when we said goodbye I'd done the one decent thing I've ever done and I didn't care what happened. You think this situation surprises me? I could've told you when I saw Shaw's body lying in the doorway the killing would be pinned on whoever was left standing. I was left standing. What does surprise me is your being here. What's the point?"

"What's the point?! You must think very little of me if you think once I found out you were vilified, instead of receiving a reduced sentence for saving several people's lives, including mine, I wouldn't try to help you."

"Help me? Go home, Elaine. Don't go back in that prison, because whoever did this and is covering it up is still there. Go home, please! Don't get involved. It's not worth it. I'm certainly not."

Before Elaine could reply, the Acting Supervisor, Lieutenant Percy, came in and whispered in her ear he needed to see her. She exited with him while Billy sat, impassive.

"Elaine," he said, "I'm not real happy with you. You aren't supposed to be here. We checked. Captain Pepper was contacted, and she says to give you access to Billy until after the trial. You want to tell me what's going on?"

"I really don't have time right now," Elaine said. "Next visit, okay? But call the captain back and thank her for me."

"Okay. I'll let it go for now, but next visit, make time for me first, or there will be no access to this inmate. Only because I know you, I'm letting this visit continue. You understand me clearly?"

"I do, and thanks. How much time do I have?" Elaine asked as she turned to go.

"Count is in forty minutes. You can have until then. An officer will be outside the door, looking through the window at all times. Just motion if you want out early. He'll come and get the inmate #997543."

Elaine opened the door and went back to sit across from Billy. He sat perfectly still, though his eyes penetrated hers.

"Tell me what happened in the last months to get you thrown in here, accused of murder, and the other Lifers shipped out of state?" Elaine requested in as pleasant a voice as she could muster.

"Sure. You saw them put us flat on our faces, arms outstretched, in order to search and cuff us. Right?"

"Right. And I know Damien was alive when I left."

"He sure was, but after they took you to safety, I apparently jumped up, took a shank out of my pocket, and slit his throat," Billy said in too calm a tone.

Elaine decided she might as well get the biggest elephant out of the room first so she asked. "Did you?"

He looked pained. "Just go home. Please. I had a pinochle game going, and there was a game show on TV in the dayroom. I want to get back to them before lunch."

She knew he was just trying to provoke her, because he knew just how much she hated this common inmate pastime. Billy never indulged.

"Look, if I'm going to help you, I need to know what happened after I left that day."

"I don't want any help, especially yours," Billy responded.

"I guess I'll just have to keep coming back every day and we will sit here until you do. I have Captain Pepper's permission, so if the officers have to drag you out, it will be done. However, it seems like a precious waste of time when they could be playing pinochle and watching game shows."

Billy's expression softened then, until she actually thought he might smile, but he didn't. He changed position in the chair, as though trying to loosen the chains and get as comfortable as he could. Elaine waited patiently for what seemed a great deal of time, though it was probably not more than a few minutes. Finally he began to recite the story he'd played over and over in his head, day and night for over half a year.

"The S.W.A.T. team came in. As the team leader yelled at us to get down and assume the position, two officers ordered to get you the hell out of there. Damien was on his knees where I put him, and I remember several of the S.W.A.T. team rushing him. I couldn't see who was doing what because I was positioned on the floor in such a way that it kept me from seeing Damien or those who went to him. The next thing I knew I'd been frisked, cuffed, yanked up and drug out the door. My buddies experienced the same. We couldn't see behind us, but there were three blue suits around Damien and he did not leave when we did. I was thrown in segregation and left without a soul talking to me for two weeks. Then they popped me in the orange suit, cuffed, shackled me, and threw me on the bus. I've been here ever since.

"Three days after arriving, they sent a public defender who must be all of 25. I could tell immediately she hated 'my kind'. She informed me I was being charged with two counts of murder and told me who the victims were. Told me I should plead guilty so I might not get a life sentence—which is when I knew she didn't know what she was doing—and told me she'd be back before the trial to ask me questions. She left, and I've sat here since thinking how ironic life is. That's enough for now. They just called count, and I'm hungry." Billy rose as he spoke.

Elaine rose also. As she did, the officer came in and took Billy out. Elaine walked back to the front desk to find the name of the public defender for Billy's case.

The front desk officer told her Billy's public defender was named Heather Graves and she could be found in the next building over. Elaine thanked him.

It was a pleasant fall day. Leaves from the large oaks and maples covered the sidewalks and streets. Elaine cherished this season. Spring never seemed like the season of rebirth to her. Autumn did. She couldn't explain it. The air was crisp and clean. Kicking leaves, Elaine thought how upset Richard would be she hadn't come back to work. She expected a serious phone message from him when she got home, but for now she kept shuffling through the leaves to the courthouse.

Heather was in her office, or rather their office, as four public defenders crowded in a room that would have been too small for one profit-minded criminal attorney. They had a receptionist, so when Elaine asked to speak to Heather, she went and got her. Heather looked up from her mountains of paperwork and

71

walked over to greet Elaine with a puzzled expression. In the time it took her to get to Elaine, Elaine had sized her up. She had to agree with Billy. Heather would not do at all. Pretty in a hard sort of way, dressed in a too short, tight black skirt, with a tight jacket over a blouse cut too low to do anything but scream sex instead of confidence to any accused man assigned to her.

But her expression told Elaine she was putting in her time until she could join a moneymaking law firm and get the hell away from defending poor people. She looked bored and arrogant.

Elaine put out her hand and introduced herself. "I've come to find out the status of Billy Robison's case. Could I have a few minutes of your time to discuss it?"

Heather told Elaine she couldn't discuss any case without the defendant's permission.

Elaine showed her the scribbled release of information form she'd had Billy sign before coming. Heather sighed and reluctantly led the way to her desk, then went across the room to find an extra chair.

Elaine waited silently, knowing the curiosity was killing the woman. Elaine determined even though this lawyer had Billy's life in her hands, she didn't have a clue who he was.

They sat until Heather finally spoke and asked Elaine why she was so concerned with this particular case. Disgusted by the fact Heather really didn't know which case they were talking about, Elaine responded, "Well, the man saved my life and I don't think he's guilty."

Heather rose, went to a file cabinet, and pawed through it. She finally gave up and asked the receptionist/filing clerk for Billy's jacket, which Elaine recognized from hiring him as a tutor years before.

These men's lives were in their jackets, their criminal files; the last word on who, what and where their lives played out. How scary knowing one slip of a typist's finger or one report included by a vindictive counselor or officer in that jacket could add years to an inmate's sentence or move him to another location for no reason; or give him a public defender who didn't care about him.

Elaine remained quiet, a trait she had picked up in prison and one she knew gave great distress to others. Heather combed through Billy's file, obviously trying to acquaint herself with the case and figure out how Billy, a convicted murderer accused of two more, could have saved this lady's life. Elaine let her sweat until finally Heather looked up and said, "What is your relationship with this man?"

Elaine thought of just getting up and walking out, not wanting to share any details with Ms. Graves, but knew that was probably not the best move to make. She patiently filled the defender in on her version of what happened during the riot and waited for a reaction.

"Well, this really doesn't change anything. You saw nothing related to the two murders and the only person you're relying on to tell the truth is a convicted murderer. The best I can hope to get for him is murder one with possibility of parole. He's lucky he won't be executed. He killed an officer!"

"Killed an officer. Wow. And that from his supposed defense attorney. Don't worry, Ms. Graves. I'm going to find Billy a good attorney and you won't have to worry about this case anymore," Elaine said, and walked out.

∞

She was waiting for Daniel when he came home a few hours later. He kissed her, put down his briefcase and made himself a drink. Tension was high and Daniel knew something was wrong.

Never the coward, her preoccupied husband turned to Elaine and said, "And how was your day? Weren't you starting classes today?"

"I was thinking about it, but I found out from the Captain

that Billy Robinson was accused of two murders and all the lifers who worked to save us have been shipped out of state. You know something about all this?"

"I knew. But I was not about to shatter the fragile state you were in by telling you and seeing you jump in to save these hardened criminals. You can't do anything, anyway. I was trying to protect you."

"Wrong. You were trying to make it easier to dump me somewhere safe so you wouldn't miss a day's work. For once in your life, admit it."

"Fine. You're right. I never wanted you working in that prison and you know it. We don't need the money, and it makes me angry you would put your life in jeopardy—and even more angry you plan on going back inside and doing it again. You really aren't a very fast learner, Elaine."

"Really? Well, I'm getting faster as we speak. You will be happy to know I'm not going back in."

For a moment Daniel looked relieved, until he saw the set of her jaw and the flash of her eyes. "Instead with all this money you have set aside for me to play tennis, join a country club or bake cookies for the grandchildren, I'm going to pay for the best lawyer for Billy. And with all my free time I'm going to help that lawyer make sure Billy does not do more time for crimes he didn't commit and maybe in the process find out who really killed Damien and Officer DeLory. I'm going to bed now. Please sleep in the guest room, as you have an early flight and I'm really tired."

Elaine went upstairs, shaking a bit, took the hottest shower she could stand, and climbed into bed feeling lonely. She waited, hoping Daniel would come in and say he was sorry and hold her until she fell asleep.

No such luck. Before she dozed off, she heard the guest bedroom door slam shut.

Chapter 9

After a strong cup of coffee around nine the following morning, Elaine began calling judges, senators and others she knew in power to find an excellent criminal defense lawyer. She hadn't told them what she needed one for but by midday her ears were ringing. She assumed everyone contacted was talking about "that little bleeding heart liberal Elaine," and what trouble she had gotten herself into now. She made four phone calls to personal sources she considered the brightest and the best. Each begged off when she told them who they'd be defending and what the charges were. So much for "everyone deserving a fair defense under the law."

From the phone book she finally came up with one impressive name. A criminal defense lawyer, not well known, whom she knew actually cared about his clients. Based on her few encounters at civil rights events, she knew this attorney wasn't opposed to helping the underdog or getting his shirt bloodied. He didn't believe all criminals were monsters. His name was Tony Williams.

Tony Williams was an African American from Fresno, California. He'd seen trouble when he was young, and probably could just as easily be sitting behind bars as defending those who were, except for support and luck along the way to passing the Bar.

He was perfect, and she thought he needed the money and name recognition he'd receive if he won the case. With any luck, he'd also have a private investigator on staff who could get started looking for the real killers right away.

When she called, Tony answered so she set an appointment for two p.m. He didn't ask what she wanted, just made time to see her. She liked that.

Since she had a few hours to kill, Elaine called Richard. "It's Elaine. Can you talk or do you want me to call you back?"

The pause seemed interminable before his perturbed voice said, "No, I'm on my lunch break. Elaine. What in the world are you up to?"

"Billy didn't kill anyone. He saved our lives, and I intend to prove it. I can't do that if I'm teaching in the prison eight hours a day. I'm sorry, I know this puts you in a bind, but I don't see I have a choice."

Always logical, Richard queried, "And just why do you think he's innocent, Elaine?"

"I know you think an emotion is not nearly enough to hang my hat on, but I will get more. What else can I say, except I still want to go riding, unless you're too angry and won't take me."

"You know darn well I don't mix work with pleasure. I can't say I support what you're doing, and I hate to see you exhaust your energies this way, but I'll pick you up on Sunday at seven a.m. if you want to ride."

"Thanks, Richard. I'll be ready, and I promise not to speak a word about what I'm doing."

"Then you've got a deal. I've got to go. See you Sunday." Richard hung up without a goodbye.

Elaine was actually pleased. She'd thought he'd be angrier, and the fun of another trail ride a real long shot. Feeling better now, she grabbed her keys and purse. The conversation had lasted longer than she'd thought, and she needed to hurry to get to Tony Williams' office on time.

She found the corner of Elm and 13th without much trouble, even though she wasn't terribly familiar with Everett. She stayed pretty much out of the cities, except for Monroe where the prisons were, and Seattle, emerald jewel of Washington, where she dined, shopped, went to the theatre, and hunted for antiques.

Looking at the old house, its law office shingle hung outside on a post, Elaine assured herself Daniel could certainly afford *this* guy, having informed her busy husband this investigation was going to be added to his bill. In the past few days their phone calls consisted of pleasantries. They simply avoided the subject of Billy. Which wasn't difficult. After all, avoidance was one of Daniel's strong suits.

She liked the feel of Tony's building as she walked through the fallen oak leaves, past a rickety gate, and knocked on a door that matched the age of the house, a hundred years at least. Williams answered the door. He might have been 5'8", was in excellent shape and his eyes, set in the fine structure of a deep ebony face, were sharp as tacks, seeing everything, but not moving much while doing so.

This man's manners were, Elaine noted, from the Old South: part charming, though a bit sardonic. Elaine shook his hand, and he led the way, almost bowing, toward a table in the kitchen which probably served for eating as well as meeting clients.

Once seated, he sat down and, using her own tactic, simply sat and waited for her to talk. Realizing she had met her match in that department, Elaine launched into a detailed account of the riot, her vacation and what she found upon return. She wanted to hire him to represent Billy and the lifers who'd been transferred unjustly, and she wanted to begin right away. "I'll be glad to pay for a private investigator and any other professionals you think we'll need."

Mr. Williams thought about it for a few minutes without saying anything. Then he said he wanted to use a private investigator he trusted –one he always worked with. He stood, left the room, and returned wearing a jaunty tweed hat that suited him quite well.

"Now I'm a private investigator. Elaine, I am all things to my clients. You need to know that up front. I have no help and am not sure I would hire additional help if I had the money. I like and trust my own work. I even type!"

Once she was done laughing (the best medicine she'd been given in over six months), Elaine reached over and shook Tony's hand. "You definitely have a deal. The only condition is you allow me to play an active role, okay?"

"Don't get in my way. Don't second-guess me, and don't do anything without clearing it with me first, and we have a deal. Strike out on your own, and I'm off the case. My blood pressure is good for a middle-aged black man and I like to keep it that way."

They spent the next four hours going over the case, with Tony asking copious questions. Elaine didn't understand the relevance of some questions, but she was impressed enough not to ask. Finally, around six p.m., having had nothing to sustain them but coffee, Tony said he had enough material for now, but would like to see Elaine bright and early Monday, to continue the discussion.

"Thank you, Mr. Williams. I will be here by eight. Are we going to go see Billy Monday? Should I call and make an appointment? When can we get that Heather Graves out of the picture? Do you think I should start talking to some of the people who were inside that day? Do we have a good case? Shall I start making a list of all the lifers shipped out because of this? Is there anything I can work on tonight that might help things along? May I call you Tony?"

Williams stared at her while she was talking and for a full minute after she'd finished. She could feel color rushing to her cheeks which gave her ample time to realize her mistake. But four hours suppressing all those questions was simply too long for Elaine.

"Goodbye, Elaine. Go do something unrelated to this case until we talk next. I mean that, sincerely." As he spoke, they were moving toward the door, and Elaine suddenly found herself outside it, standing on the chipped cement porch as Mr. Williams gently closed the door in her face.

Elaine walked down the aged steps, out the gate and drove away. She didn't know where to go, finally deciding on her daughter's house. She knew Theresa would be home, since it was a school day and she had children to take care of. Besides, hugs were definitely something Elaine could use, and she always got an ample amount from the little ones.

Her daughter seemed surprised and a little worried seeing her this time of day, but they hugged and went into the family room where the grandchildren were relaxing after finishing their dinner. They ran to hug and greet her. Elaine sat on the floor with the dog, the children, and all their homework papers, as they all talked at once. Theresa made tea. Elaine concentrated on nothing but how blessed she felt to be part of such a great family, even forgiving Daniel somewhat, since he had helped make it.

All good things must come to an end. And even though Theresa let her give the children baths, help with their school work and read to them before bedtime, by eight o'clock Elaine was exhausted and returned downstairs to say goodbye.

By this time Theresa's husband came home. They exchanged pleasantries and Elaine left, sensing they thought Mom had probably "lost it," but given their own concerns, didn't really need to know about it. She got two more hugs and "love yous," which they never parted without saying, and went out to her car, still trying not to think about the case.

At home, she spent two more hours cleaning up her old saddle and tack, thankful she'd something to look forward to. Finally, around eleven, after a light supper and a soak in the hot tub, she crawled into bed, hoping to sleep without dreams.

Her prayers were answered and Elaine woke refreshed and "eager to greet the day," as Richard always proclaimed each morning of a week long trail ride. Monday, she made her way to Tony's where she found the door of his office ajar. He was slumped over papers at the same table where they had worked two days prior. At first she thought something bad had happened, but as she surveyed the scene from the open doorway, she heard snoring and saw his chest rise and fall rhythmically. He'd apparently worked all night. Now she was sure she'd found the right person to get Billy out of this mess.

She let herself in and after banging a few pots, juggled a few cups and waited patiently for the coffee to finish brewing. Apparently unconcerned at her presence in his house, Tony got up, stretched, said good morning. Then wandered off to the bathroom. He reentered about ten minutes later looking as he had the day before, except clean-shaven and wearing fresh clothes.

Elaine hid her nervousness by reading his notes. She was pleased the notes dealt with Billy's case. Which probably meant he didn't have any other cases, which she really didn't want to think at the moment. They took their seats, and Tony began questioning her, or rather interrogating her well into the morning. He then asked Elaine to call the jail and see when they could meet with Billy and his public defender.

Billy, not surprisingly, was available, as there was next to nothing for prisoners to do in jail, even though those kept for years could have been attending school. Heather agreed to meet them at one p.m., so in the meantime Elaine invited Mr. Williams to lunch. Nearly starved herself, she was getting a bit light-headed.

Tony suggested walking to lunch and then the jail. Elaine thought this an excellent idea; every muscle in her body was crying out for exercise. Until she stood up, she hadn't realized how cramped she felt, sitting straight and still like a schoolgirl hoping to impress the teacher with her focused attention span.

Mr. Williams was worth the effort she decided. His questions seemed random, but once analyzed, they tied themselves into a picture of what he was examining most specifically. He gleaned information of that awful day she hadn't remembered. He was good, and Elaine felt better and better.

He grabbed his briefcase, she got her purse, and they walked the two blocks to a little café called Morning Do. Tony was obviously a regular; several folks greeted him and the owner/ waiter brought him black coffee before they sat down.

"Hey, Mouthpiece," the waiter said, as Elaine and Tony arranged themselves and their belongings at an old country table that looked like it had been used in a slaughterhouse in earlier days. "How's it hanging?"

"Fine," Tony mumbled. "I'll have my usual. The lady probably needs a menu."

They ate then walked a few more blocks to the jail. Again, people seemed to know and like attorney Williams. They were ushered into the same stark room where Elaine previously met with Billy.

He wore the same disinterested, bored expression as Elaine introduced him to his new lawyer. They shook hands and everyone sat down.

Tony busied himself getting things from his briefcase while Elaine asked Billy if he was being treated all right. Both men looked up, and Elaine felt some bonding male allegiance. She decided to be quiet.

Mr. Williams began, asking Billy to again detail every moment of that fateful day. Elaine could tell as the clock ticked on, he was impressed with Mr. Williams' insightful questions. He sat up straighter, became more animated.

Heather stopped by, almost an hour late, handed over Billy's case file and left. She'd done no work on it.

Finally, with count only minutes away, Tony told Billy he would come back tomorrow and asked him to remember anything, no matter how insignificant, he might have overlooked.

When they left the courthouse Tony said goodbye at Elaine's car. Finally as an afterthought attorney Williams gave Elaine permission to call him by his first name. Feeling dismissed, she

81

drove away, determined to find out where the other lifers who had helped her had been sent. It wasn't hard. Having friends with access to such information on OBITS, the Offender Based Inmate Tracking System, made it a speedy exercise. Since she still had energy and time, and wasn't expected anywhere, it seemed a good idea to burn one more man-made bridge and visit the family of one of the inmates sent away because of her.

She'd known Shawn Brayson since she first started working at the prison. He was doing life for his part in killing a gas station attendant. He had already served over twenty years which was a typical life sentence in Washington. At the two-decade mark, if an inmate showed reform through programming, he'd be allowed to start a two-to-five-year progress toward release, go to a less secure prison and be given a job outside the walls. He would get more attention from counselors in order to have an approved place to go and a job upon his release.

D.O.C. had done none of this for Shawn, even though he was convicted for assault, not murder one. The sentence indicated Shawn's partner did the killing, even though his own actions led an innocent person to lose his life.

But his was a special case. In Washington prisons an inmate is allowed to marry and have conjugal visits, which Shawn had done. He and his wife, a former guard, had produced two children. His delayed release probably was due to marrying a guard, a powerful reason to 'slow walk' help for him in D.O.C.'s way of thinking.

Elaine thought Shawn deserved parole, and had felt that way for years. He'd received an education, completed a lot of community service and been an exemplary inmate for two decades. The educational staff felt him parole-able; he was one she particularly worried about becoming despondent.

Elaine knew his wife and little boys from the family events at the prison. His wife was a nice woman who was raising well-mannered children. At least that's what it looked like to someone not personally involved. And Shawn lived for them, for when he would be released so he could become a 'real' Dad.

With full knowledge that as an employee of D.O.C. she was to have no contact with felons or their families, Elaine went to Janet Brayson's home. If she ran into an ex-felon she was to report the occurrence (something no one actually did). However, she rationalized her contact by saying it was actually a professional visit—which was really begging the truth, but it made her feel better as she approached the house and knocked on the front door.

"Janet? Hello, it's Elaine Bennett. I know Shawn from the reformatory. Do you remember me?" Elaine stood on the steps of a dilapidated house in need of a man's touch.

"Yes, I remember you. You're a teacher. What do you want?" Janet asked in a suspicious voice as she peered out from behind the locked screen door.

"I need to talk with you about Shawn being transferred. I didn't know about it and now I do, I want to help get him back. May I come in, please?"

Janet unlocked the screen door and swung it open so Elaine could precede her into the small, but very neat living room. Elaine assumed the boys were in school this time of day, or possibly after-school sports, as both were fine athletes. Shawn never ceased bragging about their prowess. "I don't need much of your time," Elaine went on, "but I need to know what Shawn told you about the day of the riot. I've hired a lawyer to clean up this mess and see the real murderers of the officer and Damien caught."

"I can't believe this is happening to us," Janet said. Her movements betrayed her stress. Although she had invited Elaine to sit, she wandered from chair to chair, picking up toys, flattening pillows. "He tried to help you and the others he respected, and now look what's happened! He was supposed to be out in five years this Christmas, and now he says they have revoked his parole status. Do you have any idea what that means? Under the old SRA guidelines they can keep him forever, and we are both afraid the parole board will."

She paused to offer Elaine something to drink, then resumed her pacing and monologue, which Elaine was reluctant to interrupt. Elaine could tell she needed to talk and felt the least she could do was listen.

"He's in Walla Walla now, a place he said he'd rather die than go back to. You know how it is there, Elaine. The Reformatory was bad enough, but in Walla Walla he has to fight just to stay alive. The one time I've been able to visit I was glad I didn't take the kids. He had a black eye and a split lip. You know he's not a fighter, but he has no choice. All the computer skills he has and they won't let him near one. He has to pick up garbage from the grounds, just like he did when he first was incarcerated 20 years ago. I don't know what to tell our sons. They know their father did a terrible crime and had to be punished. But they have also been taught forgiveness, and they can't figure out where that comes in," she said sadly.

"I tell them he helped other people, and how that was a good thing, so they think their dad should be rewarded, not punished further. They're angrier than I've ever seen them. Their grades have dropped and Joey got in a fight last week. I moved here to be near Shawn. I left family and friends. I never regretted my decision because I knew he changed and deserves another chance, and because I love him. But I don't know if I can keep going, and I don't know what else to do. I have no friends. My family disowned me years ago."

Janet seemed to be winding down, and Elaine felt the children might be coming home any minute. The best thing would be to get her calm enough to greet them.

Elaine went over, gave her a hug. To her great relief Janet returned it. She cried and cried and held on. Then she straightened up, went to the bathroom. When she returned she was very calm.

"Look," Elaine said, "I know you need to get ready for your

boys to come home."

"Yes, a neighbor is bringing them in a few minutes."

"I'm going to leave, but before I do, I need you to understand I'm going to help straighten this injustice out. Okay? But I need you to help me. Can you do that?"

"Yes, anything. What can I do?"

"Shawn calls every night, right?"

"Yes," his wife said, eyes wide and brimming with an expectation Elaine hoped she'd deliver on.

"You must tell him to write exactly what he remembers of that day, even if he stays up all night. Where everyone was, who did what, what he was doing at all times. Then he needs to send it to you immediately. And tell him to use all his stamps, if he has to, so it gets here faster. You can tell him it's for me, but have him send it to you. Then call me as soon as it gets here. Also tell him to get Attorney Tony Williams and me on his visiting list ASAP. Can you do all that?"

"Yes, but you know they'll be listening to our call and checking his mail."

"We don't care. We're not asking him to do anything wrong, so by law they shouldn't confiscate or stop any communication. If they try, we'll fight when and if it occurs. I'm going to go before the boys get home. Do you need anything? I know you counted on Shawn's 48 cents an hour paycheck. Are you okay for money?"

"We're fine for now. The holidays might be skimpy, but we've been there before. I can always get help from Matthew House if we really need it."

Elaine gave her one more hug, her phone number, said goodbye. She made a mental note to put Janet and the children on her Christmas list. She caught herself remembering she wasn't supposed to give gifts to inmates or their families, and then crossed another 'sin' off her guilt list. It was always easy to give to strangers, she thought, but this year was going to be personal. It might actually feel more real.

It was 4:00 p.m. when she drove away. Realizing she was starving, she decided to frequent a small Mexican restaurant called Ixtapas. It was special and so were the people who ran it. This immigrant family had come from Ixtapa, Mexico, and had started one small restaurant with family fifteen years ago. Elaine had seen them work to make it a success, and now they brought more family over and had a chain of restaurants serving good authentic food, reasonably priced and served by friendly, courteous people.

This was her turf now and she was greeted like a favorite guest. Over dinner and a nice glass of Merlot she mentally recounted efforts thus far and assessed what still needed to be done. By the time she got home, Daniel was watching TV and she joined him. They got in the hot tub, then got ready for bed, talking only about trivial things. They slept together companionably. It was a start, she supposed, though of what she was not really sure.

By the end of the week, Elaine was exhausted trying to keep up with Tony. She thought she had energy, but this man wore her down. Mornings were spent working on the case. Afternoons were spent with Billy, preparing his testimony or following leads that might help. D.O.C. parts were the hardest. No one wanted to give information or access to it. Pepper had informed Elaine by phone the lawyers said she couldn't talk with her anymore. Her colleagues weren't returning phone calls, either, and the college had placed her on leave.

By Saturday night she was looking forward to another trail ride. Daniel had left the country and she had finished her weekly calls with her daughter and son. She got her gear and a lunch together (including a flask of dandelion brandy, as the weather had turned quite chilly), and thought about calling Richard to confirm. Elaine decided against it, thinking if he wasn't riding (which wouldn't be like him) or didn't want her along (he had ample reason not to) he wouldn't have to tell her on the phone. She would simply get up early tomorrow morning, be ready, and wait to see.

Chapter 10

Richard was there promptly at seven, Elaine waiting on the front porch. She threw her tack in the trailer and joined him, a mug of hot coffee in her hand. She saw his own cup steaming away in the cup holder. Off they went.

"Where are we going to ride today?" she ventured, not really caring, just wanting to hear another voice.

"I thought we would go up to Pilchuck and ride the Glass Works. I had a rather hard week and don't feel like driving over the pass. Okay with you?"

"Absolutely. I'm just glad to be going. What horse am I riding today? I didn't look."

"The same old nag you had last week. I don't think you can handle anything more since you aren't putting much energy or time into riding."

"Ouch. Go ahead and say what you want, but I promised I wouldn't talk shop, either your work or mine, and I won't unless you initiate it."

"Not right now. I just want to have a good ride, exercise my horses and enjoy the day."

"Sounds good. I brought some brandy to take the edge off. Do you want some?"

With the first smiles of the morning in place, they sat back and enjoyed the drive to Arlington, parked the trailer, tacked up the horses, and began a ride Elaine always enjoyed.

Pilchuck School grounds are certainly not like the prison grounds. Pilchuck is a glassblowing camp. Elaine liked seeing it every time they rode there, and always told herself someday she'd spend a summer as a student. Elaine thought the founder was the famous glassblower, Dale Chihuly. The campus sat on about fifty wooded acres and was dotted by little tree houses. Students built them to live in during the summer while they attended classes. Some were one story, some two. The first time Elaine rode these grounds, years ago when she had her own horse, Richard neglected to tell her about the school. As she rode through what she thought was land graced with dense cedars, pines and elder trees, she began to see fairylike dwellings built right up in the big old cedar trees. A fanciful sight, up one hill, down the next, tree house after tree house coming into view, as though by magic. Elaine thought fleetingly she'd arrived in a real fairyland. The students decorated the homes with bits of blown glass. The dwellings hosted glass chimes tinkling from open doorways and windows. Pieces shimmered in open windows and on handmade tables. Glass bottles were set on stumps. Glass kites swung from trees.

Since they usually rode Pilchuck in late fall and early winter, when it was too wet and cold to ride high country and the school was closed, all the little homes were deserted. The sounds were those of forest, glass, and horses. Riders never broke the silence with idle chatter when they rode this seemingly holy place. Each time Elaine came, she rode with anticipation of seeing what new and different glass works graced the woods. Sometimes a statue made from glass sat on an old fence post. There were globes of red, green, blue, yellow, purple shining in dense forest areas. Truly a special place, she loved it. Just being here healed her bruised soul.

Elaine abruptly stopped her reverie when she almost lost her seat. The two horses reached a large grassy meadow, where riders let their horses run free. Depending on his mood, Richard sometimes gave riders a head's up before putting his horse into a canter. Sometimes there would be no warning.

The horses surged forward and Elaine felt her neck strained

back, her legs come up to the horse's neck, and then she experienced the surge of a thousand pounds of equine muscle plunging ahead while her horse tried to catch the other galloping horse. She decided to pay attention.

Planting legs firmly into the running horse, she pulled gently back on the reins, and regained a modicum of control, or as Richard was wont to say, she "stopped being a passenger and became a rider." It was glorious—to take the tension, stress, and worry out of one's mind, a full gallop on a good horse was the only way to go. One had to free the mind to stay in control of a beast ten times your weight. Physically you made every muscle work with the horse.

Elaine never wanted to stop, but seeing thick forest ahead, she knew she had to. Richard worked his horse back to a trot, then a walk, and then to a halt. She did the same with her horse. They reached the end of the clearing in unison, and as the horses stood blowing, settled in to savor the crisp air, the warmth of the horses, the companionship that always followed such exertion.

"I'll take a little brandy in my coffee if you have it," Richard said.

"I will too." Elaine reached back, unzipped her fanny pack and drew out the leather flask. Richard poured coffee into the lid of his thermos and Elaine added a healthy jigger of brandy. They took turns sipping until the cup was empty. Well, almost: Richard always gave a bit to the gods for taking good care of the riders and their trusty steeds.

He recapped the thermos, picked up the reins and moved the horses out. For the next hour or so, they rode at a steady pace through dense woods until they came out onto the Pilchuck school grounds.

The main building was impressive. Grand in scale, and almost every wall glass. Looking inside, a visitor could see the workings of glassblowing and imagine the artists creating magnificent vases, chandeliers, windows and artworks; pieces of which were sometimes there, resting quietly like treasure under the sea.

Someday Elaine would make something beautiful also. Now she wasn't working, why not?

Past the main building was a lovely lake with mossy banks, a deck, and swans. Amazingly, these delicate creatures floated and bobbed atop the water. Elaine had no idea how they stayed alive during the winter, but they were always there, seemingly unconcerned and stately in their graceful presence. She hated leaving this area, but accepted another hour of climbing before lunch.

Elaine kicked her horse, as she had once again been dawdling. She caught up to Richard's horse as they started up a narrow trail to the top of Mount Pilchuck.

"What a view."

As many times as she'd seen it, Elaine still relished reaching the top. "You can see three hundred and sixty degrees, and every direction holds something more beautiful than the last."

"Yup," was all she got as a response. Richard was off his horse, loosening his cinch and taking his pack down before Elaine finished gawking. She didn't care. She sat there, taking it all in. Finally following suit, she spread her long oil duster on the ground and began to set out her food. She noticed Richard was again indulging in a bit of the whiskey. She didn't mind at all. In fact, she was happy to contribute something to the day. She gave Richard gas money, but sometimes wished she'd more to offer. He, however, was independent, and didn't seem bothered by his guest most of the time. "I would be here anyway," he always told her.

After Richard finished eating, he stood up to stretch. He sipped his drink and watched three deer halfway down the northern side. Elaine watched with him as she ate, drank, and enjoyed the warmth of a lukewarm sun. Finally Richard looked at his watch and quickly ended their recess. They remounted their horses and started down the mountain at a pretty good clip.

Elaine never argued, even if she felt justified, when on

horseback in country. She was a novice and what they did could be dangerous. She followed and was happy to do so, even though her butt and back were protesting as the miles blew by.

Finally they reached the rig and climbed off. Richard had been wise: The sky was darkening. It was only about five p.m. He hadn't worried about darkness overtaking them, but rather thunder, lightning, and rain. Quickly untacking, they blanketed the sweaty horses, got them in the horse trailer and jumped in the truck, beating the downpour by seconds.

Comfortably ensconced inside the cab, Richard asked, "If you have any brandy left, I could stand a little more."

Elaine poured, but with some foreboding. He never drank and drove. What they had consumed on the trail, they had worked off hours ago. So if he drank now, it was because he didn't plan on driving for a while. Which meant he wanted to talk to her.

She was right.

"Elaine, I want to know what you are up to and why you aren't coming back to work. I have heard all kinds of rumors, some I'm not happy about. I figure I'd better ask you straight up."

"I have to—"

Before Elaine could continue, they heard rapping on the driver's window and almost immediately one on Elaine's side. She jumped. Richard reached under his seat for the pistol he kept there. He knew whoever was outside couldn't see in very well, so he slid the gun under his coat lying across the seat.

Elaine made no move. She'd seen him pull the gun once before in the high country when hunters approached camp. They'd been menacing-looking mule types, but after seeing the gun, had chosen to keep moving. From her training Elaine knew when the hair on the back of your neck goes up, and it was up now, you should pay attention to your senses. Her senses told her whoever was outside the truck meant them harm.

Slowly Richard cracked his window. "Hey, Ed. What are you doing and who's that over on Elaine's side of the truck?"

Ed crossed his arms over the wet window frame. "Hell, that's just Larry. He thought he'd say hi to Elaine. We saw two horses' rumps in the back of the trailer and knew you guys usually ride together. Hi, Elaine. Good to see you again."

"Hi, Ed," Elaine said, trying to get her heart out of her throat as she too rolled down her window. Ed was a Gate 7 officer from the prison.

While Elaine spoke to Larry, Richard slowly withdrew his hand from under his slicker, as he watched Ed smile and peer inside the truck. "Yeah, we're just out looking for a good place to hunt deer when we saw your rig. You know the season opens next week."

"I don't think I'm going until my sons can join me. We'll probably go east of the mountains for a few days," Richard answered.

Larry reached through Elaine's window and rubbed her shoulder, pulling her toward him in what Elaine supposed was an attempted hug. "Damn, Elaine, we sure are sorry about what happened to you guys, and we're sure glad to see you again. When you coming back? The students miss you. All they have to look at is this old cowboy, and he's purdy ugly."

Withdrawing from Larry's embrace as best she could, Elaine said, "I really don't know." She'd never liked either officer, and wasn't going to say more than she had to.

"Hey, we miss you. But, you know, we've been hearing some ugly rumors 'bout how you're trying to get that bastard Billy Robison out from under killing our friend and a guy who always looked after your cute little ass."

This bit of unwelcome news came in a hostile voice from Ed.

Richard sat up straight and turned the ignition; the truck engine sprang to life (something this twenty-year-old truck didn't always do)

"Okay, guys. Wish I could have a beer with you," Richard

said nodding towards the bottles each held in their hands, "but my ponies are getting cold and you know how I feel about my ponies. I'll catch you tomorrow."

The men had no choice but to back up if they didn't want their muddy boots run over, which allowed Richard and Elaine time to roll up windows and move onto the main highway and away from what felt like a very dangerous situation.

"So, is that what you wanted to talk with me about?" Elaine asked, as she finished her brandy and the rest of Richard's.

"Yup, but not anymore. I need to do more thinking on the subject. I'll just drop you off, take care of the horses, and get myself some dinner," Richard replied in a voice Elaine knew meant the subject was closed.

When she got in her house and out of her wet things, she sat and thought about what had just happened and what it might mean. Finally, she decided to call Tony and get his opinion.

He answered on the first ring. "Williams & Williams Law Firm. May I help you?"

"The first thing you can do is tell me why the name of your firm is Williams & Williams. You're it, right?" Elaine asked.

"I wondered how long it would take you. Yes, I'm it. The other Williams is in honor of my father. He was a sharecropper and sacrificed a lot for me. So this is how I remember him."

"That's really nice, Tony. Really nice. Listen, do you have a minute?"

"Sure. What's up?"

"Well, maybe it's nothing, but I went riding today with my friend Richard. I think he wanted to talk about the case, but before he could, two rather nasty guards interrupted us and I think threatened me. Then Richard wouldn't talk about it anymore. It was rather strange."

"What I want you to do is to write down exactly what occurred. You know by now how detailed I want it, don't you?"

"Yes, but don't you want to hear about it now?" Elaine needed someone to vent to, but it wasn't going to be Tony.

"Tomorrow's soon enough, but write it out as you would an incident report in the prison. You understand?"

"Yes, I've got it. Thanks for listening. I'll see you tomorrow."

There was silence, as Tony seemed to be thinking, but without further ado he hung up and Elaine got to work.

The following day dawned bright and clear, one of those pristine fall days that smacked of pumpkins and apple cider. Elaine wondered as she dressed how her grandchildren were doing and thought about taking them to a pumpkin patch and corn maze over the weekend. Life, for her, was too serious lately. She vowed to balance it with happier events.

She called her daughter and made plans to keep the children the next Saturday. Maybe she couldn't enroll in Glassblowing School, but she could make time for a day of being a grandmother.

Assured of at least one nice thing to look forward to, she checked her date book for Monday and, seeing nothing, decided to go to Tony's office early.

Lawyer Williams was where he always was, even though he couldn't have expected her so soon. Dressed and seated at his desk/kitchen table, coffee in hand, poring over reams of paper. "Good morning," she chirped, "did you have a good weekend?"

"Fine. Let's see the report."

So much for finding out what Tony did when she wasn't there, she thought, as she dug the typed memo out of her briefcase and handed it to him. He read as she helped herself to fresh coffee and sat down to wait.

"I need you to take Shawn's wife up to Walla Walla to see him one day this week," he said abruptly. "She gets Wednesdays off, and her neighbor has offered to take care of the boys while she's gone. It will be a long day, but it's important. I've already made visiting arrangements for the two of you. You will get two hours in the afternoon. I'd go myself, but I have an arraignment that day and can't reschedule."

Interesting, Elaine thought. She's actually learning something about him: he had at least one other case. But when had he talked to Janet? He didn't know they'd been in touch. With a sigh, she decided there was a lot she didn't know and wasn't going to as long as Tony was her lawyer of choice. And he was, so there it was.

"Sure, Wednesday's fine. It's not like I have a life, or a job anymore. I'm free as a bird. I'll call her and make arrangements. So far she hasn't gotten me a written statement about what happened that day from Shawn."

"That's the primary reason you're going," Tony snapped. "D.O.C. stopped the letter. They said that by writing it he was trying to incite a riot, so they wouldn't release it."

"What a joke!" Elaine exclaimed. "Nothing would surprise me anymore. This cover-up is amazing, I don't care what anyone says. That's what it must be, especially after what those jerks said yesterday."

"Don't know yet. I need to study it more. I'll let you know. I do think you need to watch your back from now on. I'm not trying to scare you, but obviously you've upset some people who carry guns."

Elaine caught her breath. "You don't think someone's going to hurt me, do you?"

"Elaine, get real. You're claiming a convicted murderer is innocent and going to great lengths to prove it. If he didn't do it, who did? You must have thought about this problem. Why was there a shank next to the dead officer's body? Who was closest to Damien when his throat was cut? You need to stop concentrating on just the facts, ma'am. This isn't some stupid *Dragnet* show. Look down the road at implications you must draw if you seriously want to free Billy!"

Elaine said nothing. Tony got up to get more coffee, then looked at her ashen face. "Let's get some breakfast."

They walked to the restaurant, and by the time they got there, Elaine had thought of things she could reasonably converse about over eggs and ham. "I'm really in over my head, aren't I?" Elaine asked quietly.

"You may well be. Now is the time to cut and run if you want to. No one will think less of you. I don't think you can go back and work in the prison, at least that place, but you can resume your life as you knew it and work somewhere else. To tell you the truth, that's what I think you should do."

Elaine looked at Tony and considered what he was saying. She was as scared as she'd been facing Damien in that hot, smelly prison classroom. She didn't like the feeling, and momentarily thought of Dr. Duncan, who'd be most willing to give her something to calm her. A glass of wine or a few shots of brandy didn't sound bad either.

"No. I can't pretend I don't owe those men, especially Billy, for saving my life. I'll be careful. Maybe I'll get the big dog I've been wanting. Who knows, maybe I'll get a gun. Everyone else seems to have them." Elaine laughed, trying to lighten her mood and Tony's so they'd get back on task.

"Look, Elaine. I'm not playing around here. You've pissed off some not-so-nice people and they aren't going to look the other way when we start to point fingers. This could get dangerous. It may already be. I will stay with the case. They are not going to deter me. You pay me and I'll keep you posted by email and phone as to my progress; but I think you might want to back off. I can lend Shawn's wife my car and she can go up to see him alone. You don't really need to be visible. In fact, the more I think about it, the more I like the idea."

"No, I'm taking her, and I'm coming down here every day. I'm going to testify and be in that courtroom and I don't want to talk about this anymore. I'm done eating."

She hadn't touched a thing.

"Okay, but let me know if you change your mind."

The walk back to Williams & Williams was a long one, and once there, Elaine begged off further work, saying she had some things to take care of and would be back after lunch.

She drove to Edmonds and sat looking at the water trying to decide whether to get on the ferry or not. She didn't really have time, but a boat ride might be exactly what she needed. The Edmonds ferry dock wasn't crowded so she decided to ride over and back. She could always call Tony if she was going to be late.

She drove on, parked and walked to the side of the deck. Facing the islands she noticed the day was turning out to be mild and the sun was bright. Fog had burned off, except for what was called tulle fog, which lay low and mysterious over the water. Perfect for this ominous Halloween season.

Elaine realized she wasn't quite so sure of herself and the direction of her life as she'd led Tony to believe. She also knew if she continued fighting for what she believed was right, she was going to make some unpleasant changes in the way she lived. She wasn't selfish enough to put her grandchildren in danger, so the Saturday excursion at the pumpkin patch would be cancelled. No more trail rides, as Richard was obviously being harassed at work, she realized belatedly. She would get a big, well-trained guard dog. The gun idea seemed too farfetched to contemplate seriously, but she wouldn't disregard the idea completely.

Should she tell Daniel about all this, or leave him in the dark? That she would have to ponder, but she had time, as he was not expected home until Friday.

The ferry ride calmed her. She was ready to continue her original plan to right this injustice perpetrated on Billy and the others.

With her goal firmly in mind, Elaine drove back to her lawyer's office. She walked in, took a seat across from Tony and began reading what he tossed across the table. They ate again and went to see Billy. She was home by five o'clock, planning to call kennels and pick up a trained dog that day.

When she reached the garage she was surprised to see Daniel's car. The engine was still warm so she knew he hadn't beaten her home by much, but she was still curious why he would be there at all.

Chapter 11

"Daniel?" she called out. "Hello? What are you doing home? Did your story peter out? Where are you?"

"In here," came a stern voice from the living room.

"Is something wrong?" Elaine inquired, going to pour herself a large glass of something red.

"Richard called yesterday, Elaine. He got my number from the office and filled me in on how he thinks you may be in danger trying to save this convicted murderer, Billy. He thought I should know, in case I had any influence on you, and could get you to give up this insane quest. I flew home in the middle of a very important meeting to try, although as I told him, I think you'd listen to him sooner than me."

"Look, I appreciate your taking time from your busy schedule, but I don't see this as a major issue. I'm going to get a big dog, I'd been planning on doing that anyway, since I'm alone so much of the time. But that has nothing to do with Billy. In fact, I don't appreciate Richard going behind my back. Also, in case you and Richard forgot, that convicted murderer saved his and my life. Or doesn't that mean anything in the scheme of things?"

"Of course it does but Richard is a good friend to you, Elaine. You should listen to him about this if you won't listen to me."

"He never bothered to talk about this with me. But I plan to talk with him very soon about calling you as though I'm some witless child!"

"So nothing I say is going to stop you from proceeding with this?" Daniel asked.

"No. In case you and your friend Richard haven't thought

about it, the pressure being put on me indicates Billy is innocent and a cover-up is occurring."

"Elaine, no one is happier than me that Billy and the others put their lives on the line for you. But let's face it, those guys have done enough bad things. That's why they're in prison. Some of them should probably live out their lives in prison. Why not just call it a good deed and let it go?" Daniel's voice was rising to a level Elaine didn't like.

"I can't do that," she said in a quiet voice, hoping to defuse his rising anger. "Believe me, just this morning I wished I could. Yes, these men did terrible things and they're being punished for their crimes. But to let them be punished for doing good, when it was done to save my life, is not something I can live with. I simply couldn't look at myself in the mirror if I did. Why can't you understand that?"

"Because I can't. Even your good buddy, who's spent thirty years with these gangsters, can't. Elaine, look. I'm flying back tonight. I'm behind on the story as it is, because I came home to try to talk some sense into you. But I'm begging you. Please let this go! We almost lost you six months ago. Don't make us go through that kind of worry again. It's not fair to your family or me."

As he said this, Daniel poured himself and Elaine another glass of wine and approached so that all six feet of him towered over her intensely.

"Let me ask *you* a question. If this were a story you were involved with, would you quit because you might be in danger?" Elaine craned her neck to speak up at him.

"Damn, that's not fair!"

"Yes, it is. Every time you go on a story, I worry. I'm sure the children do too, but we never try to stop you, because we know stories are a part of who you are. Well, this case is a part of who I am, and I'd like, just once, your support. If I can't get it, I will continue anyway, because it is a part of who I am. You're just going to have to live with that."

"Fine. Then I'm out of here. You do what you want, but don't be surprised if I'm not around much. Call if you need something, but I don't want to watch you get hurt, or worse, over a bunch of convicted criminals. You won't win this case, Elaine. There is not a chance in hell. From what Richard told me, you are taking on D.O.C., the blue wall of custody and any staff member in there who wants to keep his job. All you're doing is wasting your time and my money trying."

With that, he grabbed his overnight bag which was sitting next to the door and left, slamming the door behind him.

Shaken, Elaine drank her wine and watched the sun set from the huge bay window. It was too late to call dog kennels. Fortified with a second glass in hand, she decided to call Richard and have it out with him.

"Richard, it's Elaine," she said when he answered the phone, "I need to talk with you. I've been drinking a bit so I'd like you to come over here. Think you could manage that?"

"I'll be right there."

Thirty minutes later, about the time it took to grab a jacket and drive over, Richard pulled up in front of the house. She let him in and led the way to the shadowy living room. The sun had set, and she hadn't bothered to turn on the lights as she waited.

Facing him across the dim room Elaine said: "How could you, Richard? How could you call my husband like I was some, misguided child who needed a spanking? I thought we were friends, dear friends. I thought you respected me."

"I do respect you, and I care for you a great deal, probably more than I should, since you have a husband, but Elaine, you need to understand what you are doing is dangerous and I'm not going to stand by and watch you get your head bashed in by some stupid guard."

"Oh, so you think Billy didn't kill anyone and custody is involved in a cover-up?"

"Stop it, Elaine. Stop being so naive. Your twenty years is nothing compared to my thirty. You were never in a riot before. That was my third! I've seen men raped and murdered. I was there when they were still riding hog motorcycles around the big yard and writing books about the place, like *Concrete Jungle*. Hell, I'm quoted in the book, I think. That prison has been like a Disneyland since you got there. Everyone cleaned up his act and because there were good programs, the animals were happy and calm. So the guards were happy. The pendulum swung back, just like I knew it would. Now the animals are unhappy and bored, which makes the officers mean. That's what you witnessed the day of the riot and it's only gotten worse in the last six months. So what if Damien got his throat slit? I'm sorry Officer Shaw died, but so did a lot of officers in other areas. Who cares who did it? It's over. Trying to make it right won't change anything."

"Billy saved your life! So did those lifers. Doesn't that mean anything to you? I always admired you. I thought you were the most honorable person I knew. How can you just let this go? It's wrong and I'm ashamed you're considering it."

With that, Elaine busied herself turning on lights and pouring a drink. "Would you like something, Richard?" she asked.

"Yes, some of that Scotch I see back behind the bar. Pour it straight up." He moved to the couch, sat down heavily, and crossed his booted feet. Elaine sat beside him and passed him his drink. After a couple of sips, Richard turned toward her and said, "Look. Maybe those guys aren't getting a fair deal. I don't much like it, but I've seen too much to think I can change the system, or to think you can either. I'm very serious when I say you are really pissing some people off and they're not going to let this drop if you don't let it go. These are dangerous men and they aren't locked up. Please, I'm asking you nicely, let this go."

"We can go riding. Hell, I'll retire and we can take off. Just leave. Go see the world. We could do the Pacific Crest Trail on horseback, from Canada to Mexico, like we always talk about.

You and I know doing a section a couple weeks each summer is never going to get it done. I don't know what kind of permanent companion I'd make, but we get along pretty good when we're together, and I know you aren't happy here."

As he said all this, Richard looked around her beautiful home and then back at her.

"Even if you don't want to go down the road with me— sometimes I think you do and then sometimes I think you don't—I beg you to leave this case alone, for your own sake. I don't think I can protect you as I've tried to do both in the prison and on the trail. There are too many of them; it runs too deep, goes too high, and they're serious about hushing up what happened in there."

Elaine turned toward him with a sad smile. "You, my friend, are one of the dearest, most wonderful people I know. I love your company and trust you with my life; I actually have at times. I can't 'do personal' right now, but I sure hope you'll make the offer again when this is all over. I mean that. As far as this case is concerned, I can't walk away. Maybe I haven't seen enough terrible stuff. Maybe that's why. I actually wish I could leave, but I would go back to drinking, pills, sitting on a stupid island, waiting for my family to show up now and then and pat me on the head to make sure I'm still there and not getting in trouble.

"You didn't know that's what I was doing those months when I was gone, did you? It took everything I had to come back and pick up my life. And such as it is, my Nevada Daddy taught me you have to play the hand you're dealt and this is it. I don't like it much, but there you are. Please, *please* help me solve these atrocious crimes so we can both move on with our lives. Please?"

Richard downed the Scotch, stood up, and looked at Elaine, still on the couch, looking like she might have lost her best friend.

"I can't. It's not me, Elaine. I'm a hedonist. You know that. I seek pleasure, not pain. Moreover, you are asking me to betray

105

people, some of whom I go back years with, inside and out. You're asking too much. I don't think you know how much trouble you are bringing on yourself. Let's go riding Sunday and talk more. Okay?"

"Aren't you worried about hanging out with me?"

"You are still my favorite partner in the world, and I'm loyal to my friends, another reason I can't help you, Elaine. I'm not afraid of these fools for myself, or for you when I'm with you, but if you don't change your mind, I can't always protect you and that, I assure you, is when bad things will happen."

"Did I tell you I'm getting a guard dog tomorrow?"

Richard scoffed. "Just don't bring the stupid thing with you on Sunday. I don't want him scaring the horses. I'll be here about seven a.m."

With that, Richard gave her a kiss on the cheek (which was more, she realized, than she had gotten from Daniel), and left.

The next morning she called Tony and told him she wouldn't be in that day because she was going to look for a guard dog. She said she and Janet would still be leaving the following morning to see Shawn in Walla Walla. Tony snickered when she mentioned the dog; he didn't like dogs and didn't want them around his office.

Elaine still thought it an excellent idea so she drove toward Winthrop and the breeder who'd told her over the phone he had the perfect dog. He hadn't actually asked about her specific situation, but she was confident when she told him, he would be able to match her with a good companion and a bit of safety all rolled into one darling puppy.

When she arrived at the breeders office she knocked on the screen door. A man looked up from behind a desk.

"Jim?" she inquired.

He nodded slightly.

"I'm Elaine. I called you about the dog?"

"Please come in. I'll take you to see the dogs, but first I'd

106

like to get a profile so we make a good match. Right offhand I'm thinking of Scout, a two-year-old, highly intelligent young male I think would be an excellent match for a single woman like yourself."

"Well, I'm not really single, but I'm alone a lot," she answered.

"This dog is absolutely beautiful. Here's a picture."

"Wow, he looks like Rin Tin Tin. I always wanted a dog just like this when I was a child. Can I see him now?"

"First I need to ask you a few questions, just for our records. Okay?" Jim said searching for a pen in the desk drawer.

"Shoot. What do you want to know?"

"Well, do you own your home and will Scout have a place to run? We don't let our dogs go just anywhere. I'm sure you can appreciate that."

"Oh, of course. Yes, I have a beautiful home, with beachfront access in Mukilteo. I jog a lot and wanted the dog to run with me."

"Excellent, excellent. Now, why did you decide you wanted a dog at this particular time?"

"Well, I teach in prison. A few months ago I was taken hostage in a riot. Some inmates helped me escape, but now Department of Corrections is accusing one of them of killing two people during the riot. I don't believe he did it, so I hired a lawyer to look into the case. This has made some of the guards furious so I am nervous. I think maybe a guard dog might make me feel more secure as I continue with my investigation."

Jim's mouth fell open halfway through Elaine's explanation. He smacked it shut and collected himself as he quickly yanked back the picture of Scout and put it in its file. Looking across at this demure, seemingly sane woman, he reassessed the situation, got up, went back to his filing cabinet, and returned with another picture of a German shepherd.

At least that's what Elaine thought it might have been at one time. Whereas Scout's fur had been silver, touched with shades of black and his countenance proud and wise, this dog looked like he was barely awake. No, take that back—barely alive. He had fur, but it was stringy and thin. He was lying down rather than standing like Scout, and it looked like that might be his only comfortable position. All in all he didn't emanate confidence.

"What happened to Scout being my perfect new friend?" Elaine queried.

"You know, he is very young and squirrelly and probably can't be counted on all the time. Yogi here is a sure thing. Used to be a police dog, shot twice in the line of duty. Good dog. Sound dog. Just the dog for what you describe as your, um, lifestyle?"

Elaine understood. This man was afraid she was going to get his precious Scout killed, so he was "knocking off" on her a used version of a guard dog.

Fine. She decided to check out Yogi. Who was she to ridicule anyone getting up in age? Her fiftieth birthday had been last spring. "Let's see him."

Jim looked relieved. He took her out back where various cages were lined up. The barking began immediately as Elaine looked in each kennel. After they'd exhausted all cages, Jim rounded the corner and started calling, "Yogi, Yogi."

Out of the woods came the biggest, slowest dog Elaine had ever seen. His picture didn't do him justice. His fur was matted. He smelled bad. And he didn't seem too impressed with her either.

He did come on command, in his own sweet time, but then lay down at Jim's feet, looking back from whence he'd come. Elaine bent down to pet him and turned his head to look into his eyes.

She was a goner. His eyes were as clear as any puppy's and had a depth of knowledge she knew was valuable. Getting up, she said, "I'll take him—but not until you bathe and groom him. Is it a deal?"

"I'll do it right now. Why don't you go into Winthrop? It's

only a couple miles north. Get some lunch, and I'll have Yogi ready in two hours." He sounded relieved.

"Sounds like a plan," she said, gingerly petting Yogi's head. She looked back before they were out of sight of the dog. He was still staring out into a fathomless place she knew nothing about.

She enjoyed Winthrop, another old stomping ground for those who took trail riding seriously. Winthrop was a gateway to wonderful trailheads in to the high country. She drove around a bit after eating a sandwich at a favorite tavern, breathing in the memories and hoping for new ones in the years to come. After two hours passed, she drove back down the winding road to pick up her new dog.

This time Yogi looked much better. Checking the dog's papers Elaine discovered it was seven years old. In dog years, that would make them about the same age. She liked that.

Elaine also discovered Yogi was a female. She liked that too. She was pretty sick of men lately. It would be good to have another female for company. Females were more open-minded, sensitive, understanding. Yes, this would be a good match. To hell with gorgeous Scout. Who needed him, his muscles and cocky look of confidence?

She paid Jim a hefty price. Then again, Yogi had papers. The dog jumped willingly into the car's small back seat and fell sound asleep before they left the breeder's long driveway. Elaine smiled. The dog slept until they got home, jumped out, squatted in the bushes and followed Elaine inside as though she knew it was her house.

After checking each room, Yogi apparently decided she liked sleeping by the front door best, where she curled up and slept some more.

Yogi was exactly where she'd left her when Elaine got back from the store with food. She followed Elaine into the kitchen to eat and drink from her new bowls. After dinner, Yogi stood at the back door until Elaine put a leash on and they descended to the beach. Elaine wasn't ready to jog so she took Yogi off leash and simply walked along the water's edge. At one point Yogi veered off an embankment, apparently did her duty, and reappeared beside Elaine, without missing a step.

Elaine decided she liked her, but she wasn't convinced this dog could protect her. She looked over the hill for a vicious guard dog. Still, there was always the option of a gun if Elaine really started feeling afraid. For now she liked the company and enjoyed Yogi curling up beside her bed that night. She made good decisions, she thought, and she didn't care what other people thought.

Chapter 12

Janet Brayson was good company on the trip to Walla Walla. She was calm and composed today, unlike the last time Elaine spoke to her. She dressed nicely and turned out to be interesting.

"It looks like we are going to have good weather for the trip," Elaine volunteered as Janet got in the car.

"Yes, I'm really happy it turned out that way. Thank you for driving."

"No problem. If we get a statement of any kind from Shawn, written or verbal, about what happened that day, it will be well worth it for me."

"He says he will do it, but I don't know if they're going to let you write anything, or let him write something and hand it to you. You know how they are about anything exchanging hands."

"I know. We'll just play it by ear. That's all we can do. I called Captain Pepper and asked her to get authorization, but she never called back. So I don't know if anyone will allow it or not."

"Captain Pepper was always good to me and Shawn. That's one of the reasons I didn't want him transferred. If one of the children was sick, Shawn got to talk to him on the phone a little more, and his letters and cards got here faster than normal."

"I guess I've put her in a bad spot, stirring up all this trouble for her with the S.W.A.T. team but I just don't see how else all this could have happened since you and I know these lifers didn't do it."

"It's going to be impossible to prove. You know that, don't you? They've closed ranks and I can promise you D.O.C. is not above vengeance if you do something they don't like. After Shawn and I got married, he was beaten up by guards, his letters were torn up, and they kept his store from him and turned his cell every week for months. I got terrible crank calls until I finally moved and changed the number. It all stopped after a few months, but this is much more serious. I'm worried about your involvement. Aren't you?"

"Oh, I didn't tell you–I got some protection." As if on cue, Yogi sat up in the backseat and stuck her head between them.

Janet screamed. Elaine turned the wheel sharply, and Yogi barked. "I'm so sorry Janet. Yogi's a little deaf. It also takes awhile to wake her up some times. Then other times she's really alert. Kind of like me I guess." Elaine shushed Yogi while she reassured Janet.

After she got the car under control, Janet quieted down and Yogi shut up, Elaine decided it was time for the Northwest's cure for anything, a cafe latté. She pulled into an espresso stand, got their drinks, and by the time they were on the road again, Janet and Yogi were fast friends.

"You really think the people who actually committed the murders could be officers?" Elaine inquired as they burned up farmland miles.

"Oh yes! Some of the officers I worked with were just criminals who hadn't been caught. They bring in the drugs and other contraband all the time. They talk trash constantly and play really nasty tricks on the weaker inmates. Some of them come to the job mad at the world for having no control over their own lives, so with power sanctioned to use on people in cages, they misuse it. I saw a lot of that. Actually that's how Shawn and I met. He was helping a smaller inmate get up after several officers left him bleeding in the showers"

"You know, working in education, I was somewhat sheltered from all that, but I didn't think abuse happened very often," Elaine said, still not really believing it could be as vicious an environment as Janet described.

"Well, it's not my job to convince you how broken the

corrections system is, but I have no respect for it, I can tell you that. When I started, I did. I thought it would be a good use of my sociology degree; I could start as a guard and work to become a counselor as soon as I passed tests."

"Well–referring to D.O.C. guards who have been promoted to 'counselor' as trained counselors is a stretch. You probably would have been the first advisor with any kind of college degree."

"They're just guards who got a promotion for sticking with the stinking job a while; not making waves in D.O.C., and not getting caught doing anything that would embarrass the department. I learned that." Janet sighed.

"I don't like our system of punishment. I think it's capricious and arbitrary. I've traveled enough to prisons in other countries to know there are better ideas out there; but the last few years I've gotten tired of trying to convince D.O.C.. I've started to think this huge bureaucracy just doesn't want to change. There's a lot of money involved. It's big business. I don't know," Elaine admitted. "Maybe I'm just getting old."

"You're not old. And you obviously haven't stopped caring or we wouldn't be here today."

"I know, but that's just because this is such a travesty. Billy and the others saved my life. I can't walk away from that debt. But the D.O.C. system is a different story. I wrote my dissertation on how wasted the funds are. No one read it. I've spoken all over the world on how changes can be made. Other countries have changed, but not the great U.S. of A. We seem bent on punishment instead of rehabilitation. And we let the inmate back amongst us, more dysfunctional than when he went inside."

"Now, that doesn't always happen. Like with Shawn. But he worked hard at helping himself, with little in the way of opportunity. Most guys don't have that kind of determination or confidence. They would rather watch TV, play pinochle or lift weights. And that's fine with D.O.C.. It drives me crazy–while we have their attention by keeping them in prison, we should give them incentive to improve themselves, not just let them vegetate. It's so stupid."

"Yes, it is. And when you put the shit they get from guards on top of that, you really have a sick system."

"Okay. Then what should it look like?" Elaine decided there was nothing like a long car ride to bring two strangers into conversation they would never think of having over coffee.

"Don't think I haven't pondered, discussed, and prayed on this topic," Janet answered. "Remember, I have two sons whose father is an incarcerated felon. If I don't work twice as hard countering that stigma, I could have more trouble with my boys than I already do. It has to start with fair sentencing. Three strikes you're out is insane. You rob a pizza driver, after two priors at the age of 22, and you go to prison for the rest of your life. It takes away all hope. Why should any person try to change?

"Without hope this 22-year-old wreaks havoc while doing time and makes it horrible for everyone. And the super max prisons have got to go. No other country in the world has prisons where people are never let out of cages. It's inhuman. Our prisoners are more violent than any others in the world. We make them that way because of our treatment of them the first time they screw up, and because of drugs."

"We don't try to help them when they're young and impressionable. We isolate and alienate, making the problem worse. Oh, we have little programs that help maybe one percent of the total population, D.O.C. and the media tout to the public so they can say, 'See, we try to help these fools, but you just can't help people who won't help themselves!'"

"I think we need to take children away from their neglectful parents and never let them return. I hate the foster care system. The old orphanage system was actually better. The children at least got to go to the same schools as public school children and stay with their siblings. We had a good orphanage where I grew up. There were private homes built around a big building on ten acres. The children lived in these homes, twelve to a house, with the same state worker couple as surrogate parents, until the child turned eighteen. And the children went to our schools. We used to go to their homes for parties. They came to ours. And they were never given back to the biological parents, though the parents could visit. Society worries too much about the parents and too little about the children. That's why the vicious cycle of abuse continues."

"I like that. I also like some privately funded rehab programs. And not the ones where the state just hires outside companies to bring in incompetent guards and treatment personnel because it saves money; but real programs like Delancey Street, where the residents actually help themselves and each other prior to completion. These types of programs have an eighty-five percent success rate instead of the dismal twenty percent which is all D.O.C. can claim. If community members would provide the money to these types of programs, instead of bureaucracies that are mired down in nepotism and graft, we could reduce crime plenty, I know we could! Wow," Elaine laughed, "I'm really getting wound up."

"Maybe we should give it a rest. We're getting close. The prison is out in the middle of nowhere and we can't visit until one p.m. I know a decent place for lunch. It's just a Denny's, but it's good and cheap. And I'm buying, since you drove."

Elaine felt unexpectedly humbled by this offer. She knew the Braysons had almost nothing to live on. She'd found over the years these gestures of generosity were common among those who had the least, and rare from those with ample funds stockpiled for themselves. When she was with her wealthy friends, it was always splitting the check to the last penny. She found it an ugly, embarrassing practice which meant, of course, she usually ended up offering to pay, which amazingly didn't shame them but rather seemed to make them happy.

"Okay, but I'm getting the tip."

"Fair enough," Janet said as she returned Elaine's smile. "Turn up here."

Elaine hated Walla Walla. Even though it was the same era as her prison, with stone walls and granite turrets, it was not gracefully built on a high, cedar-laced mountain. Instead, it sat sadly on flatland, surrounded by weeds and scraggly second-growth firs. The entranceway wasn't curved with flowers and rhododendrons lining the driveway, instead was sullen and naked. Its sidewalks and paths were barren of shrub that might conceal a weapon or drugs, but it was oppressive in its preventive sterility.

They both knew the drill: Stop and identify yourself to the tower guard before parking. Leave all valuables, except identification, in the locked vehicle. Inform officers you were locking a pet inside the car. Proceed to the main building, go in, and wait for the desk officer to take your identification. Proceed to the scanner. Wait in the line for your turn to go through what looked like an airport scanner, but was actually many times more powerful. Submit to either a visual body scan or, if the buzzer rang, a pat-down by an officer who took you to a separate room.

Elaine and Janet passed through security easily, but many others were not fortunate. Waiting in line, Elaine almost gagged on the competing perfumes emanating from the lonely, unattractive women who had gotten on some inmate's visitor's list, exploited for sex, money or drugs while the prisoner professed undying love for the female and laughed at her with his partners in the card room after the visit. The system made Elaine sick. And though it looked to her like Janet and Shawn had made a go of it, Elaine didn't like felons who found women in personal ads, married, had babies, and then let the taxpayers support them, in most cases for the rest of their lives. To her, it was another example of a system not only ridiculous, but lining lots of lazy pockets.

The visiting room was crowded. Babies and toddlers cried

tiredly when they should have been home taking naps or playing with toys. Elaine wasn't against legitimate parenting programs, where the incarcerated father took a class, learned tools, and was allowed quality time with a child he'd created outside the walls. She was in favor of educational programs where the incarcerated father read or taught the child something. But that was not what went on with most of these families. The woman wanted to be with her man. The children were fed junk food from vending machines and told to shut up while Mom and Dad copped a feel under the table.

Now Elaine remembered why she hated family events. Most of the mothers knew less about parenting than the dads. The children were pawns. If Mom was unhappy, she would threaten not to bring the child to see Daddy. Dad would promise anything to get another visit from a child to hold and to be powerful and have control over, if only for a few hours. Elaine starred at the macabre scene, feeling anxious and guilty. Yogi was sitting unattended in the car. The guards knew the dog was there and she had rolled down the window and left water, but she felt neglectful. Questioning her involvement in this entire venture Elaine needed to stay on task mentally so she turned her focus back to the inmates. There were exceptions to the stupid inmate rule, and Elaine admired the incarcerated fathers who would never dream of letting children come inside a nasty prison for their own gratification. But for the most part it was a bad scene and turned Elaine's stomach as they were buzzed into the old theatre used as a visiting room.

The inmates hadn't been allowed in yet. Their fate was worse than the visitors. They were cavity searched. Elaine often wondered what officer could stand doing such a repulsive job. However, Elaine knew searches were necessary, and should be done as each inmate exited. Drugs, weapons, and other forms of contraband would be discovered, swallowed during a stolen kiss, attached to a tooth with floss, to be later regurgitated, pushed up

117

a rectum in a balloon or jabbed into skin, as in the case of needles later used for tattooing or as part of a shank.

Elaine knew little was 'in housed' this way. The search was done mostly to humiliate. A large percent of contraband was brought in by staff, as was the case during her riot, thanks to Raylyn.

After what seemed like hours, but was actually about fifteen minutes of Shawn's precious allotted two hours, #99437 walked in and came over to sit at the tables. Both the tables and the hard uncomfortable metal stools were bolted to the floor. Elaine looked around at the elderly visitors, probably parents, and decided if they could sit on these things without complaining, she could too.

No one was allowed to touch, but everyone did anyway. The one guard behind glass could do little about a hundred people greeting loved ones. He would eventually speak into his goose-necked mike and order everyone to separate and sit. Of course, by that time, anything going to be passed, had been.

"Hi, Dr. Bennett," Shawn said after he and Janet had broken their embrace and sat down. "I can't believe you came all this way to see me. Thanks for bringing Janet."

"You're welcome. I'm going to leave you two alone, but first I need to know if you were able to write what you saw happen during the riot. They wouldn't let me bring in paper and pencil."

"I wrote it, but the only way I got it done was in my vocational class with Mr. Johnson. I told him what I needed to do. He said he was a friend of yours and would help. After I wrote it, I gave it to him. He's going to meet you at the exit and give it to you. It's about twenty pages long and it's pretty rough. You know I'm no writer."

"I remember Bob Johnson. He does workshops at our Correctional Education Association conferences. I hate to get him involved in this, taking something out for an inmate that hasn't been screened, but..."

"Look, I tried three times to mail the report and each time custody confiscated it, saying I was violating Section 302 of the penal code, which as you know states I was trying to cause a riot. They tore up my cell twice, trying to pin something on me so they can throw me in solitary. If they do that I lose my visits." Shawn's voice rose.

Janet put her hand on his arm. "Please, honey, calm down. She's trying to help you."

"I'm sorry, but I was on my way out. Now I'm back in this stinkin' prison with no end in sight. I know you're trying to help, but I can't afford to get in trouble while my lawyer works on my appeal." Shawn stared at Elaine with eyes filled with such pain Elaine dropped her gaze.

"I didn't get a chance to thank you for saving my life," she said. "I know what you and the others did that day. This is the only way I know to thank you. Can you understand?"

"I understand, and thank you for the gesture. I've seen you do some pretty amazing things to change an inmate for the better. That's the only reason I'm helping you now. But do you really know what you're doing? You're going up against D.O.C.. I have nightmares about how stupid that is. They were asking me why you were here before I came in. They know something's up, and I'm the one who has to go back in there and not answer their questions."

"You're right. All I can do is promise you I won't quit until there's a new trial and I've done everything I can to get you guys back where you were, or better. But I can't do it without your help. If you tell me to tear up the report Johnson gives me, I will. I won't involve you. I'm asking a lot and I'm not the one who has to go back in there."

"No, I've gone as far as I can, but I want my sons to know I've changed and I am an honorable man who stands up for what he knows is right. I'd just appreciate it, Elaine, if you'd watch out for them and Janet. This whole thing is going to get bad and I can't do a damn thing from here to protect my family. You understand?"

"I understand perfectly. I'd already decided to do as much as Janet will allow. You married a very strong woman. She wouldn't let me pay for lunch!"

"Well, we wanted to buy lunch. We talked about it, and we appreciate what you're trying to do," Shawn said as he glanced with pride at Janet.

As Elaine rose, the officer ordered her to resume her seat or state where she was going. She gestured toward the exit door. "I'll be waiting in the car. See you at three. You two have a good visit."

Elaine left the room and went to sit in the car. She thought maybe she'd take a nap because she hadn't slept well and the drive was a long one. She'd closed her eyes when a rap on the window startled her. She saw blue, rolled the window down, and waited.

A young officer said, "Ma'am, you can't stay here. No one is allowed to wait in their car."

Not surprised, Elaine asked him to tell a visitor named Janet Brayson to meet her at the bottom of the road off the prison grounds, where she'd be at three p.m. She knew custody would never allow her to drive back up.

"No problem, ma'am. Thank you."

Elaine found a pull out for cars, used, it seemed, by plenty of tired people before her. She let Yogi out for a few minutes and returned to the car to resume their naps. Right at three o'clock Johnson drove up beside her and rolled down his window.

"Hey, Elaine, I thought you'd be getting too old to stir up as much trouble as I hear you're doing."

"I didn't ask for this, but I can't let innocent people get punished for something they didn't do, especially when they were saving my butt. You'd do the same thing, Bob."

"I don't know, Elaine. You and I always pushed the envelope when it came to D.O.C., but this is serious stuff. Even way out here, I hear about it."

"Do you have something for me?"

Bob passed a manila envelope from his window to hers. "You know, if D.O.C. pushes it, I'm going to have to tell them I got this report from Shawn and then you will be involved. Speak now, or forever hold your peace," Elaine said.

"I thought before I showed up today and I hope it doesn't come to that. But if I ever get stuck in a room with a bunch of pissed-off inmates, and a few brave souls have the courage to get my sorry ass out, I'll regret not doing this. Besides, I'm sick of watching Shawn get manhandled for no reason. He's a nice guy. I try to keep him out at school with me as much as possible, but when I'm not here, they really give him grief."

"I wish there was more I could do. I don't know how the other lifers who helped me are holding up. I appreciate what you've done and I'll try to keep your name out of this. I just can't believe officers killed one of their own. I know they would kill Damien given a chance, but Shaw?"

"I'm hearing Shaw was getting ready to talk about all the shit the S.W.A.T. team was up to. It was an opportune time to shut him up. So they took it."

"What kind of shit?"

"This is just inmate talk, but they're saying your little S.W.A.T. team had a drug business going from the inside out that was bringing in over $10,000 a month to each of the players. Nice little supplement to their crummy paychecks, wouldn't you say? And worth killing for, if you had to, I suppose. Good thing I don't care about money. I have my sailboat to live on. I can afford the beer to go with it. Don't need much else."

"You know this information helps me, even if we can't confirm it. Can I give you my home number and have you keep me posted with anything else you come across?"

"Sure, Elaine. I was thinking about retiring this year anyway. I'm sick of the bullshit. Twenty-five years of this crap is enough. But you watch yourself. If your ears aren't ringing, they should be. Remember, these guys are trained with weapons and they love using them."

"I'll be careful, and thanks. You're truly one of the good guys, and I miss seeing you. Too bad we don't have our CEA conferences anymore. We had some good times, didn't we? Raburn break dancing, Garcia's toupee falling in his beer. The good old days, huh?"

"Yeah, when we had decent administrators who weren't jockeying for position in Olympia."

"Look, I see Janet, Shawn's wife, coming. I don't want to compromise your job any more than I have. You should probably not be here."

"Okay, Elaine. I admire what you're doing, even if I think you're crazy for doing it. You're quite a lady. Always have been, in my book."

"I love you too. Now get out of here, but call me with any news. I'll take inmate talk, especially since, as we both know, it's usually true."

"Bye."

"I want a trip on your boat someday!"

"You've got it." Bob drove off just as Janet came within earshot.

"Was that Shawn's teacher?"

"Yeah. Neat guy. He's watching out for Shawn as best he can."

"You ready to hit the road?"

"Sure." Elaine knew from listening to the men all these years parting was excruciatingly painful. One of you was going back to a cage. The other back in society to struggle against prejudice and stigma of being a criminal's spouse. Elaine decided it was probably best to let Janet reminisce on the way home and she would concentrate on driving the dark wet roads. Yogi had already been out twice, so she was good to go.

Janet went to sleep so Elaine didn't stop for dinner. They arrived at the Braysons' front door at around eleven at night.

"Did you get that report you wanted? I forgot to ask," Janet said sleepily as she pulled on her jacket.

"I got it, and let's try to keep it between you and me. Okay?"

"I don't tell anybody anything anymore. Makes for a rather lonely life, but it protects Shawn and the boys better."

"I enjoyed the trip with you and get some rest. I probably won't be in touch unless I have to, because I don't want anyone placing you in this mess. You can call me if you want."

"Thanks and I want you to know we both appreciate what you're trying to do. Shawn said to tell you he was sorry he acted like a jerk."

"No need. He's trying to protect what little he has to love. I understand completely. Good night."

"Good night."

Elaine waited until Janet got inside and turned the porch light off. Then she drove away, envious of the embraces the two little boys gave their Mom as the front door closed.

Chapter 13

Elaine was anxious to share with Lawyer Williams information she'd received from Shawn and Bob, but she feared he might be asleep. The rain hadn't followed her west of the Cascades; the evening was mild and the moon and stars shone brightly. Distracted thinking about the case, she went inside, grabbed her old Dr. Zhivago coat and walked immediately down the back steps to the beach with Yogi. She didn't bother to leash her, since the dog stayed right beside her except to do her duty in the bushes. Yogi was anxious to get out, since she'd been in the car since early morning. Elaine pulled into the garage and opened the car door for Yogi who immediately took off for the beach. Elaine closed her own car door and proceeded confidently behind her.

Years before Elaine read a book, *The Gift of Fear* and gave it to all her female friends and daughter. It was about dealing with danger without becoming afraid. She thought of it now, because as she walked beside the ocean, something bothered her and she couldn't figure out what.

She looked down and saw fresh footprints in the sand leading back toward the stairs. Something wasn't right. All the years she'd walked out here, she'd never seen footprints.

Yogi returned to her side, pushing her with her body away from the stairs. She growled. The fur along her back was raised, and her head alert. Elaine decided not to challenge her feeling, nor what the dog was telling her. She turned and bolted toward the neighbors' lights a distance down the beach.

She pounded on the door until the retired couple she knew vaguely let her in. After they called the police, she sat down with a steaming cup of coffee to wait for the response team. Feeling a little silly after she'd calmed down, Elaine made small talk. "I'm sorry to have startled you. I'm sure there's nothing to be frightened of. I think I just got worked up over nothing, and the dog's actions probably didn't help. Why don't I go back to my house and wait for the police so you two can get to bed?" She rose to leave.

"That's ridiculous, Elaine," the wife said. "We wouldn't think of it. The dispatcher told you not to return until they've gone in and made sure everything is okay." The husband nodded emphatically.

While they bustled around, making more coffee and offering her coffee cake (which she politely declined three times), Elaine felt envious of their companionable silences and quiet conversation. They liked each other, liked being with each other, knew each other in a way unusual to her fast-paced, career-driven generation. She wondered what Daniel would think of her calling the police over something seemingly silly, or if she'd even tell him. Why open herself up to constant, unrelenting criticism of what she was doing for these lifers?

When the police arrived, they didn't seem anxious to go back to the house with her. The sergeant had a lot of questions. "Mrs. Bennett, do you or your husband have enemies that you know about?"

"What are you trying to say?" Elaine asked, growing more nervous.

"When did you get home tonight? Did you come in the house alone?"

"Yes, I came home alone. My husband is out of town. My watchdog is a good one," she decided to add in Yogi's defense, "Nothing seemed wrong."

"What did you do after entering the home?"

"I was too keyed up to sleep and the dog needed to go out, so I grabbed my coat and went out the back door to go for a walk on the beach."

"Did you see anyone, hear anything?"

"No. Not until I saw footprints and Yogi came back, clearly aggravated by something. I decided not to return until the house was checked."

"A wise move. Someone was in your house. There may have been more than one person and it looks like they were searching for something. We think we interrupted them."

"Oh, dear," the neighbor exclaimed and sat down heavily at the news.

"It's okay, Ma'am. These aren't random thieves or robbers casing houses. These men were after something specific." The detective said all this staring at Elaine as though he knew she wasn't being straight with him. And, of course, she wasn't.

Elaine decided to play dumb if for no other reason than she didn't want to explain the whole story to town police. In previous encounters, she'd found them to be more like Keystone Cops than real policemen. Because she lacked confidence in their competence, as well as feared they might be buddies with D.O.C. employees, she asked if they could go back to her home and let her neighbors go to bed, since it was approaching two a.m.

"You sure you want to go back there? It's quite a mess!"

"I'm sure, as long as you say whoever was there is gone."

"Yeah. They were probably scared, being caught in the act and all. We saw the car speed away. Of course we didn't know it was the suspect's car at the time."

Elaine congratulated herself at deciding not to confide in these bozos, who wouldn't stop a car speeding away from the scene of a possible home invasion in the middle of the night.

"Were you able to get a plate number or at least a description?" Elaine asked sweetly.

"Err..., no, ma'am. We know it was a truck, but it was dark and my men concentrated on your house."

"Of course, Officer." Elaine had just demoted him, but he didn't seem to notice she had done so sarcastically.

Elaine thanked her neighbors, apologized for bothering them, and went back to her house with the police. Yogi pushed past her and entered first. Elaine watched the dog's reaction, then followed. On a quick appraisal, it wasn't nearly as bad as the cops led her to believe. Pillows and couch cushions were thrown around. Lamps turned over. The damage was mostly confined to her study where papers were everywhere. This reaffirmed, to Elaine's mind, what the perps were after.

She told the police she was fine, signed all their paperwork and showed them to the door. If Yogi felt safe, so did she. Yogi had already gone to sleep, obviously not distressed by the destruction of private property the way humans were.

The police tried their macho best to frighten her, by telling her to leave until her husband could come home and presumably protect her. Elaine wondered how these guys would function in the riot she had lived through, keeping her head while all crumbled around her. Not well, she decided.

She did need to notify Daniel. After all, it was his home too. She sat at her desk, rummaged through the mess to find a pen and paper, and wrote:

Dear Daniel,

I'd hate for you to find the house this way, if you get home before the housekeeper arrives. I will call her in the morning. She has her own key. Hopefully she can clean this up, and by the time you return, all will be in order.

I'm going into Everett to rent an apartment, one that will take my dog. It's not that I'm frightened to stay out here alone, I just don't want to. I will leave it to you whether you want to rent or sell while we are sorting out our lives and what now seems to be a long-distance relationship. I won't make a decision until after Billy's trial. I have no idea when that might be. I will keep you posted.

As soon as I find a place, I'll call you and invite you over. I'm fine, really. Try not to worry about me, and I'll do

the same about you.
Love,
Elaine
P.S. Please don't tell the children until I do. I'm going to say I need to be closer to the courthouse, etc., during the trial and since you travel so much, it's just easier. Actually when I think about it, it's true.

Elaine packed clothes, cosmetics, gear for riding and food for Yogi. She was surprised when finished how much she really didn't want.

As the sun glared through her windows at the break of a new day, she got in her sweet little car, with her friend Yogi in the back, checked to see the prized manila envelope was securely under the passenger seat where she'd left it, and drove away.

While driving she made two calls. One was left on her housekeeper's answering machine, knowing Martha would be at the house to put things in order, first thing. The second was to Tony Williams.

"I hope I didn't wake you."

"Of course not."

It had become a game where she tried to catch Williams sleeping like a real person, and his not allowing it.

"Look. I need to come to the office and speak with you. The good news is I have Shawn's incident report. The bad news is someone tried to take it back while ransacking my house, so I'm looking for a new place to stay. I've been thinking about doing it anyway. I saw a For Rent sign on a little house in your neighborhood. Thought I'd check it out."

There was total silence. Finally: "Okay. I'll see you when you get here." Click.

☙❧

Elaine walked into Tony's office. This early in the morning it really looked like he lived there. Clothes were spread out. Dirty dishes lay in the sink. Coffee was brewing, which she knew was in honor of her visit.

Elaine sat at the table while Tony got her a cup. "You all right?"

"Yes, thank you."

"Okay. Let's hear what happened from the beginning, please, but leave out the color of the leaves on the trees on the drive over, okay?"

"You don't need to be sarcastic. I think that stories should be told in detail."

"I know. Please?"

Elaine brought Tony up to snuff while he sat looking out the window at a somewhat hazy morning sky. Finally Elaine looked expectantly at him.

"You sure stay busy, Elaine! Billy has been helping me understand how you function, but I must say, it seems every time we meet, there's another surprise in store for me. Do you ever have down time?"

"You ask me that? I have yet to catch you asleep not at this table, or eat without doing at least three other things at the same time. Look, here's Shawn's statement." She threw it down on the table.

"Okay, fine. Let's just get on with what we need to do. I called the company handling the house you're thinking about renting. Even though it's early, we can go see it now if you want."

"I want. I'd like to be settled in by dinner time."

"Of course you would," Tony responded with a dash of sarcasm, but she was too tired to spar with him. Even the coffee wasn't keeping her Type A personality afloat. She slowly put her arms back into her coat and stumbled down the street after him.

The rental agent was waiting outside. He and Tony exchanged pleasantries while he unlocked the front door and ushered them inside. "The last tenant was a single woman, and an artist, so you'll see evidence of decorating all over."

It was fabulous! Every room was painted a vibrant green or yellow or red. The old country kitchen had a bit of all three. The parlor, the green room, had a wonderful old freestanding stove and huge bay windows covered with tulle and silk drapes with Italian woven threads complementing rugs laid over exquisite hardwood floors.

The rooms upstairs were painted again with greens, but accented with mauve and gold. Everything was small compared to what Elaine was used to, but that made it cozy and safe. She loved it and knew it was perfect for now. It was also extremely clean, which was a definite prerequisite to her way of thinking. "I'll take it."

Both men looked at her with contempt. She really didn't care.

"Elaine, you don't know what he is asking, or if it's available," Tony asked with more condescension than she liked.

"True," she responded to the landlord, ignoring Tony, wishing she hadn't brought him with her. "So tell me."

A half hour later she'd signed a six month lease, paid first, last and a pet deposit, received the keys and ushered both gentlemen out the door with great aplomb, at least in her mind, which was all that counted.

She retrieved her dog and possessions from the car and returned to the house. She loved it even after a more in-depth inspection. The last tenant left the previous week so the utilities were still on, including phone. She spent another hour putting everything in her name. By then she was starting to run down, so she left to buy the bed of her dreams, bedding and some groceries.

It took some doing to get what she wanted delivered by six p.m., but when she threatened to walk out, it suddenly became possible. By now it was early afternoon. She ate fast food, which she hated, bought groceries and returned home to wait for deliveries. Even a washer and dryer were later delivered that day, placed in the cutest little pantry Elaine had ever seen. The kitchen led out to a small fenced backyard, perfect for Yogi's needs.

It was overgrown. Apparently the artist's touch hadn't extended to the outside, but Elaine didn't care. She sat on the old broken stoop, watching Yogi and drinking her hundredth cup of coffee, thinking how satisfying it would be to clean up the yard. A grand old apple tree loomed importantly in the middle of lush grass crawling out to the fence. The old wooden fence bordered blueberries, roses, lilacs and evergreen bushes in desperate need of shaping and a good trim; creating a feeling of privacy between herself and her neighbors.

Finally the bed arrived. She splurged on an adjustable one so her head and legs could go up and down. Sometimes her back and calves needed relief. It was a double, but seemed big placed in the middle of the largest bedroom. She'd already washed the linen, so after the delivery men left, Elaine took pleasure in making up the bed with mauve and green sheets, pillowcases and an inviting down comforter. She hung complementing towels in the bathroom; took a long bath in the claw-foot tub with Yogi lying near the door; struggled into a comfortable old nightgown and crawled into bed.

She knew she'd locked all the doors, but chuckled to herself she probably wasn't in much danger since no one except Tony knew where she was. And she was quite sure he'd had enough of her for one day.

As she dropped into a deep, exhausted sleep, she remembered being in Paris when, wandering around alone, she followed a group of uniformed children into an old cathedral and couldn't find her way out. She passed room after room of crypts, every stairway leading to others. All night she dreamt of wandering in that old Gothic church, and woke still trying to escape, as a mean old French priest yelled at her and pointed, as though to say "Get out," something she would gladly do if each corridor hadn't kept turning into a dead end lined with walls of dead people.

Chapter 14

Elaine was disoriented at first after opening her eyes. Green walls? Mauve curtains? She sat up and looked around; recognizing only Yogi, who stared back at her, until the fog in her mind cleared and she remembered all that occurred during the previous twenty-four hours. Stretching, she realized her back didn't ache the way it usually did. Good bed, she thought as she located the bathroom and turned on the shower. Glancing at her travel clock on the old windowsill, she realized she'd over slept. She couldn't remember when her body had last allowed her that luxury without a wake-up to use the bathroom or get a drink of water.

That reminded her, the dog probably needed a walk. She turned off the steaming water and went down to the back door where Yogi stood politely, looking out yearningly at the yard.

"I'm sorry, old girl. It's been a while since I had to meet anyone's physical needs but my own." Realizing how suggestive that sounded, she chuckled and opened the back door for the rather desperate dog. Enjoying the morning mist, Elaine dawdled another minute and decided she would brew a cup of coffee to take with her while she dressed.

Waiting for coffee to brew, she ate some cereal and a peach, mesmerized by how little she missed the opulent lifestyle. Cautioning herself not to be naïve in terms of the upkeep of an old home and lack of a hot tub, which might really present a problem, she grabbed her coffee and ascended the stairs, admiring the architecture and bright colors.

Showered, dressed and back down in the kitchen, Elaine

scavenged a piece of paper from her purse and made a list of what she'd need from her 'last home' and all she'd need to still buy. The previous owner hadn't been generous enough to leave furniture, though Elaine couldn't help wondering what it would look like. She'd quite a bit at the big house she could take; antique stuff her little grandmother had brought from Italy, she remembered sitting on as a child, and other things her dear Aunt Rosie recently left her when she passed away.

The only person who owned a truck and might help her move was Richard. And she knew it might take a couple of men, so he would need to see if Harry would be willing to help. Elaine decided to find him so they could move items that afternoon. She knew Richard frequently left the prison grounds for lunch, so she decided to try and catch him at Fred Meyer's. He loved their fried chicken. And if luck and timing were with her, she'd pick up the other stuff she needed at Freddy's at the same time.

She called Yogi back in, showed her where the food was, patted her on the head with an admonition to bite anyone who tried to break into this home, and locked the door. It was almost eleven when she reached Monroe. It seemed weird not to be taking a right turn off the old Snohomish/Monroe highway up to the prison complex, but she kept going into town and onto busy Highway 2 where the Fred Meyer store sat between the old and the new.

Poor little Monroe. A few years ago it was known as the gateway to the Cascades and was a small cowboy town with pretty good fairgrounds and some quaint shops and markets.

Now it was one big traffic jam. The city council had gotten greedy and not protected their sweet little city. Yuppies from Seattle discovered it and flooded the roadways with cars, trucks, campers, boats, and every sort of recreation vehicle. Urbanites with money were now building monstrous 'country homes' commuting back and forth into the city. On weekends it was even worse. The traffic clogged Highway 2 all the way to the mountain recreation sites. It was sad; but some called it progress. Elaine was in no position to stop it, although she wished she could.

This time of day the roads weren't too bad, being the middle of the week. She grabbed a cart in Freddies and went to the little restaurant to see if Richard was in a booth watching people come and go. He wasn't, so she went to gather all the items necessary to make a house a home. She hadn't seen a microwave in the kitchen so she invested in a small one.

This Fred Meyer store wasn't all that big and was laid out so Elaine could shop, go back to the food court, and shop some more until 11:45 when she saw her old partner sitting, eating and staring at the world. The sight of him warmed her. He was such a good partner, but she knew he wasn't going to be happy when he heard what she'd say.

"Good morning, Richard," Elaine called as she left her cart and climbed onto a stool next to him.

"My goodness, Elaine!" Richard wiped his mouth on a paper napkin, like a kid caught stealing cookies. "It's good to see you." He looked around and saw all the items in her heavily laden cart. "Elaine, have you finally left Daniel and that mausoleum you two call a home?" he asked with expectation written all over his face.

"Well, something like that, I suppose, but probably not quite the way you might be thinking."

"What does that mean?" Richard responded in a voice that suggested maybe he really didn't want more information and would rather go back to eating his chicken.

"Now, you have to promise you won't get mad or lecture me. I just don't need it."

"What good would it do? Just tell me before my lunchtime is over."

"All right. But remember your promise." She took a deep breath. "Our house was broken into night before last. They were looking for some papers dealing with Billy's case and the riot."

Richard's shoulders rose and fell as he kept chewing; even

135

though she couldn't hear the sighing going on, it was impossible to miss.

"Look, I don't want any help dealing with this case or the trial, but I was hoping you and Harry might assist me move a few pieces of furniture over to the house I rented. And by the way, how are you?"

"You're too much, Elaine. You really are. What does your husband think of all this having to move in the middle of the night?"

"Daniel hasn't been home since the last time we rode, and I told him about working on the case. He lives where he works or on the road. He doesn't think much of my decision-making either, I suppose; but I didn't come here to be judged or questioned. I just need a couple of friends. If that's too hard, then forget it."

Elaine got up to leave, angry, frustrated and near those damn tears that came at the worst possible times. Richard grabbed her arm and stood too, not letting go. "Just calm down. You always overreact when someone's trying to get information. Of course I'll help you, and Harry will too. We were just going to hit the taverns and get something to eat after work anyway. We'll meet you at your old place at four. Have a six-pack waiting."

Elaine was so relieved, she reached out and gave him a hug. "Thank you, thank you!"

"Now I've got to go explain to all the eyes watching why you and I were embracing in a public place. You sure don't make my life easy. But actually, I was planning on calling you anyway. I want the truth to come out, I don't want you hurt, so count on me helping and being around. Got that?" He lifted her chin and looked her in the eyes with a serious look, while Elaine smiled back at him.

"I'll see you at four. Oh, what kind of beer?"

"Get that Mexican Dos XX stuff you like. It's kind of grown on me."

"You've got it. I'm buying dinner when we're done, and no arguing. See you."

Elaine returned to pushing her cart with a more definite spring in her walk than she'd had walking up to him. She knew Richard worried how the hell he was going to keep her from hurting herself, at least on his watch, which was all he could control in life. She felt somewhat guilty. He was sixty plus years. But she brought color to his life and right now in his dismal black-and-white existence that must mean something.

His wife had passed on. The children were grown and busy. He enjoyed trail riding. If he had to go out on a limb to help her, he should. What could this damn system do to him anymore? He should tell them all to put the job where the sun don't shine! She knew he'd actually been wanting to for years.

His old buddies had retired or died in the harness. Richard shouldn't go out that way. She might be a blessing in disguise; a reason to leave; a reason to move on.

Elaine finished her shopping, took it home and put it away, relieved that Richard was back in her corner as a friend and partner, and more importantly as someone who knew that what she was doing was the right thing to do. He wasn't the kind who chased windmills. He considered himself a hedonist, he had once told her, and that might be true in terms of his own life and pleasures, but she knew he was conservative and slow to act if there wasn't something he could directly see was important.

When finally satisfied with her domestic work, there remained an hour before she needed to meet Richard and hopefully Harry at the old house. She decided to drive over and catch up with Tony. She thought he might still be at the jail with Billy, so she took a seat on the stoop. She was still there when he came walking back, briefcase in hand, so deep in thought he almost tripped over her as he got out his keys. "Jesus, Elaine. Don't ever sneak up on a stressed-out guy!"

"Excuse me, but I think you ran into me. What's so serious you can't see where you are going, anyway?"

"For one thing, what Shawn wrote in his report. Thank God

those guys who trashed your house didn't find it or you, or I'm quite sure both of you would be dead by now. If what he claims happened actually did, there's a cover-up going on that certain people wouldn't hesitate to kill to keep covered. Now get inside. You and I don't need to be standing around like sitting ducks for anyone who might take a shot at us."

Tony practically dragged Elaine into the office and closed the door, looking out through the window after securely locking the door behind them.

"I'll make some coffee while I'm here, but I can't stay. I have a couple of friends helping me move furniture later."

"Well, you might ask them to spend the night. I'm not sure you're safe, even in the new house, though I don't suppose anyone has read Shawn's report, right?"

"His teacher did, but he's on our side and we can contact him for more help."

"This is not good, Elaine. Not good at all. If what Shawn says is true, the entire S.W.A.T. team knew what went down. Some of them are the murderers, and it was done to protect a drug ring that was making a lot of people on the inside a lot of money, including some of them. I'm serious when I say people will kill to keep this quiet."

"Are you serious? You're telling me that all twelve officers are dirty?"

"And possibly more than just the S.W.A.T. team who rescued you. Quite a few more, and higher in rank. This is big, Elaine, and dangerous!"

"What can we do? How will we help Billy and the others without getting killed, Tony?"

"I don't know yet. Did Janet read Shawn's report?"

"No, she slept on the way back and then it was so late she just wanted to go inside, check on her sons and go to bed. She had to work the next day."

"That's good. So it's just you, Shawn, the teacher, and me—we

138

think. If that's the case, we can buy some time," Tony said, pacing and rubbing his head. "But that can't be. Someone knew you had something or else why would they ransack your home?"

"I don't know, but you're scaring me!"

"Good. It's about time you took this situation and me seriously."

"I have taken you and this situation seriously!" Elaine responded with frustrated indignation. "I don't think there is anything so far I could have changed. Do you think I'm enjoying this?"

"Of course not. I'm sorry if I suggested anything to that effect. I just think you take chances most reasonable people wouldn't."

"Oh, so now I'm not a reasonable person?"

"Let's just change the subject. I'm starting to think you are the lawyer, and I'm not enjoying the cross-examination much."

"Fine."

"Look, Elaine, there is one more inmate, now at McNeil Island, who Billy tells me might have seen or heard something that could help us. Do you know Rodney Smith?"

"Of course. He was a great tutor, serving life. Really good athlete and helpful to me."

"Well, they shipped him to McNeil after the riot, and I would like to have an incident report from him also, but I don't know how to get to him without alerting D.O.C. and the people who might be involved in this mess."

Elaine thought for a moment, and then her eyes lit up. There was someone who would help without even asking why. "Mike Medly, the GED instructor—he can do it! I'll call him tonight and ask."

"No!"

"What do you mean, no? They aren't going to allow me into McNeil."

"I'm concerned your phones are tapped. Call from a payphone to his home. That would be safest. Can you do that?"

"I haven't used a pay phone since college. I'm not sure I know how."

"Go to Fred Meyer. Buy a phone card and use the pay phone inside the main doors where they keep the carts. You pick up the receiver, insert the card and follow the directions. Okay, Elaine?"

Elaine was growing tired of Tony at this point. Besides, she was already late. Elaine gave him a dirty look and left.

Taking Yogi, she drove to her beautiful former home overlooking the Sound and waited for Richard and Harry. She didn't want to go in alone. They weren't far behind, and without any chatter they scooped up the items Elaine chose and placed them carefully in the bed of Richard's truck.

Elaine watched, enjoying the memories she was taking from the house that no longer held any pull on her emotions. There was the hardback rocker which only a small person like her Italian grandmother could have fit in. It was now one of Elaine's favorite places to relax. There was a black leather settee she had scrimped and saved to buy when she and Daniel first got married, and where she reclined and daydreamed about life.

A horse lamp, half price from Molback's, an old rocking chair and very comfortable footstool upholstered in purple velvet that would work with the colors in her new home: An old sideboard, from which she carefully removed her mother-in-law's china and silver. The sideboard had been her fraternal grandmother's and her father had refinished it for her. There was a wall in her parlor where it would shine, filled with memorabilia important to her. Her grandmother's cedar hope chest, again refinished by her dad, would fit perfectly at the end of her bed and give her extra room for linens and such.

Finally, her desk, computer, printer, and they were done. Good thing, too, as the truck was full, and she didn't want to impose on them for a second load.

She knew exactly where she wanted everything to go, had foreseen it in her mind's eye. That part of the move went quickly;

so smoothly she received a compliment from Harry. "You're different from other women I've helped in the past. Sure you don't want to switch things around twelve more times?"

"Thanks, but no thanks," she answered laughing. "I'd rather go eat. It's almost seven and I'm starved. Plus it's my treat. Where do you guys want to go?"

"Well, if you are asking me," Harry answered, "I like Buzz Inn. Not too far. They have good cow and drinks are cheap. How's that sound?" He turned to Richard.

"Sounds great. There's one here in Everett on Colby.

Dinner was filled with good food, good drink, and light conversation, which Elaine was grateful for. She wasn't interested in getting Harry involved in the legal mess she was embroiled in, and figured he felt the same way by his lack of curiosity about her move, unemployment and her life in general. Richard was astute enough to just let it go. They laughed about old times at work or conferences and each took turns telling war stories, embellished or not.

She gave them hugs when they let her off at her new residence and watched her open the door, greet Yogi, who seemed calm, and close the door once safely inside.

It was fun and relaxing putting away the treasurers into drawers and nooks and crannies this old house offered at every turn. She remembered her dorm room in college, from a time when men and women students lived separately, and the luxury of a single room; where she could think and look at her own things, hung on the old steam radiator or placed on wooden shelves held up by decorator bricks. It had all been so beautiful, fresh, young feeling. She felt that way now, full of hope and expectations. She'd no idea for what, but it was the kind of feeling she'd had as a child on Christmas Eve or before a birthday.

Somewhere along the years she'd lost that keen expectation— except, she had to admit, the nights before her rides. But she felt it here, in this old house. She liked it a lot. Honestly, most of her Christmases and birthdays had turned out to be terrible disappointments. The fighting between her parents always put a damper and placed guilt on the small girl who each time believed everything would turn out differently. And riding horses was great, but there was always the end of the day.

Here she felt the refuge she had been searching for and she slept well, without dreams or awakening. Refreshed when she awoke she remembered she was going to see her grandchildren that afternoon. It was her grandson's eighth birthday today. She'd get him a great present and wander over to bask in the family.

They hadn't seen Yogi yet. It would be fun to see how they reacted to the dog, and her to them. The only kink would come when it was time for explanations, which she wasn't excited about fielding. Too bad, she thought. For god sakes, she was a mature woman who didn't have to account to her children for what she did with her life.

It would be interesting to see if Daniel showed up. He'd told their daughter he might make it. Elaine knew if he'd gone home he would have found the empty house and the note. That in itself could make for another interesting conversation. She was rested. She was up for it, as much as she'd ever be. She only wondered if talking to her would make him miss his flight back to the war in Iraq.

It was his choice. She was just glad he was still generous with money. Of course, it was her money too. She must keep remembering that and stop feeling as though she owed Daniel. Even he didn't think that way. Well, she couldn't completely erase how she had been raised, even when she wished she could. Guilt was guilt, and if she allowed it to rear its ugly head, she had it in deuces. What girl raised in the 60s didn't? All her friends did to different degrees. Oh sure, some had burned their bras and protested the Vietnam War. Some had tried free love. There was an oxymoron for a woman. Love was never free. And some like

Elaine had gone to college instead of letting finding a man and getting married be their ultimate reason for having been born.

But she knew, all these hard years later, that the 70's so-called freedoms were extremely dangerous. In fact some freedoms had been deadly. What the women of the 70s had achieved came with an increased rate of stroke, heart disease and ulcers. Now, some of these women who fought for those freedoms found themselves raising their grandchildren because their daughters decided freedom meant placing careers ahead of everything else. It seemed modern women wanted to have their cake and eat it too. Young women still wanted to have children, but no longer saw children as their first priorities. Somehow, Elaine's generation had given out mixed messages. And as is true, every generation takes what suits them and ignores the rest of any message.

Her generation danced at Haight-Ashbury to make the world a better place for all women. They protested against the horror and injustice of a man's' world, in hopes that the next generation of women would take it one step further. That one step hadn't happened yet. The fight for freedom didn't imply women should have it all. However that's what some young women seemed to take from it. In reality, the fight was for a woman's right to choose. Not just reproductive issues. The right to choose applied to everything; career, family, religion—even things as trivial as clothing. Sadly what had been lost was the responsibility inherent in choice. No matter what the choice, one should never forget the choice has to be made freely and then cherished and protected.

If it was to be children, then fine. If not, that was fine too. If it was to be a man, fine. If not, okay. If they wanted to rise to the head of the corporate ladder, so be it, to break through that glass ceiling along the way—but to keep female characteristics and strengths, not adopt a man's. Use compassion and fairness in dealings. See the big picture and strive to attain it, not just assume the violent, territorial attributes so common to ambitious males.

As she sat drinking her coffee and watching her dog roam the bushes, she thought of friends she used to know, still knew; and some who had died along the female 'trail of tears.' There was Sarah, married to Mark; so bright and touchingly beautiful. She'd stayed home because he told her to and raised lovely children.

Then Mark found a younger version of Sarah who made him feel virile as she could no longer do, because she no longer was. She had nothing. He had ruined her self-esteem and she was now at an age where she had little earning power because she had no education. He gave her no money, as the children were grown; and all the cooking, cleaning, washing, serving, chauffeuring, doctoring, gardening, raising children weren't worth financial compensation, not in this society. Sarah died, as Elaine watched, of a broken heart; even though the medical determination was chronic colon disease.

The truth was Sarah couldn't figure out what to live for. Men her age wanted the sweet young thing. Her own children were busy. She was too old to be desired in the workplace. She was poor and ashamed to work at minimum wage jobs. Her friends, including Elaine, had struggled to find their own place which took quality time not spent with her. And she was no longer half of a couple, which had been the whole of her.

Then there was Christy, the opposite of Sarah in their generation. The consummate bra burner, war protester, feminist writer; accomplished, well-traveled and now totally ignored by the next generation who didn't want to hear her message of responsible sex, patriotic duty, community service, which she subscribed to and practiced during her adult years. Now she was Elaine's age; had no family, no audience and became just another broken heart, because again all the decent men her age still wanted the young honeys.

The saddest part, to Elaine's way of thinking, was that these women still wanted the men their age at all. These would be men who in a few more years would need lots of care. Well, there was a saying that "old women take care of old men." It seemed to make sense if you had been together for decades that you continued to take care of each other, but to do it with a stranger seemed like one more form of servitude.

Maybe she was just lucky, or keeping the middle of the road balancing game she'd always had to play, would now give her the greatest freedom of all—a sense of peace within herself and by herself. She felt that way now, but how long would it last? Would she get lonely? Would she want someone in her bed permanently, or at least when she felt like it, ever again?

Looking at her watch, she knew this was not the time to decide. Her coffee was cold and Yogi was staring at her, as though to say, "Could I please go in to sleep now?" And she only had two hours before her grandson's party.

Elaine couldn't account for her melancholy both at the party and after it was over. It was a great party for an eight-year-old. Her daughter, always creative, had arranged for them all to go to a racetrack, where the kids and parents could drive actual race cars in safety but with a real sense of speed. Everyone was very nice to her, but Elaine felt old and a bit disconnected. She had done all this and it had been a great time. She was glad she'd provided a loving, safe environment for her children. She supposed she was sad because there was no one else there close in age. Nothing was really wrong, but nothing was right either.

Daniel never showed up, to no one's surprise, but their present was a big hit. As soon as she could, she made excuses and left feeling relieved they were all too occupied to ask questions. She had a reprieve and was happy for it. They had liked her dog and her dog's excellent manners, but she could tell Yogi, also, was relieved to get away from the loud noise and fast movements of children and their normal age-appropriate activities.

She decided to go back to her former house one more time.

There were a few odds and ends she wanted to bring to her new home. As she approached the house, she became aware more lights were shining brightly from windows than she had left on. Unlocking the door, she allowed Yogi to precede her inside the house. When they got to the living room, Yogi growled and set herself between Elaine and a figure who sat facing the ocean window. The clink in a glass informed her it was her husband.

"Daniel, we missed you at the party, but our present was a sensational success," she said.

"I wasn't really in much of a mood for a party after I came here to change and found your rather brief note."

"I'm sorry about that. Truly I am. A lot happened quickly, and I'm just now catching up myself. I rather thought you might have called my cell phone before now. I would have filled you in."

"It's hard to call from Iraq, Elaine. I thought when I got home, my wife would still be living here and we could catch up then. My mistake!" He sounded bitter and petulant.

"I think if you made a mistake, it was to think I could sit here unemployed day after day and wait for you to visit. Come on, Daniel! This has become more like a hotel than a home. Admit it!"

"I want you to travel with me. I think if you do, we will become close again."

"Thanks, but my idea of a romantic vacation isn't going to the Far East while you leave me alone and go off on assignment. Living here's scary enough."

"What are you talking about?" Daniel answered with exasperation.

"Our house being broken into—that's why I moved and why I have this wonderful dog. Didn't you read my note?"

Daniel glanced at Yogi, now lying in front of Elaine's feet as she sat across from Daniel. "I admit, I didn't read the note too thoroughly. I was too damn mad. Nice to know, I've been replaced by a German shepherd. When'd we get broken into?"

"Earlier this week. I was out on the beach when they got in the house."

"My God, Elaine." Daniel rose, grabbed her out of her chair and hugged her, as Yogi got to her feet and growled menacingly. "This has something to do with that damn case, doesn't it?"

"I'm not really sure. It might," Elaine answered in a quiet voice.

"That's it! You can't keep putting yourself in danger like this. I forbid it!"

"You don't have a say in the matter," Elaine said as she pulled away, patted Yogi to calm her, and resumed her seat.

He glared at her. "That's just fine. I give up, Elaine. But I don't want a divorce. Actually, if you keep this up, I may not need one, since you'll probably make me a widower. If you need me, call the office. Otherwise, Merry Christmas. Please call me when this idiocy is over and we can talk reasonably about our future together. If we have one."

She hadn't noticed the packed duffel bag beside his chair, but wasn't surprised by it or his storming out and slamming the door behind him, one more time.

Without the interest, enthusiasm, or energy to sit and examine their relationship, Elaine gathered the items she'd come for, locked up, and drove back to her new home. She was relieved to arrive without incident and discover a gift basket on the porch filled with wine, cheese and crackers.

An enclosed note read, "I decided if we're destined to be neighbors, I might as well be more welcoming." It was signed "Williams."

Chuckling at the sentiment, Elaine took the basket inside, let the dog out for a minute, and locked up. She checked for messages, found none. She slept soundly for a second night in a row.

She'd made it through another week of her new life. Elaine was pleased this Sunday she'd a horseback ride planned with

Richard. Saturday she would do laundry, grocery shopping and catch up on some of the legal material from Tony she'd fallen behind on. She hadn't been to see Billy for five days, but figured he was in good hands with Tony and that her presence might not be wanted.

After a good Saturday and a great Sunday, Elaine realized she was right in feeling that Tony, and perhaps Billy, no longer wanted her directly involved. Sitting in Tony's office, he started in with: "Elaine, I think it best you disassociate yourself from Billy's case. I'm his lawyer now and I like to work alone."

"I can still visit and bring him things to help do the time."

"No, I want him off limits until the trial. Being personally involved with him is going to muddy the waters. Do you agree?"

"I suppose, but without a job, how do you expect me to keep busy until the trial?" Elaine asked, a touch of desperation creeping into her voice.

"Billy and I talked about that, and we think it would help if you use your professional contacts in Olympia and see if you can't get some support for an independent investigation. Pressure from a couple senators might help blow this cover-up out of the water before Billy ever gets to court. How does that sound?"

"Not bad, but aren't you just afraid that I'm in a dangerous situation and are trying to protect me?"

"That's not true, at least on my part. You're a grown woman with an excellent education and a good mind. As far as I'm concerned, you can take care of yourself. My mother did and her life was a lot harder than yours will ever be. I see no reason to coddle you. If Billy does, that's his problem; but you need to understand your presence puts him in danger."

"Fine. I give up for now, but I want written reports every week. And to be able to call and meet for a meal now and then."

"The reports are no problem, but shred them after you read them. I'd hate the other side to know what I have planned, and we know your dwellings are targets. No phone, no meals. You're going to have to trust me on this, Elaine, or I can't do the job you are paying me good money to do."

"Some neighbor you've turned out to be!" she joked. "I might as well have moved to Seattle where I could go to plays and the opera while I'm sitting on my hands for the next, what, four months?"

"I think the trial will take place in January. I'm quite aware it's only November, but I didn't ask you to move here. I honestly think blanketing the powers that be in Olympia could help a lot. Look, I have loads to do today, so I have to get back to it. Are you going to be okay?"

Now she felt angry, but the logic of the situation reached her, so Elaine walked home, wondering who she should make appointments with at the state capital before the day was out.

Damn, she had never called Medley at McNeil. She thought she'd better skip that or have Williams do it. She wasn't as brave as she previously thought.

Chapter 15

"Senator Suvall, please," Elaine told the staffer who answered the phone. "This is Elaine Bennett calling."

"Hello, Elaine. It's Jessica. Do you remember me? I attended your last prison graduation ceremony at the Reformatory. I'm the senator's political assistant."

"Of course. How are you, Jessica?"

"I'm fine, but we need to find $14 million before the next session convenes or some of Ollie's pet projects aren't going to make it out of the senate."

"I'm sorry to hear that. How is the Senator?"

"He's fine. We really enjoy coming out to the prison. Are you calling about some upcoming event?"

"Not this time. Actually I need a half hour with the Senator as soon as possible. I will come there at his convenience."

"Oh—" Jessica hesitated. "Do you think it's something I could assist you with?"

"Thanks, but not this time. I need to talk directly and privately with Ollie."

"He is in committee all day today, tomorrow, and Wednesday. What about Thursday at ten a.m.? By then he should be ready to slow down somewhat. He could give you thirty minutes."

"That sounds great. Where do I come to, his office?"

"Yes. I can give directions if you need them."

"No, I think I remember, but I'll call if I get lost. Thanks so much. I'll look forward to seeing you also."

"Great, we'll see you then." Jessica hung up

"Okay," Elaine said out loud. "That takes care of Thursday.

Now to fill my calendar for Tuesday, Wednesday and Friday." She made a few more phone calls, left messages, and decided she did feel like Christmas shopping. She called an old friend who was usually available and they spent the rest of the day and evening in Pioneer Square, ending with an excellent fish dinner and wine at the Wharf.

Thursday arrived quickly. No other senators or aides returned her phone calls. Elaine decided it was best to test the waters with Ollie first. He was her favorite, a small town guy who had few political aspirations, which was good because he was constantly pissing important people off with his blunt talk and hard line in support of the underrepresented citizens of the state. But time after time, he got reelected. Elaine thought sometimes people who would normally never go to the polls only voted for Ollie. And he was worth it. He got things done.

She enjoyed the drive down with Yogi. She liked having the dog because she talked to her and stopped for her, and in exchange received undying loyalty and affection. No judgments, no criticism, no chastising. Just love.

She found the office, a wonderful wood-paneled room inside the Rotunda on the third floor of the ornate Capitol Building. Early to a fault, she stopped and got a latté while wandering around until her appointed time. Finally she went in, exchanged cordialities with Jessica and was ushered into Ollie's office, where he sat with his huge feet on the desk, talking intently on the phone.

"No, I don't care what Senator Smith wants. I'm not going to change my mind on this. My vote stands. I have to go. Give him my best." He hung up without another word and came around the desk to gather Elaine in a huge bear hug, typical of the man. Ollie truly liked people and he let them know it. And he loved his job. The pressure didn't seem to affect him, a good fight to him was just another challenge to meet and win. He was the perfect Jimmy Stewart politician, except he was real flesh and blood, and there was a lot of him. He stood 6'5," all solid muscle. An 'old Scot', though not that old, he had bushy eyebrows and wonderful curly hair, which gave him another two inches he didn't need.

Afraid he was going to twirl her five-foot frame in circles like something from *The Sound of Music*, Elaine pushed away and straightened her suit. "Goodness Ollie. I'm glad to see you too!"

"Elaine, Elaine, Elaine. Sit, sit. Did Jessica offer you something to drink?"

"Of course I did, Senator, but it's a good thing she refused, or she'd be wearing it right about now," Jessica laughed. "Would you like something, Elaine?"

"No thanks, I just finished enough caffeine to keep me going until tomorrow."

"Senator?"

"No, I'm fine."

"You've got half an hour undisturbed," Jessica said with her beatific smile and left, closing the door firmly behind her.

"What's up, Elaine?" Ollie asked. "Jessica made your message sound somewhat urgent."

"Urgent may be too strong a word, but important is not. Remember the riot in the reformatory I got caught up in a little over a year ago?"

"Of course. We're still trying to figure out who owes who. You know about the state liability because of the deaths and injuries. Christ! That is a mess! You must have been scared shit....sorry."

"I *was* scared shitless. No other word to describe it. But do you know who did what to whom and how all that is playing out?"

"Not really, except the inmates responsible are in custody— not that they weren't already—and the book will be thrown at them."

"Don't start throwing things just yet. Ollie, is this room secured? And can I count on you to keep what I'm going to tell you confidential?"

153

"Our offices are all swept regularly. Sad, huh? But that's twenty-first century politics. And as to my discretion, I give you my word, and I hope you know it's my bond."

"I do. Look, those inmates being punished are innocent. I wouldn't be here today if those men hadn't saved my life and the lives of the other educators caught there that day."

Ollie sat and gaped at Elaine's bold, seemingly heretical declaration. "You want me to believe that everything told to me as Chairperson of the Criminal Justice committee was fabricated? That the testimony by the Department of Corrections Secretary was all a lie?"

"I wish it weren't so, but I was there. And there is an extensive cover-up being perpetrated to keep you and the public from knowing the truth."

"Come on, Elaine. You know I like you and I admire the hell out of the work you do with those guys, but aren't you exaggerating something here?"

"I wish I were, but I was there. I know what went down, and I have it all written out, safe with my lawyer, in case something happens to me."

"Lawyer? Danger? What'd I miss here? Start from the beginning." Even though her half hour was up, Senator Suvall picked up the phone and instructed Jessica to hold his calls and cancel all his appointments for the rest of the afternoon. He brooked no argument, although Elaine could hear protestation in the background.

After another hour of attempting to recap the incident, with Senator Suvall constantly interrupting, Elaine still hadn't gotten very far. He suddenly stood up and announced, "We're getting out of here."

It was fine with Elaine, so she allowed him to bustle her past a curious secretary and out to his car. He drove. She sat. He said nothing until they were miles from the capital. Elaine had visions of his career ended when journalists snapped pictures of him and 'some woman' entering a hotel/restaurant in the middle of the day. However, it wasn't her reputation at stake, and he did seem to be paying attention and taking her seriously, so she followed into a nice lounge at the back of the nearly empty café.

"Okay. Start where you left off," he growled as he ordered himself a gin and tonic and a coffee with brandy for her.

"Well, after Billy agreed to help me—" she left out his declaration of love, having half convinced herself she'd heard it wrong or misunderstood— "he left and we waited. With the pizza came the S.W.A.T. team and everyone was rescued except me, as Damien had dragged me over to the administrative offices."

"I'm with you so far—everything you've said matches the written statements of the staff and the S.W.A.T. team, except they never mentioned an inmate helping them."

"Of course not. If they had, you might want to know why they have that same inmate up on murder charges."

"Let's order something to eat," Ollie suggested. Elaine agreed. She had nowhere else to go. And she was starting to think Tony and Billy's plan to get her out of the way might actually bear a very influential and important ally.

After lunch and another drink she was relaxed and growing quite animated about her subject. "When everyone else in my building, thanks to Billy, was evacuated, the lifers, who have now all been transferred and punished if they speak the truth, led by Billy, went back to the administrative office, regained control, subdued Damien, and only then did the S.W.A.T. team reappear. They made all the inmates lie on the floor, and were kicking and cuffing them. Damien was alive while all this was occurring. They ushered me out at the same time."

"Well, maybe he resisted. Maybe they had to shoot him. Lots of maybes in here, Elaine."

"Sure there are, but if you read the report, Damien's throat was slashed, as was Officer DeLory's, outside the building door. That's how they're getting away with saying Billy did it. It's absurd, and a more than perfunctory investigation by an agency outside D.O.C. would conclude this is all nonsense. That's why I'm telling you there is something terribly wrong with this picture."

"Why are you in the middle of all this, if I might inquire?"

"Because I went back to work, expecting to thank Billy and the others, and hoping maybe some time had been taken off their sentences. Instead I was confronted with Billy being tried for a murder and the other men having been shipped out. I can't live with that. They saved my life. So I quit, and am now working full-time trying to get this mess straightened out."

"Well, that answers the question as to why you think you're in danger." This senator was nothing if not fast on his feet, Elaine thought, as she tried to remember if there was anything she hadn't told him.

"There is no reason for the inmates to have slit Officer DeLory's throat," she added. "The inmates liked him, and he shouldn't have been out there. His assigned post at the time was Gate 7. Officers might have wanted to shut up Damien. In fact, we're starting to find out information that suggests a very sophisticated drug/prostitution ring was being operated from inside. Damien might have been a kingpin. Our sources also claim that members of the S.W.A.T. team were involved and making millions from the enterprise."

"You've got to be kidding!"

"I'm not kidding, Ollie, and neither is my lawyer. Billy's trial starts in January and it will all come out then if some agency doesn't intervene before his date." It was starting to sink in to the Senator that all the ramifications surrounding the riot had done nothing to give the citizens a feeling of confidence and safety; that the adverse publicity of state employees involved in drugs and prostitution inside a maximum state penitentiary might lead to a whole new slate of politicians come election day. And to be fair to Ollie, he was likely trying to figure out how to do the right thing. Elaine was willing to give him that much credit until he showed her differently.

By four o'clock, realizing she was going to hit the traffic going home and that poor Yogi was waiting in her car, Elaine suggested Ollie sleep on everything and they get together again soon once he had.

Poor Ollie acted as though, if only he could sit there a while longer, he could find a solution. Or that if he never left at all, he wouldn't have to. But he paid the bill, slowly got up, and they drove back to her car in silence.

Elaine asked him to wait while she went to her car and let out her dog. Yogi dashed madly to the nearest strip of grass. Afterwards, she went back to where Senator Suvall was sitting, his huge arms draped over the steering wheel, staring blankly out the window. Elaine gave him her cell number but asked him not to share it with anyone, adding she had been threatened and her house trashed so she'd had to move. She added she would be anxiously awaiting his call, and left. It took six long hours to get back to Everett.

On Sunday Richard's rig pulled up at nine a.m. It was nice to be starting out later as the cold November mornings were relentless until about ten a.m., which was usually when they were tacking up the horses. Maybe it was old age, but the cold was really starting to penetrate her bones. Still, she felt exhilarated as she climbed in the truck cab and smiled at her friend. "Morning," she cheerfully greeted him.

Richard looked almost as serious as he had the day of the riot, when he'd been tied up and unable to help himself or her. "I think we'll just make it a short ride out on the Burke Gilman Trail in Woodinville and then go have lunch at that tavern where we can tie up the horses. Sound okay to you?"

"Um, sure. Sounds fine," Elaine answered, feeling like a balloon from which the air was starting to seep. She knew better than to press. The truck ride was quiet except for some old Willie Nelson tunes playing on the tape deck. The trail ride was quiet, too, except for the clip-clop of the horses' hooves on the frozen ground and periodic noises produced by a cyclist or jogger whizzing by. Finally, they tied up at the tavern, loosened the cinches, removed their chaps and walked in the back door.

Always greeted warmly by the locals who loved the horses and felt free to pet and feed them carrots, Elaine and Richard sat facing each other near the old potbelly stove. Looking around, Elaine could still see evidence of the high times from the night before. Lots of peanut shells on the floor, beer bottles tipped over in plants and behind window curtains, and the floor still sticky from the drinks that hadn't made it into the patrons' mouths. She didn't care. This little country dive was a place of refuge and relaxation with good memories from rides past. She hoped she'd have another after today, but wasn't confident.

"You want your usual, Elaine? I'll order," Richard said.

"Sure."

Richard went to the bar/restaurant desk and placed their requests, paid and then went off the bathroom. Elaine decided to do the same. When she returned, Richard was back, nursing a beer. Her red wine was waiting, warmly inviting, as she sat back down and took a sip.

The tension was so sharp, it felt like icicles she had seen hanging in the shade on the way here. "That was a good ride," she commented. "Just enough for such a frosty day."

No response.

"Are you all ready for Christmas? Are you going back to Wyoming to see your sister again this year?"

"No."

"Okay, that's enough—I won't be able to eat the delicious fries I assume you ordered for me, if you don't tell me what's wrong."

"There's really nothing wrong. I just had to make some decisions that were hard, and I need to figure out how to explain them so you'll understand them correctly."

"That doesn't tell me much. Why don't you just start? I'm

sure once you do, that glib tongue of yours will follow along nicely." Maybe her attempt at light humor was starting to punch through that leathery exterior, because Richard smiled.

"Okay. Here's the deal. I've been asking questions inside, and as hard as it is for me to accept, I have come to believe there *is* a cover-up going on and that Billy did not kill anyone."

"Wow. That's a big declaration. I know better than to ask how you found this out and from whom, but can't say I'm not thrilled you've finally accepted the truth."

"Actually, truth be damned. I've seen a lot of corruption in that insane asylum. And I've always let it pass, or told whoever was doing to keep it away from me. But I can't turn away from this."

"Really? What makes this time different?"

"I thought a lot about that and I think there are two reasons. One is you. The other is Billy. I care about you, and Billy saved my life. I don't take that lightly. I can't."

Elaine was relieved that their food arrived just then. They busied themselves with catsup and salt and settled in to eat; while new ideas floated in their heads along with the ramifications their airing might cause for both.

Finally, with nothing left to eat and second drinks set before them, they looked up and smiled and spoke at the same time, which made them laugh.

"What do you want to do now, Richard?" Elaine asked quietly. "And remember what is happening is dangerous. I'm living proof. Plus your job is at stake, and you don't have a rich spouse." She could tell as soon as she said the last part it had been a stupid and insensitive thing to say. Not that Richard cared about money, but she could tell sometimes he didn't appreciate having to be so careful about the same fifty dollars.

"I'm sorry. That was a really stupid thing to say. I'm just nervous, and I don't know quite how to handle the situation. Only once before has a man said he wanted to do something dangerous

159

for me because he cared about me, and all that did was cause him grief. I care too much about you to let that happen. But I know you could be a great help and I also know you are a man who can take care of himself. I'm really confused and not making much sense."

Elaine sipped her second glass of wine for something to do besides babble.

Richard started laughing that wonderful deep rich laugh of his. He got up and grabbed his chaps and started for the back door. Now she knew she'd made a complete fool of herself, again, and followed after him. He was mounting his horse as she dragged herself up.

And he was still laughing, which was starting to be quite irritating, as she followed him down the road. By the time they got back on the trail and could ride side by side, she was getting quite peeved. They had spoken personally and all he could do was laugh at her? Fine, she decided. She was not going to be the first one to talk again. Let's see how he deals with that.

As they were untacking and putting the horses and gear away, Richard finally deemed it time to speak. Well, this should be interesting, Elaine fumed, as he approached her side of the trailer and walked in front so she had no place to go.

"Look, Elaine. I'm not some schoolboy who has a crush on a teenage girl. I'm not some lonely cowboy who would like to get in your pants. I'm your friend and partner and my sense of injustice is almost as high as yours, but not quite. So be it. I want to speak with the lawyer you hired for Billy, let's just leave it like that for now. We'll keep riding, but not till after the holidays. I do need to get away to my sister's ranch. Maybe wrangling and real country folk will help me think. Okay?"

Elaine brushed past and got in the truck. Richard did the same. The long road home was filled with old time country music. Elaine dug in her purse and handed him Tony's card before she pecked him on the cheek. He squeezed her hand and she went in her house, light-headed from the wine, cold air, brisk ride and concern

160

she felt for putting in motion so many balls she couldn't control. After a long afternoon nap, fully dressed, she felt better. Examining what had happened again on this afternoon's trip, sitting before her potbellied stove with Yogi and all the presents she needed to wrap, she accepted once again that all of the men she was purportedly close to had either left her because she was impossible to be with or bonded together and excluded her from their midst.

She made herself promise to call some women friends in the morning and hang around them as much as she could during the holidays. They and family were all she wanted until the next year. Men were stupid and impossible except for her son, and as he got older, he'd probably get just like the rest.

But her plans were interrupted by the mail the next day. It was from the Netherlands, news she had been awarded a Lifetime Achievement Award for her work with Correctional Education. They wanted her to give a speech at the upcoming conference. The only problem was the International CEA conference was being held in the Netherlands and was taking place in two days' time. She sarcastically thanked her previous employer for not forwarding her mail. Now she would miss the biggest honor of her life.

She paced her little kitchen, letter in hand, for what seemed like hours, Yogi's eyes following her back and forth. Finally she decided she needed to vent and since she'd sworn off men, she called her friend Jill, who owned a company called Vintage Travelers. Her clientele were rich, 'mature' people who wanted safe, classy traveling experiences.

Hearing the stress in her friend's voice, Jill left the running of her agency to someone else and drove from Edmonds to Everett to be with her. Elaine had been there plenty of times for her. Elaine hadn't said what was wrong on the phone, but good friends picked up on such vibes and came running.

They hugged, and Jill, always the fashion critic, took a tour

161

of her surroundings before settling in front of the fire, drinking her wine and eyeing the dog. She'd never been an animal lover, but this one seemed docile. At least he kept his distance and was quiet.

"Okay. What's going on?" Jill bluntly queried

Elaine spent well over a half a bottle of a smooth Merlot, with Jill doing most of the drinking, catching her friend up. Since Jill hadn't known about the move, until hearing the new address, catching up took a while. She'd known about the riot and Elaine's time away, but thought everything was fine. Was she surprised!

"Let me see if I'm caught up," Jill jumped in, when Elaine paused long enough to sip. "You quit your job, left your husband, hired a lawyer to defend the murderer who saved your life, and you're not too sure there aren't people out to hurt you. Is that about all of it?"

"Yes, I think so."

"And tonight you are unhappy because your mail didn't get to you in a timely manner, as you said, so you could go to a conference and receive an award."

"Yes, if I'd known a month ago maybe I could have gone. It would have meant a great deal to me."

"In case you forget, I'm the one who was looking at Buddhist temples in Japan while you were trying to get into their prisons. I was also the one who flew over the Great Divide with you and made you go on an ice walk at Banff, or you would have spent the entire week listening to dull speeches."

"Well, it doesn't matter now. What are you doing for Christmas?" Elaine asked. Jill wasn't married and had a very attentive 'friend.' He took her to plays, operas, ballet. He had money and loved to spend it on her. She was worth it—interesting and charming, men loved being with her.

"Jim and I leave the day after tomorrow for Morocco. I'm looking forward to some warm weather."

"Well, let me give you your present now. I just finished

wrapping it. Open it so I can see if you like it."

"I'm sure I will. Oh, Elaine this is lovely. You know which outfit it goes with, don't you?"

"Of course, the Black silk with the mauve running through it."

"This scarf is fantastic!"

Elaine felt more cheerful, with a friend there who'd liked the present. "Do you want something to eat?"

"I'm sorry. I have to get back to the business. With us leaving before Christmas I have a million things to do."

"I'm sorry I dragged you away, but I'm glad you came. I feel much better about everything,"

"I'm glad, but I think you are going to feel better if you come pick up your tickets to the Netherlands at the agency tomorrow."

"What are you talking about? It's too late. Isn't it?"

"Of course not. While you were talking, I was making your itinerary in my head, and you have plenty of time. I'll give you until tomorrow night to shop and find someplace for that beast. You still have a passport, don't you?"

"Yes."

"Great," Jill said as they rose. "I need you in the office at nine a.m. Can you do that?"

Elaine grabbed Jill for a hug as she struggled into her big wool cape, and they both got wrapped up in it. "You're the one who is fantastic. Can you really do this? What if I don't have enough money?"

"Sweetheart," Jill said in her best Mae West accent, "that's what credit cards are for. Go now, deal with the consequences later. Please. I want you to get that award. God knows you deserve it. I'm just a little concerned about that 'some people may be trying to harm me' part of your story. If you don't do this, you have to stay at my home over the holidays or I'm going to call Daniel. And you know I will. I don't have so many friends I can afford to lose one."

"I'll do it. I'm already starting to write what I'll say in my head. I'm really excited about this. Thank heavens I called you. This is going to be a great Christmas after all!"

The rest of the night into the wee hours of the morning Elaine spent packing and thinking about seeing her old friends at the international conference. Huh, she thought. Daniel wasn't the only one who had people and places to visit.

Chapter 16

Tuesday came quickly. At seven she took a shuttle to the airport. Tony reluctantly agreed to take care of her dog. He wasn't thrilled, but Elaine could tell he was relieved she was getting out of Dodge. He had enough to worry about, she figured, besides some ditzy she-devil. Elaine had learned years ago there were serious differences between men and women, and race was certainly an issue in relationships. She'd also learned it needn't be a bad thing. It just needed to be addressed so that it never hung around like the elephant in the room no one looked at. Mr. Williams was a great lawyer, she'd decided back a few months. He was also uncomfortable around strong women. She wasn't sure yet if it was strong white women or all women in general, but she'd figure it out at some point. It interested her.

The plane left for New York at nine a.m. She was checked in, had a hot espresso and ticket in hand, and at least an hour until boarding. She had hoped for the downtime, because she hadn't yet told her husband or children she would not be home for Christmas. Presents for the children and her family, including Daniel, she'd left under their tree on a short visit a few days before, but she hadn't planned on leaving the country.

The night before she'd watched a favorite old movie when she couldn't sleep, *Shirley Valentine*. She always gained courage from the middle-aged woman's jaunt to freedom. The 'high' of Shirley's escapade was still with her. She felt strong, young and very romantic. It wasn't a sexual feeling, but a 'high adventure' kind of tingling Elaine savored as she reached for her phone and placed her first call.

"Good morning, Theresa, how are the children?"

"They're fine, Mom. Why are you calling so early?" Elaine could hear the TV and homey sounds of children in the background. "I need to update you on my holiday plans. I just found out I'm the recipient of the highest honor my organization, CEA, can give, and I need to be there to receive it so I can't make it over on Christmas Day. I'm sorry, but you have the presents, and I'm sure with Dan's large family there, you won't even know I'm not present. And when I return, we can get together."

"Mom, what kind of conference is held over Christmas?"

"Actually, the conference starts tomorrow, but I want to stay around and play tourist. I've never been to this particular conference site before."

"Where is this conference, Tibet?" her daughter asked jokingly.

"It's held in Holland."

"Holland! Mom, why didn't you tell us about this earlier?"

"I told you, my mail just caught up with me from work, so I couldn't. Jill talked me into it yesterday. You know, my friend Jill with the travel agency?"

"Mom, this is crazy! The children will be disappointed, and I think Dad is going to be here. I thought you and he should spend some time together, since you haven't been getting along very well."

"Oh, how long did your father say he can stay?"

"Well, just overnight, but still...."

"No, sweetheart. Just don't go there, okay? I know it's hard for you to understand, but overnight, with a huge celebration as the backdrop, is not a good venue for your dad and me to talk, much less work out our issues. But it's okay. I am really excited about the trip and the honor. Please be happy for me, and have a wonderful Christmas with your family. Make every moment count. It all goes by so quickly."

166

"Mom, I think you're being selfish and unreasonable. Now we have to worry about you. You'll do anything for attention, I swear. First, the riot, now this."

"Do you hear yourself? Do you think I wanted to be nearly killed in a prison riot?"

"You didn't have to work there! Dad said so many times."

"Look, honey, I'm going to say goodbye now. I love you and I'm not doing this to make anyone worry. You only get one life, and I plan on living every day of mine to the fullest. I suggest you do the same. Please give everyone my best wishes, and have a great Christmas. Call me anytime. I'll keep my cell phone on. Love you. Bye."

With her dialing hand shaking, Elaine next called her son. He always seemed more accepting of his wayward mother's plans. "Rob, it's Mama. How are you?"

"Asleep, that's how. What's up, Mom?" he asked drowsily.

"I'm at the airport on my way to the Netherlands. Isn't that exciting?"

"Sure, but why? Why so sudden?"

"It's actually a very nice reason." She proceeded to tell him about the award, her absence from the Christmas brunch and the suddenness caused by the mail snafu.

"That's actually cool. Congratulations, Mom. I'm proud of you. I'd go with you if you'd given me notice."

"Oh, that would have been wonderful. I'm going to stay ten days if you want to join me. I would love it." Her son had traveled on conference trips with her before, and was a good companion, but just as her hopes soared, they fell quickly.

"I can't. I promised Theresa and the kids I'd be there on Christmas Day, then I leave that night for a ski trip in Vail with Pete and Jeff. I'm sorry, Mom."

"That's fine. I'm glad you have something fun to do. Your present is under your sister's tree. You're so hard to shop for, but I hope you like it. I think she's mad at me, but oh well."

167

"Mom, you taught me to live life to the fullest with your work, your trips, horseback riding and CEA, and I think you're doing the right thing. Have a great time. Go find some more windmills to fight. Now that you aren't working in the prison, you probably need more Don Quixote causes, don't you?"

Rob knew she wasn't working, but nothing about the legal case and all that was going on around it. Elaine saw no reason to worry him. "You've got it, buddy. Thanks for the vote of confidence and words of support. I need them just now."

"I'm not saying don't be careful, Mama, because I know you will, so have a great time."

"Thanks, sweetheart. Merry Christmas. I love you."

"Love you too, Mama. Bye."

"Goodbye, son," Elaine answered quietly, tears forming at their conversation.

Now for the call to Daniel. Hoping she would get his voice mail, she waited as it rang. Her prayer was answered. "Daniel, Merry almost Christmas and Happy New Year," she said quickly. "My plans for the holidays have changed. I'll be in the Netherlands for a CEA conference. I'm really excited about it, but sorry we won't see each other at Theresa's. I'd love to get together after the new year and talk if you want, but you decide. Be safe and remember, I do love you," Elaine said, relaxing her shoulders and unclenching her hands as she put the phone away.

Thirty years, and in all that time she'd never spent a Christmas away from Daniel or the children, but she knew in her heart she was doing the right thing. Just at the moment between hesitation and bravery came the boarding call for her flight.

She had no further time to think, thank God. Gathering up her briefcase, purse and shoulder bag, she got in line, comforted by the mass of bodies moving beside her on their way to another place than where they were.

Elaine hadn't heard from Richard before she left, but Tony told her he'd made an appointment to sit down with him after the holidays. As Elaine crossed herself, a Catholic thing she did on all takeoffs and landings, she remembered when she and Richard had traveled to San Francisco for a grant they were engaged in, and he'd laughed at her superstition. There was no one to laugh at her now, and for just a second, she felt desolate.

Once the plane banked and the pilot announced all the flight notices, she felt better, now in the 'no turning around zone'. She decided to get her briefcase out from under the seat and work on her speech.

After several starts, stops, cross-outs and the requisite glass of wine (after lunch, of course, at least on the East Coast), Elaine had what she felt was a passable draft of a ten-minute speech. She was quite pleased with the avenue she'd taken.

She wanted to address those who actually worked with the inmates in a security environment. She knew full well many of those in the audience would be bureaucrats, but they could follow along and get from it what they could. She missed 'her inmates.' She missed her colleagues, and in these few minutes tomorrow, she wanted to express all they meant to her. She felt confident she'd accomplished her goal.

She cuddled into the same Dr. Zhivago coat she'd worn during the riot and watched some pointless movie until she slept and was awakened by the rapid descent into Kennedy Airport. She quickly blessed herself, said a little prayer, and gathered herself for the jog to her connection.

This was one of the many parts of flying she hated. The airlines always put the connections so far away you really had to race to make your next flight. Elaine's back was not up to such a feat, and she knew that by tonight her spine would let her know it. But what the heck, this was probably the last time she'd be going on such an adventure. And she did have a big bottle of Advil. She could make it, and so she did.

They were calling last boarding when she dragged her luggage down the walkway to the plane, but barely there was good enough in this sport, so she smiled at the ticket agent who scowled back. Once, on a trip alone to Paris for a conference, she'd read the ticket wrong; and upon showing it to the authorities, had been lectured in caustic French as they showed her the tiny number one stuck behind the staple that indicated 12:30, not 2:30 p.m. She made that flight and she made this one.

This was starting to feel fun, like being in the high country on horseback when the last rig pulled away and you had nothing but your horse to take you across the mountain range where you hoped a horse trailer would pick you up a week later. There was no turning back and with that thought came peace and calm.

She was on her way and feeling great about everything.

Jill had called the chair of the conference and told him Elaine would be coming, so he could add her to the program. Mr. Olsen, an old friend of Elaine's, a funny Dutchman, seemed thrilled. He said he would personally pick Elaine up at the train station in Leyden for the conference.

It was a challenge to figure out which train to take from the airport in Amsterdam, but she managed and now was safely attached to her old friend and feeling relieved. With her arm tucked under his elbow, he guided her out to a waiting taxi and took her to the hotel to change. She only had an hour before addressing the luncheon. Was she prepared? Her friend wanted to know.

"Of course, Robert. I'd never let you down. You know that."

"But on such short notice I can't believe you could put all this together!" he said in grave, accented English.

"Well, I did, and here I am and so excited."

"Good. We will talk later. I hope you like this hotel. Knowing you, I thought you would like something in the University district. Yes?"

"Yes!"

"Okay. I'll wait downstairs. You hurry. I'm playing hooky from my duties."

It was a wonderful room in a very old building. Heavy drapery cushioned huge windows over old-fashioned heaters. The view was of the river, surrounding the cutest little town Elaine had ever seen.

Small shops with the brick lined canal smiled up at her through open windows, even though it was cold. Outdoor heaters were prevalent, where bicyclists, mingling thickly with cars, sped every which way. But no gawking, she reminded herself. It was eleven a.m. She would speak at 12:30, and she had no idea how long the drive was.

She quickly showered and changed into a wonderful gray tweed tailored suit, with a little white blouse. She combed her hair, and put on pearls all while going over the draft speech she wrote on the flight over. Then she hastily tucked the speech into her purse and went downstairs to meet Robert, who hugged her and immediately started dragging her into another taxi.

What an audience and what a place! This building had the Old World charm Elaine craved in her own life. But there was no time to explore and wonder. Robert immediately led her up to a raised dais, in a room quickly filling with people. She was introduced to the current president of the European branch of their American CEA organization. He was from Russia and his English was not good. However, pleasantries were pleasantries in any tongue and so it went until she'd met the other six people on the stage and was seated.

For the first time, the enormity of the event hit her. Her speech didn't seem appropriate. It was sentimental and schmaltzy. It smacked of disrespect for authority and disdain for anyone not a correctional educator.

What was she going to do? She couldn't write another speech, and she was not capable of improvising. She took out the notes from her purse and perused them again, trying to find a new perspective from the audience's point of view.

It wasn't that inflammatory, she decided. Anyway, they were

the ones who'd asked her to speak, so they must know she wasn't going to sugarcoat why they were all here. She calmed herself with a drink of water. Besides, most of the audience might not be bilingual, like the gentleman to her right, so they wouldn't understand her anyway.

She rose to accept the beautiful plaque, after listening to all the nice things that were said about her. She shook her old friend's hand. Then she began to speak.

"Ladies and gentlemen, fellow correctional educators and guests. My life has been blessed in many ways, few more special than by the years I have spent as a Correctional Educator. For those who aren't a part of Corrections as an educator here today that statement may seem strange. What could possibly be so charming and meaningful about working in an old smelly building without enough equipment, materials or support with a group of individuals society sees as less than adequate or desirable?

"And *doing* this job year after year, decade after decade must certainly indicate a *failing* on the part of a person not willing to strive for more. We know that is how others see us. Don't we want a 'real' job? Or maybe we just can't get one?"

I learned over the years that it is those who have *never* crawled into the belly of the beast, our United States prisons, who cannot understand the beauty that resides there amidst the horror; but it is they, my friends, who have missed an opportunity to see the face of God. For within each of our prisons is the evidence of man's humanity to man, not just the *in*humanity the media bombards the public with:

"To see a big tattooed criminal, with hair to his chest and mid-back, escorted to school by another equally dangerous looking man and told to sit in a seat until he learns to read is to witness God touching two faces."

"To watch big burly-looking men of all racial backgrounds work side by side to hang crepe paper, blow up balloons and hang them with bits of tape for a graduation ceremony for other inmates, knowing that if they choose to attend the graduation ceremony, they'll be humiliated by cavity searches, both entering and exiting the visiting room, but who will do it anyway, is to see the humbleness that God wants all of us to master.

"To watch mean-looking dudes of all ages play softball and gently make sure that the old guy with the limp not only hits the ball, but makes it completely around the bases is to touch the face of God."

"To be teaching a class for serious gang-bangers who are seventeen, eighteen, nineteen years old with nothing to lose, because some fool sentenced them to forty years for three drug crimes and having no custody within a mile. Then to have an inmate teaching assistant hand you a straightedge razor one of the students stole from the barbershop and was intending to use on someone, maybe you, is to be touched by God."

"To watch with pleasure as one of your inmate literacy tutors works intently one-on-one with an illiterate inmate on a Saturday or Sunday in a little broom closet turned tutoring room, when both could have been pursuing their own pleasure, is to watch God in their faces."

"To watch as a man, angry because you have just fired him as a tutor, lift his mask so you see the murderer's face beneath for just an instant but choose, instead of more violence, to put the mask back on and walk away, is to be graced by God."

"To see a twenty-two-year-old leave prison with a GED certificate, a Job Readiness Certificate, a Parenting certificate and a vocational certificate tucked neatly and proudly in a folder under his arm after serving five straight, which was no walk in a park, now finally armed with the tools he should have had *before* he entered is to see God's smile on that young man's face."

"To have a black student ask if you are Muslim because you dress discreetly, or a Native American ask if you are Native because you have knowledge of his culture, or a Hispanic man ask if you are Hispanic because you make faltering attempts at his beautiful language, an Anglo student tell you that as a young teacher you remind him of his wife or girlfriend and, as you get older, of his mother, when you advise, lecture or chastise that same man, gives a simple life great value. God helped you offer each one something hopeful as they searched desperately inside the belly of the beast for something to hold onto."

"To have an officer, inmate or staff member ask you to speak to a troubled inmate, because they thought he might listen to you graces your life as powerfully as the beautiful setting sun does as you leave for home after a long day 'inside.'"

"God, whatever form each of us thinks that God takes, encourages us in our lives to help those who need help, to teach those who were left behind in life, to save those who cannot save themselves. And God teaches us we are not to judge the sins of others unless we have no sin ourselves. Those of us who teach in correctional environments or assist those who do rise above the petty self-indulgent lives of many people we share this earth with. As correctional educators we actually work to make our country and the world better, if only for a little while."

"My professional career, spent with those considered 'damaged,' spans thirty-five years. It never brought me fame nor fortune and most likely won't for you either; in fact, when I finally, after ten long years, finished my expensive doctorate, I called my son who has always championed my endeavors. His profession is one where work is done with large amounts of money. I told him I would be making ten thousand dollars more because I'd finished, and he said, 'Fantastic, Mom! Ten thousand dollars more a month will really make a difference in your retirement.' It was my sad duty to tell him, 'No, son, ten thousand dollars more a *year*.'

"But my work has given me a sense of peace and pride in a job well done, because my time was spent helping those who morality tells us need us most. There is great comfort and satisfaction in that thought. My only complaint is that this lifetime of achievement, if indeed I am worthy of such a statement, has gone by too quickly."

"If I may humbly offer any advice from my many years it is this: As you work, play, laugh, and maybe cry in your endeavors, never think you are alone. We are a unique group of people and we are *loyal* because we share a common bond, the bond of humanity and the desire to leave this world a little better than we found it. We hate injustice so strongly that we give time, energy, blood, sweat and tears to the unheralded cause of assisting those who, for reasons we do not judge, need help."

"When there is a hurricane, people give. When there is an earthquake, people give. But so many only give from a distance and only occasionally—when the media tells them to and only if the cause is politically correct. We in correctional education have chosen, or been chosen, to give 'up close and personal' it seems like, within a set of circumstances that would crush lesser human beings, to the lepers of society. The job will never bring earthly glory!"

"If you are in correctional education for any other reason than to really help in the passionate dedicated manner I have described, then get out: You will do more harm than good to those who must reside in cages. But if you are listening to me today with a heart that hears the cries of the incarcerated and wants to answer those cries with enlightenment through education, then I commend you and offer you my sincere thanks for all that you do, and for this award today."

"Not many people are as fortunate as I to be acknowledged for their lifetime of work by people whom they respect and admire. I pray that I am worthy of such acclaim, and that I may still be of service in the years ahead. I want to be. Just seeing all of you here, struggling against the same old enemies of budget and support restraints, makes me envious that I am no longer at present able to fight the good fight, but must settle for a sideline seat."

"There is so much energy and insight here today, I can feel it, and have heard you talking. Conference-goers are geared up to go back to their institutions and try new techniques, share new ideas, fight for more respect and money. I commend you and the Correctional Education Association that ties all of our hard work and us together."

"Thank you and peace be with us."

People were standing and clapping. She was so close to tears it was crazy. They kept on applauding and it made her wish her family was here. The rest of the luncheon was a blur. After it was over, several old friends bought her drinks in the bar. Elaine realized she hadn't eaten lunch and knew from past experiences if she didn't slow down, she wouldn't be able to attend the evening festivities. So she excused herself, called a taxi and went back to her little hotel room to rest, shower and change.

She was so proud. They'd stood for her. They'd clapped for her. All this praise made her feel powerful and strong. She now knew she could go back and fight for Billy. He wasn't just a number, he was a valuable human being. On the way back to her hotel she kept reliving the moment, savoring it like the taste of an unusually fine wine.

Her room was even more delightful than she remembered. The bathroom was quaint and charming, with the European fixtures and high ceilings. But it was the view that kept her mesmerized for over an hour. The sky was darkening. The temperature had to be dropping; but still people walked and gathered together. And as the lights came on, the canal took on a medieval quality that made Elaine think maybe she had truly stepped back in time. She could have sat there forever, just being.

Finally, she shook herself from her trance and prepared to head out for the evening. The conference banquet dinner was excellent. The speeches were great, and from past experience Elaine knew the music to follow would be even better. Many of the thousand or so conference goers would go out on their own: some back to their hotel rooms to sleep and others out on the town to party. Her own group of friends would find some large area of the conference center where they could sing and play. Oh, how she loved this aspect of the European lifestyle. Hard core types like herself who had been on executive boards that met three times a year from all over the world tended to want to be together, and the Europeans knew how to make the most of this, because of their music.

Elaine sat with a friend from Ireland as five flutes were brought out of their cases, three guitars appeared, and bongos joined to complete the ensemble. People from different countries, even continents, looked forward to jamming together each time they met. Elaine was a singer, as were thirty or forty others. The rules were simple: you drank and sang a song from your own country. Some people would sing together, some alone. You actually just started the song, and if others knew it they joined in. All the songs were in English, since Europeans, unlike Americans, knew two or more languages fluently, one always being English.

When it was her turn, Elaine decided to sing "Summer Time". She knew it well, since she had sung it to her children at bedtime when they were little. Plus she knew others would love to sing along with her after she began.

The music was charming, as always. It was dark outside which made it feel less imposing and allowed people to screw their courage to the wall when volunteering to sing the next song. The musicians seemed to know every tune, and picked up after one or two beats on songs they had probably never heard before. Oh music. The universal language.

Elaine was having the time of her life. Her song went over well. It had taken her until almost eleven p.m. to be loose enough to sing it, but she would remember the moment forever. What a night it was. She was fading fast now because of the time difference so she said her good nights and once again got into a taxi to head back to Leyden and her warm bed.

Her wake up call the following morning found Elaine a bit

disoriented and heavy-headed, but a shower soon put her right. This was the final day of the conference. She'd actually missed most of it due to faulty scheduling, but she didn't care. Workshops were not for her. She'd been to hundreds and hosted many over the years. It was fun watching young faces, so energized and emblazoned with hope to change a system that Elaine feared was irrevocably broken.

She did take in one workshop because the title in the conference packet interested her: "Are We Really So Different?" It was being led by a young Irish American who wanted to discuss the similarities and difference of inmates from country to country. The ten people in the room were from Russia, Germany, Iceland, Finland, America, Canada and the Netherlands. The participants spent an hour and a half deciding whether their offenders were similar and how their teaching was comparable. Where they differed was in the treatment of the offenders while incarcerated. Other countries were kinder and more humane than the U.S.. Education and treatment programs were more advanced, especially in Germany. Elaine felt rather depressed as she left, but decided she was doing what she could. She thought briefly about calling Williams and asking how the case and her dog were doing, but decided there was nothing she could do from the Netherlands so why bother?

Elaine figured since it was now cocktail hour she'd find her old friends in the lounge and she was correct.

"Elaine, we were just getting ready to go to Amsterdam for dinner and a night on the town. Want to join us, yes?" Robert asked, as he gave Elaine a seat at their table and a glass of wine appeared automatically.

"Yes, I'd like that very much," Elaine answered with a smile, thinking how dear these people were to her; even some she'd only met once or twice. There was a special kind of intimacy among correctional educators, one she could only explain to friends and family by referring them to old reruns of *M*A*S*H*. Her European friends' castigation of U.S. policies was always tinged with love for Americans. They loved Americans even if the American government didn't impress them.

"You go back now and dress warmly and comfortably. Yes? We may get on a boat and it will be cold outside."

"Sounds good." Elaine finished her wine and went to find a taxi.

The evening was magical. The lights, crisp winter air, cruise down the canals, getting off long enough to hit a club for a drink, dancing and wonderful jazz, kept everyone warm and exhilarated as the night ended and dawn broke. The thin sunlight reminded them, as did the boat driver who wanted to call it a night, they should get some breakfast and let the poor man go home.

Robert picked a place with all the meats, eggs, cheeses, creams and coffees one could hope for in a lifetime. Elaine ate like a lumberjack. The men laughed at what she put away, but it was all good banter and she was sorry to see it end when they waved goodbye at her door. They were going back for the final day of the conference. Elaine was going to bed. And did, until almost two p.m. the next afternoon.

She wanted to attend the closing ceremonies which were probably getting underway. So she rushed to dress and jumped into yet another taxi. She made it in time to hug, kiss on cheeks and wish goodbye to many dear friends. She knew she might not ever see them again. She felt sad as she finally sat down at a spare table to wait for Robert to finish his duties.

"Let's go, Elaine. My car is out here. It is very small, but we do not have a long drive." Robert had come down from his hotel room with his luggage. "We will stop by your place, get your suitcase and be on our way. It is a good drive and we will be home in time for a late dinner. Tessa knows to wait for us."

Elaine looked at Robert and wondered if he would make it until dinner. He looked like death warmed over. His color was gray. The bags under his bloodshot eyes hung over his lined cheeks. Elaine guessed he was about 65, and today he looked every day of it.

"You don't look so good, my friend. Are you sure my company is not going to be too stressful?" Elaine offered, hoping he wouldn't take her up on her polite withdrawal from his invitation.

"No, certainly not. You are going to be my buffer when Tess takes one look at me and knows I have been out all night. She won't yell at me with you there. You must come."

"I can't live with you forever! You'll have to accept the consequences for your bad behavior eventually," Elaine teased.

"She can not stay mad with me. She knows it is my nature to live every moment. She will be over her anger by the time you leave. Come. As you and your cowboy friends say, we are burning daylight."

When they finally arrived, Tessa was waiting.

"Tessa, Tessa. How good to see you," Elaine called as she exited the tiny car and rushed to hug her friend as she came down the steps. She could never decide who was more fun, Robert or Tessa. Tessa was definitely better-looking. In fact she was drop-dead gorgeous. Probably fifty, her skin, hair, and figure were all that of a twenty-year-old, and her smile was infectious and genuine. Elaine had loved her since Robert brought her to the U.S. for one of the board meetings he attended as European delegate.

"You look marvelous, Tess. You never age a year. How do you do it?"

"Clean living, I think," she responded in a heavy French accent. "Unlike some old men who do not know how to act when allowed to leave home." This was all said as she looked over Elaine's shoulder and witnessed the wreck that had once been her husband. "But come in, Elaine. You must be tired. Please sit."

Elaine had never been to their home before and found it unpretentious and comfortable. "Thank you, but please don't be too hard on Robert. I watched him run that huge conference, and it was no small job. He has a right to be exhausted. Honestly."

Robert threw her a smile of thanks as he deposited her luggage behind a curtain that separated the small guest room from the living room. He kissed his wife tenderly, as though he had truly missed her, and vanished out of sight.

"Let me get you tea, Elaine or would you like wine?" Tessa asked.

"Tea, please. I think wine is starting to leak out of my pores, I have had so much. But the conference was well-organized and very interesting. I'm glad I came and am so grateful to you for letting me be part of your family holiday. I hope it's not too much trouble."

"Heavens, no," Tessa called back, returning with the traditional tea tray and serving items. "I'm thrilled you are here. Robert will probably sleep a lot and I have always wanted you to meet the rest of our family. Now you will."

Elaine winced slightly at the mention of family, but kept it hidden. "I'm happy to be included. Thank you again."

"I know my dear husband will be hungry as an old bear, as it is way past his dinner time, so sit and rest and I will see to the kitchen. Okay? Or you may join me. The bathroom is right there. The door facing the living room."

"I'll freshen up and join you. We need to catch up."

"Of course. Just bring your tea with you."

Chapter 17

Tessa went back into the kitchen and Elaine went to the only bathroom. It was neat and organized. Everything one could ever need was there. 'How wasteful Americans are,' she thought. She was glad she'd moved to a smaller place and she'd be proud to have people come and stay. She was glad to be out of the mausoleum she and Daniel owned.

The two women didn't get a chance to really talk until, after a very filling meal with a very tired Robert, Tessa put him to bed and returned. "I thought his head was going to fall in your excellent soup, Tessa," Elaine laughed. "He's had it, I think."

"Amazingly he will be up at eight o'clock tomorrow fit as a fiddle and anxious for the day to bring whatever it has in mind," Tessa said as she cleared the table.

The kitchen was a delight—small and efficient but still welcoming, as only kitchens that are truly used can boast of being. "Tell me, what goes on at Christmas time?" Elaine asked after Tessa had warded her off from helping and she sat nursing her tea.

"We open presents in the morning after the children and grandchildren arrive," she told Elaine who pondered how Robert's three sons, as big as him, and their families could fit into this little house. She was surprised the house was not decorated for the holidays, as she knew they were religious people. Only figures of Mary and Jesus adorned the walls, and she assumed those were there year-round.

She caught herself daydreaming and heard Tess saying that after opening presents and breakfast they all dressed warmly and attended Mass. Elaine was welcome to join them or not, as she wished.

"I'd love to go. You know, the one place I go in every country I visit is the church. It tells me a lot about the people."

"I agree," Tess responded as though translating that particular statement. "Now I'm done. I shall have some tea and you must tell me why we so unexpectedly have the pleasure of your company. And do not try to fool me by saying the honor you just received was the reason. You could have caught a plane home to be with your family. You did not. Why? I know how important they are to you."

Elaine spent three hours bringing Tessa up to speed and, by the time she finished, Tessa had opened a bottle of smooth cognac for her own nerves, if not Elaine's.

"Elaine," Tessa said finally as they sipped the cognac, "I think you are in danger and should stay with us longer. Maybe Robert gets you a job here."

Elaine giggled then laughed. What dear compassionate people they were. And whether she saw them every day or never again, they would always be some of the dearest, most precious friends she'd ever have.

"Thank you. Thank you, my dearest Tessa, but I can't stay. My home is in the United States. I would miss my family and I have to clean up this mess with Billy and the other lifers. Can you understand?" This was said with tears in her eyes, but joy and love mingled with them in her heart.

"You worry me, but I will say nothing more for now. But I'm going to share all this with Robert. He knows nothing, does he?"

"No, but don't worry him. I'm fine and really looking forward to tomorrow."

"You sleep here. I hope you will be comfortable." Tessa drew back the curtain off the living room and Elaine saw a mattress with a pillow and blankets. She kissed Tessa on the cheek, said her good nights, and closed the curtain. She undressed sitting down, folded her clothes over her suitcase, lay down, pulled up the covers and slept like a baby.

She awoke to the sounds of stomping and decided they weren't reindeer hooves, but boots shaking off snow on the porch. Dressing quickly in the other outfit she had brought, she grabbed her cosmetic bag and flew into the bathroom to prepare for the day. It was already 9:30. She skipped the luxury of a shower and lathered deodorant and Chanel instead. Deciding there was little more she could accomplish, she packed up and opened the door.

How could so many people be so quiet? Robert and Tessa's three sons sat with him in the living room; while the three daughters-in-law were busy in the kitchen with Tessa. She looked outside and solved one piece of the puzzle; at least ten children of all ages were throwing snowballs, running in circles, and working diligently on a snowman the size of their grandfather.

Once the mothers saw she was up and presentable, they went outside and allowed the children to run inside, one or two at a time, to jump on Robert. Eventually there were so many squealing, giggling bodies Robert was no longer visible. Elaine crawled up on his vacant chair to not get trampled in the mayhem. Finally, long after she had decided her dear friend was going to be killed by his own kin, he stopped pretending to struggle, and all the children let him up and gently escorted him to a chair.

Looking at the children, Elaine was spooked by how identical they were. The men were all Dutch. The women were all French. They knew their heritage, and it was simple. How interesting, so unlike American stew, she thought without judgment.

The puzzle of the missing Christmas decorations solved itself. From a back porch off the kitchen, the sons produced a large live spruce they proceeded to prop up on a handmade stand of boards in the living room. All the chairs, couch and table were pushed against the walls and the tree placed in the middle of the room.

As though orchestrated over generations, Tessa produced

boxes of lights and ornaments and after the men strung lights, each child took turns putting a special ornament on the tree as Tess handed them out while telling the history of that particular piece. The children waited patiently and quietly in the kitchen. There was no pushing or shoving. There was no whining or begging, arguing or fighting. Even the smallest was silent. The only voice heard was Tessa's.

Elaine was entranced by the ritual. Maybe she *would* move to Holland and make her family come here as well. No, she thought, it would never work, but she could enjoy this time and tell her rough bunch back home about it, and maybe some of the beauty would rub off.

After the tree was completely dressed and the boxes put away, the daughters in law served eggnog—virgin for the children, spiked for the adults—and carols were sung and toasts were made to those who could not be with them. Elaine toasted her husband and children and felt the better for it. After that, everyone went to cars, closets, pockets to retrieve beautifully wrapped gifts which they then placed under the tree or on it, depending on its size and weight.

Elaine thanked God once again for reminding her to bring presents. Her small crumpled treasures with various name tags, she put on the tree with great care. As with the dressing of the tree and the singing, the placing of gifts was done one at a time with reverence. Elaine found this delightful. She had a moment of guilt as thoughts of her own family passed through her mind. She pushed the guilty feelings away and reminded herself to call her daughter's house *late* on Christmas Day. That would take into consideration the time difference between Everett and Holland.

Elaine turned her attention back to Tessa just as she returned with the *pièce de résistance*, a delicately wrapped Nativity scene. She and the women placed it with loving care on the windowsill to announce Jesus was born and among them this wondrous day. All held hands as Robert said a prayer of thanks and peace for

186

the world.

A breakfast of fine pastries and fragrant coffee, milk, and fruit finished the celebration. Then it was time for church. This family had an extremely strong sense of family and never rushed off to community worship, but savored it as an afternoon engagement, which suited Elaine just fine. She could smell dinner cooking as everyone donned coats, hats, and gloves. Elaine borrowed galoshes from Tessa for the five block hike to the church.

Elaine definitely needed to get out, she decided as they strolled along; mothers and fathers speaking sternly to the children, who were starting to exhibit American-style tendencies like sneaking a snowball to throw at a lagging sibling, or pushing a younger one (dressed in a bulky snowsuit and just learning to walk) to topple over like a bowling pin, much to the older ones' delight. The tiring parent snatched up the little one and soothed its crying as the walk continued. Elaine wondered how these restless children would fare in a long Christmas mass.

Again, she was pleasantly surprised by their manners, patience, and maturity. After getting unwrapped from their warm outerwear, the small ones cuddled into outstretched arms, Elaine held a two-year-old miniature Robert, who couldn't care less that she was a perfect stranger and went to sleep quietly slurping his thumb.

The cathedral was beautifully decorated for Christmas, but even without the trappings this church would stand as one of the loveliest she'd ever seen. It was a true Gothic cathedral; a structure that had taken centuries to create. The architecture lent a sense of permanence and continuity as it was built long before they were born and, unless man's warlike tendencies destroyed it, would be standing long after they were gone. A Gothic church was not made to impress visitors, but to impress upon the congregation the importance of worship. Light from the stained glass windows embodied the essence of God's light.

Sitting with this precious baby asleep on her lap Elaine

remembered a statement she had read somewhere: "The church, by its beauty alone, acts as a sacrament. Like the plain and the forest, the cathedral has its atmosphere, its fragrance, its light and shadow, its chiaroscuro. The great rose with the setting sun behind it seems, in the hours of the evening, to be the sun itself, on the point of disappearing at the edge of a marvelous forest. But this is a transfigured world, where light is more dazzling than an ordinary life, and shadow more mysterious." Emile Male, a religious art scholar had written this about the Notre Dame Cathedral in 1949, but Elaine felt it fit perfectly for this cathedral on this day.

Because she held the baby, she was not expected to rise or kneel and instead was able to feel the genuine warmth of this family, a warmth she knew came from her Holy Father and Blessed Mother to whom she intently prayed as the service went through its familiar course. When it was time to take communion, Elaine handed the small Robert to his father and rose to walk the aisle to the priest. She felt cleansed. Saying over and over to herself like a mantra as she walked to the altar, "Forgive me, God, I'm not worthy to receive you, but only say the word and I shall be healed."

She felt at peace with herself as well as the world in which she resided.

Everyone was subdued on the walk home. The children were exhausted, which made it easy for dinner and the opening of the presents. The children got to go first.

It was accomplished by age, and though their gifts were fewer and less expensive than Elaine's own family exchanges, each was received with appreciation and sincere thanks. The sons and daughters in law went next. Much of the exchange was clothing, Elaine noticed: practical or pretty new things to wear, to keep warm while thinking of the giver.

Finally the children and their families took leave. It was almost midnight and a good tired was turning into a desperate

188

need for sleep before the sun rose again. Goodbyes and good wishes were exchanged, and the house seemed far too quiet after the departures, as Elaine, Tess and Robert cleared away refuse and put furniture back in place so they could sit facing the tree while completing the exchange of gifts.

Since all were experienced travelers, the gifts were light and small. People who are travelers and not tourists, travel light, but that never meant gifts were slight in meaning. The opposite was usually true. Time must be spent finding just the right thing. That was part of the rapture of the exchange. How close could you get to giving something the receiver would treasure and not put away, forgetting about the giver among the possessions one accumulated in a lifetime?

Elaine had spent great care choosing Tess and Robert's gifts. She did her shopping over the course of a year, sometimes years. The right gift was important to Elaine. Tess and Robert's gifts would have been late arriving, had she sent them as she'd planned. Another justification she thought, for having come on this grand adventure. Excited, she asked them to go first.

Robert obliged her. For a man with huge, bulky fingers, it was touching to watch him gently untie the ribbon and then spread back the tissue. It was a hat—but not just any hat. It was a dark blue wool Basque cap, more like a beret, really. It lay flat on the head and was particular to a region of France where the Basque people herded sheep and spun wool as they had for centuries.

Robert wore this kind of cap all the time, but this one was handmade by the king of the Basque hat makers. He only made one hundred a year, and they were hard to get and highly collectable. Elaine had spied Robert's head size from another cap a few years before and had commissioned this one for him. It had taken a year to arrive.

It was a good thing, because she could be here to see his surprise and appreciation. He was stunned. After lovingly turning it over and over in his large hands, he finally donned it at her insistence. It fit perfectly and he looked smashing. He got up, went to the mirror and stared. Then he let out a huge whoop and dragged Elaine out of her chair and into one of his bone-crushing bear hugs, while Tess laughed and clapped her hands.

"Put me down, you big lug. Please! You don't know your own strength."

"Never, never, never. Now you must live here with us forever so I may receive such gifts from you each year. I insist!"

"Not on your life. My bones couldn't stand it. Now stop. I want Tess to open her gift."

She knew Tessa's love of wool scarves, and this one matched the lovely blue velvet of her eyes. It too was handmade by a weaver friend of Elaine's, sprinkled generously with specks of rich gold thread. Elaine had loved it and had one made for herself. But this was definitely Tess's color and she knew it would be the finishing touch to the heavy wool coat Tessa had worn to church.

Before she opened the package, Tessa commented on its bulk and weight; Elaine mused that giving this gift allowed her room in her luggage for more gifts to take home. It had been an extra weight she would not miss. But Tess's happiness at the gift was well worth it. She spent time putting it on and admiring the finishing touch it gave to the look.

"Now, Elaine, we have only one gift for you, but we think you will like it. We hope so," Robert said, as Tess looked on with a Cheshire cat kind of grin. The present was heavy and solid. There went the weight reduction in her luggage, Elaine thought with no animosity, just curiosity. The wrapping was cloth with a ribbon bow, both of which Elaine knew she would treasure, no matter what the present turned out to be.

Then the box was opened, and Elaine was not only speechless, but crying as she saw its contents. They could not have given her a more special gift. "But how? When? How? When did you have time? When was it taken?"

It was an eight-by-ten photograph of her, shaking hands with

Robert as she received her Lifetime Achievement award only two days before. It was beautifully framed in rich mahogany, an inscription attached to the bottom. It read: "To a wonderful correctional educator and a great life traveler. From Your International Friends."

Below that was a small photo, somehow attached to the wood itself—a group shot of all the people from the sing-along that night.

Tessa brought the brandy. They toasted life, each other, correctional education, families. Then they hugged and Elaine crawled into her little annex, leaving the curtain open so she could look at the picture by the light of the Christmas tree left glowing at her request.

The next day was relaxing. The three cleaned up after the Christmas festivities, then took a leisurely drive to a favorite pub for a late afternoon dinner and songfest with the locals. Everyone liked talking to the 'pretty American woman', as Tessa kept calling her, one villager after another coming up to shake her hand and introduce himself. The liquor flowed, the music got louder, and the lies bigger.

Robert was a master of the tall tale. Except for the Irish, no one spun a yarn better than the Dutch. It became, as it always did, a sort of contest as to who could tell the largest story. Robert never took off his prized hat and Tessa received many compliments on her woolen scarf, which pleased Elaine. The trip couldn't have turned out better.

She decided to take the train back to Leyden the next day. The inn where she had stayed had been kind enough to keep the bulk of her luggage and a reservation. She was anxious to be on her own for a while. And she believed in the old adage about 'staying too long' at someone's home. She and Tessa walked arm in arm through the station while Robert parked the car. Then they all hugged, promised to write, and at long last she was alone at least until New Year's Eve, when they had decided to meet in

Amsterdam and bring the New Year in style.

She had a few days and nights left to explore Leyden, the university and perhaps some of Amsterdam. The thought of being alone pleased Elaine. She'd spoken to the family on Christmas Day. They were fine. She was fine. That was enough. Now it was her time to just be and, looking out the train at the lowlands, she sketched her itinerary in her head. The trial for Billy invaded her thoughts but she gently pushed those thoughts away. The trial would go on, with or without her

Relieved to soak in a hot bath and relax that evening in the same room she'd been given before, Elaine took time to make several journal entries about what had happened since she had arrived in this peaceful country. Before she forgot the colors, smells and sounds, she wanted to capture them for when she was an old woman, sitting in her grandmother's rocking chair by some fire warming her brittle bones and arthritic joints. Once finished, she realized she had written some twenty pages.

Good night, world, she murmured as she looked out the window from her darkened room. Sleep in peace and goodwill.

Tessa had told her about a street market where she could wander in and buy souvenirs cheaply. Robert told her about the red-light district with the marijuana cafes. That day she saw it all. She bought lovely silk scarves in the market and, because she was traveling alone, skipped the legal marijuana, but drank the coffee and watched those who were indulging. They seemed fine, before, during and long after they were done.

She and her friends had probably gotten more out-of-control drinking than these people did smoking marijuana. Why not legalize, control, and tax marijuana in the States she asked herself for the hundredth time? The government couldn't control its use. It was like Prohibition in the 1920s. Almost everyone was doing it, even if it was illegal. And Elaine was sick of seeing young American men thrown in prison for selling it.

She wandered through the Leyden campus. It was very

pretty. Tower clocks chimed the hour. Students walked and chatted along lighted sidewalks. She enjoyed their little chapel and spent some time in their library. What a wonderful place to go to university. It appeared so safe. And then, just to say she had, she walked to the red light district to see the women in the windows, beckoning their clients in the door with a flash of thigh or an exposure of breast. There was every conceivable prostitute Elaine assumed for every possible taste, because there was every kind of john. Old, young, dark, light, fat, skinny, beautiful and handsome. Ugly and plain.

No one approached her. She was not attacked. The whole scene seemed like some kind of theater production, with her and the audience as the players acting out parts.

Her feet hurt. She had a brandy in the downstairs restaurant of her small hotel and was surprised by someone speaking her name.

"Yes?"

"It's Dennie. May I sit with you?"

"Dennie, how nice to see you. Of course you may join me. I'd love it."

Dennie was the head of prison education for the province of Quebec and someone she liked. His accent was French, as that was his first language, but his English was excellent.

"What on earth are you doing here? I assumed everyone but me had rushed back to their homes."

"My wife and I are not big holiday people, and when I come so far to attend a conference, I like to stay and see the country. I know it is not likely I will return."

"I understand completely. That was one of my main motives in hanging around. What have you seen so far?"

"I'm ashamed to say I was so tired today I stayed in my room and rested. I felt good enough tonight to come down to dinner. I was just going back up when I saw you here and thought I would join you for a nightcap." He had one in hand, so Elaine continued the conversation and sipped her warm brandy slowly.

"I had a most interesting day," she offered. "I bought presents at the market, toured the university, watched people smoke pot, and strolled through the Red Light District!"

"My, you did have a full day," Dennie said with a slight laugh. "Maybe we can spend tomorrow together. What was your plan?"

"I want to go to Amsterdam, tour by boat, and wander through the famous museums and art galleries. I need to see where Anne Frank was hidden. That stop is very important before I leave. What were you thinking of doing?"

"I too wanted to go to the art galleries. I hadn't thought about a boat trip or the Frank hiding place, but it sounds interesting. Do you mind if I tag along?"

"Quite the contrary. I was enjoying being on my own after all the people at the conference, but one day seems to have been enough. I'd love the company."

Dennie finished his drink, set it down and rose, having left enough money on the table to pay for both drinks and a tip. "Then I will see you down here about nine-ish. Is that a good plan?"

"Yes, an excellent plan. See you tomorrow."

Dennie was right on time. They walked across to a tourist center and took a bus to the city. It was bitterly cold, but both knew how to travel for comfort; they wore layer upon layer of warm, removable outerwear. The driver announced where they were and the history of each site.

Elaine was surprised at the terrain of Holland, what little she'd seen. It was flat and without much in the way of trees or windmills. That had been her only disappointment. Of course, she only knew of the country from the Hans Christian Anderson books of her childhood. They disembarked right where the Amsterdam boats picked them up. Elaine was relieved the boats were completely enclosed, with warmth and libations as they comfortably wove past the intersections of this grand old city. She and Dennie liked the fact they could get off with the same ticket, see sights on land, then re-embark whenever they wanted until the last boat, which was not until midnight.

They chose one museum. Magnificent. Grand Old Masters everywhere. Seeing them all took three hours. Then, as Elaine wished, they climbed the narrow stairs to where the Franks had hidden during the Netherlands's saddest period. The idea all those people had lived for years in an area no larger than her tiny living room in Everett was extremely moving. The fact that little Anne didn't live to become the astounding woman Elaine was sure she would have been made her quiet as they exited the house.

Dennie was a sensitive soul who picked up on her mood. He suggested a warm drink and some food before they went back on the boat, the evening lights offering another perspective. There was a quaint little place right next door to the Frank hiding place and they whiled away two more hours there, talking, eating, and counting their own blessings before continuing their boat tour.

It was almost midnight when they finally made it back to their hotel, hugged and said goodbye as Dennie was off for home early the next morning. Again Elaine realized she might never see him again, but he would always have a special place in her heart from sharing such a special time together.

New Year's Eve came quickly. Elaine had checked out of her hotel in Leyden, buying a decorative tile as a souvenir. She figured out the correct train to take in a very crowded station. Arriving early afternoon, she took a taxi to the hotel Tessa and Robert had reserved and settled into another hotel room.

When she arrived, the message light on her phone was flashing. Her friends were already there and waiting down in the lounge. Donning a silk caftan she'd found in a little shop in Leyden, she went to meet them and ring in the New Year.

The following morning they took her to the airport and got her checked in. She welcomed the help as she was nursing the grandmother of all hangovers. They had drunk and eaten and danced in the streets, then had breakfast.

She slept all the way to Chicago, ran again for her connection, and arrived home the same day. Time zones were crazy, Elaine decided. But she had gone, seen, done and was now ready and eager to get home and resume her fight for Billy.

She was tired, but as Richard always said, it was a good tired.

Chapter 18

She slept for two days, getting up only to eat, clean up, and let the dog in and out. She didn't like it when Tony called as soon as she got in to say he was glad she was back so he didn't have to deal with the dog anymore. But Yogi was happy to see her, and she her Yogi. Elaine loved having her own things around, her own bed, her own answering machine- filled with messages, and a huge stack of mail.

One had to take the good with the bad. She'd learned that long ago. Christmas cards, were fun. Bills, not so great. She hadn't paid any since before marriage. It was a control issue with her husband. She supposed she'd wrap up the bills and send them along to Daniel. Or could keep them and invite him over for that talk. She thought that idea best.

She called several people to say Happy New Year. She'd talked to her children and grandchildren during the trip, so those calls were brief, just to say she was home safe and she'd see them soon. Around lunchtime she called Daniel, a cup of coffee in hand, her dog at her feet, thinking he wouldn't be around. Surprise. He was not only around, but anxious to get together. He sounded good. They agreed to have dinner that evening at the big house, as Elaine now called it, where he was staying.

"Hi, Happy New Year," Elaine offered as a very dashing looking Daniel opened the front door.

"That's just not going to cut it," he responded as he wrapped her in his arms and kissed her, quite well, she decided, on the lips. "Dinner's almost ready. You get a T-bone just like you like it, and I get my prime rib. Have a glass of Chianti while I turn the steaks."

"Great. How was Christmas for you?"

"I didn't make it to Theresa's. She wasn't happy, but I figured maybe we can go over there this weekend and open presents together. Sound okay? The grandkids would like it."

"Sounds good. They don't need to know that one or both of us has gone 'round the bend. Right?" He was in a great mood, attentive, very handsome and nice to her—making her a little nervous, actually, but as the evening went on, she began to relax and enjoy herself. He loved his tie from an exclusive shop in Amsterdam. He gave her Chanel, so she was pleased. Finally she thought she should go, and decided this was the moment he would start in. But nothing came.

For a fleeting second Elaine considered going to bed with him. She knew he would like that a lot. Their sex life had always been good, even if the foreplay and afterglow became briefer as the years went by. She would like the physical release and the closeness. But she knew if she did, she'd never leave, and she'd come too far. She believed if she did go to bed with her husband at this particular juncture in their relationship, she would be opening herself up for tirades. She wasn't ready for that.

She'd go home, take a cold shower, or whatever, and wake up alone with fewer problems. He graciously took the bills she handed him at the front door. He gave her a passionate embrace and kisses before walking her to her car. He kissed her again lightly, once she was settled at the wheel, and waited as she drove away.

Elaine felt totally confused in thinking about him, the very nice date, and what he was up to. She dwelt on it quite a bit that night and the next day. He really was a great guy and always there for her. He'd been a wonderful father and a good husband for many years, if she was honest with herself.

Elaine was looking forward to seeing him again. She called her daughter and made a date in the near future for a late family Christmas get-together at her house. It was time the family knew where she was, and she wanted Daniel's approval.

She had a lot to do: Tony had given her written reports on Billy's case and she needed to read them. Senator Suvall had left many messages and Richard called twice to say he was back and needed to see her soon. The trial date had been set for February fourteenth. Great, she thought, as she prepared her notes one more time for the hearing with Senator Suvall. It was already the second week of January and Elaine would be happy to see the month end. The weather was dismal. She allowed herself to fall into a funk, probably because of all the wining and dining and attention she'd received on her trip.

I still have a lot to be grateful for she thought. Her friends supported her, and that meant more than anything right now. She had also been invited by the Senator to speak to the Senate Committee on improving programs for transitioning felons back into society. Elaine thought the members would listen to ex-convicts more than they would her. So she'd looked up a couple of ex-felons she knew were still in the Northwest. They were out, free and clear with no parole or strings attached by D.O.C., so—albeit reluctantly—they agreed to appear.

The day of the event Elaine picked them up at a food court in South Seattle; one was a drug counselor, the other a floor installer. Both were very shy with her as she pulled out of the parking lot. Apparently being with their old instructor without bars or razor wire made them nervous. It did her, too, at first, and she wondered if she'd once again gotten into too risky a situation. After they'd been on the road a while, stopped for breakfast and conversation, the atmosphere became less constrained. They each took turns telling war stories, funny ones, nothing heavy. Elaine felt people would be surprised at the funny stories that take place in a prison.

David was grizzled looking, small in stature, funny and smart. He told how, way before she came to work in the prison and before he'd straightened out his act, he'd gotten blitzed on homemade alcohol known as 'Pruno' one night. He had taken a long rope into the big yard and, with sirens blaring, lights blinding him and amid orders to desist or be shot emanating from the tower guards, he staggered around, trying to throw a rope over the twenty-foot razor-wired topped brick wall before the guards hauled him down and threw him into solitary for six months.

The story was funny if only in the telling. It also was humorous because in the 1970s, when he pulled this stunt, the guards wouldn't shoot you if there was no imminent danger. They knew David, liked him, and just wanted him to stop. Nowadays they'd have blown him away after one warning to "lie flat on the ground and don't move." It wouldn't be a funny story now, Elaine realized. And there would have been no one to tell it.

Vincent's was a retelling of the drama class Elaine had taught so some of the guys could get their college English credits out of the way. Of course that was in the 1980s when the powers that be realized the importance of sending offenders back out into society with the tools needed to survive. The class was held on a Saturday and they were rehearsing in the chapel where the play would be performed a few weeks hence.

The play was entitled *What Ya Make It* and had been written, directed, produced and acted by some of the best students Elaine had ever worked with, inside or out. They worked hard, and she hadn't made it easy. She hadn't wanted to cheat them out of credits comparable to those they would have earned on a campus.

One dress rehearsal Vincent was playing a punk (a jerk, in laymen's terms). He was supposed to pick a fight with the 'good inmate' in the script, who was trying to help himself before release. It was important to the story the good inmate not engage in the fight but walk away. If he fought he would go to the hole, which wouldn't show he'd been rehabilitated and could walk away from meaningless aggression. During the rehearsal Vincent and the rest of the cast decided to let the fight take place in order to freak out the professor—Elaine.

200

That they did. They staged a full-fledged fight onstage with others joining in, knocking over chairs and desks. Elaine turned to the officer, a good old guy whom she could see was laughing so hard, his gut was jiggling as it hung over his invisible belt. That's when she knew they'd got her. Once she had her blood pressure under control, she saw the humor in it. Now, twenty years later, she could laugh along with Vincent.

Her own story was about her Jeep. Elaine had only been working in the prison for maybe six months. She needed a car, and the auto shop teacher talked her into a little C-J7, an off-road Jeep with soft and hard covers. He said he'd have the inmates change the tops, depending on the seasons. She loved her little candy apple red 4-Runner.

It came time to put the hardtop on, so she cleaned out the Jeep, as she knew the inmates would take anything they could use. She brought it through the back gates about eight one morning as arranged by paperwork. It was inspected with the mirrors and she left, expecting it to be ready at the end of the school day.

Next thing she knew, an officer called her out of class and escorted her down to Gate 7. Awaiting her was the Sergeant and seven very somber looking guards. Now she was nervous, but not nearly as much as when, opening his fist, the Sergeant produced two rolled cigarettes that looked like marijuana joints.

Elaine's knees buckled as the Sergeant said, "Are these yours, Dr. Bennett?"

"Of course not!" she answered with more confidence than she felt.

"We found them in your vehicle."

"You did not!" she answered, already seeing herself being dragged off to Purdy, the women's prison.

That was when they all started laughing, and the Sergeant explained the inmates working on her Jeep had found enough alfalfa hay under the floorboard to roll it in cigarette paper and sell it in the main prison. They went on to inform her the hopheads who bought it said it was the best shit they'd ever smoked.

∞

They'd arrived in Olympia well before they were expected to testify, so, since neither of the men had seen it, Elaine gave them a fairly professional tour of their state capitol. It and all it stood for had never meant much to her, but looking through the eyes of these two ex-felons, dressed nicely in suits, but wearing expressions you might see on newly arrived immigrants, she could appreciate it all the better.

Finally they went to Senator Suvall's office and, after shaking hands all around, were ushered into a small conference room to wait to speak. This delay gave them time to finalize who was speaking first, what each was responsible for addressing, and how long each had to speak. Elaine was functioning as a facilitator, but she did have one extra item she planned to address: Billy's case.

The senator didn't know she was going to do this. He'd asked her to speak about prison reform, but she was tired of lame excuses on why Billy's case hadn't been investigated. In fact, she was suspicious he hadn't informed the committee about her concerns. She would have one shot at shocking them out of their lethargy and fear of offending constituents, and thus losing votes. She had to take it.

She'd let David and Vincent explain how difficult it was to fit in, once released from prison after twenty years. She would let them detail experiences and offer solutions for others, so in the future, released felons could have more assistance in the transition process. She would then ask them to be excused and she'd speak about the cover-up.

Vincent and David looked uneasy at first, but after the committee folk spoke about how they appreciated their coming and educating them, they relaxed and did an excellent job explaining that work release and job release facilities were setups for failure, as the placement of these facilities was found in the areas of aggressive prostitution and drug dealing.

They could not use saved money or access earned money for over a month, and upon release were still expected to find transportation and jobs. Not knowing the area was a crisis waiting to happen for men who already felt like fish out of water. Using metaphors and funny examples, they had the committee listening and laughing as they shared humorous examples of mistakes made that could have caused them or others great harm.

Vincent cited the time, early in his work release, when walking in downtown Seattle, near the Hammering Man statue, someone came up beside him talking to himself. Vincent knew better than to stare, but he also knew that people talking to themselves close to you posed a great danger in prison.

There were many mentally ill people improperly placed in prisons. The man walked on, still chatting animatedly; it was only then Vincent could see he was talking on a tiny cell phone and posed no threat.

Funny, yes. Sad, also yes. Scary, but the committee ate it up. Both men had them eating out of their hands by the time they were finished. Elaine thanked them and asked them to wait outside.

Responding to the 'direct order' tone of her voice, which she felt a twinge of guilt for using, they quickly left and Elaine sat down before the committee. She told them why she was there and the action she wanted them to take. By giving them this information she placed herself in further danger.

She told them she had no choice, and left them with the veiled threat that if they took no action in the next two weeks, she'd speak about it in a public trial and to the media. They would then have to deal with the fallout. She shared she'd already lost her job. She thanked them and told them she'd be happy to come back any time and speak again. Shaking hands all around, she left.

Vincent and David were smart enough not to ask any questions. They were still riding the high of having been listened to by important people they were still innocent enough to believe had heard their message and would make great and lasting changes for the incarcerated. Elaine was more jaded, but didn't show her disdain.

She treated them to a steak dinner before dropping them off, thanking them, and saying goodbye. Elaine still had optimism some kernels of the ex-felons' message to the legislators had taken root; but more realistically, some of the bricks she'd thrown at their heads would make them smart enough to seek her out for first aid by setting up the committee she needed, before requiring help for their wounds from the press.

Billy, Richard, Daniel, the Senator, and especially Tony were going to be royally pissed off at what she'd just pulled. But that was too damn bad. She was sick of being treated like a naive child who needed to be protected. She was really angry by the time she got home and glad she had spoken up.

The trial would begin in two short weeks and they needed pressure put on the right people to make it a fair one. Elaine thought she had exerted just that pressure and felt proud of herself as she patted Yogi, in her bedroom doorway, and dropped off to sleep.

Nothing. By the time the weekend rolled around she'd heard nothing from anyone!

Suvall hadn't called to chew her out. Nothing from Tony or the others. The family was coming over for dinner Saturday. Maybe Daniel would say something then. She knew everyone had probably already heard about the meeting by now. She had a ride planned with Richard for Sunday, so maybe he would speak about the bombshell she had dropped in Olympia.

Saturday and Sunday came and went. It was great to see her grandchildren, feel their warmth as they sat on her lap and hugged her while she opened gifts. The dinner turned out great and her daughter seemed to like her new home and seemed more accepting of her life. Yogi was the hit of the evening. Daniel was still very attentive and loving toward her. He waited behind and asked if he might stay the night—only if she wanted to, of course. He had to leave to catch a flight back to Asia, but he thought the intimacy might be good for both of them.

They were married, she reasoned. She—and he, she had to assume—were lonely. She certainly didn't need to worry about getting pregnant; she knew Daniel well enough to know even if he wasn't being totally monogamous, he was physically cautious and wouldn't share anything but the intimacy and closeness she really did miss.

He was considerate. She was nervous, not about the lovemaking which she knew would be wonderful, but about letting him into her bedroom, her bed and her special sanctuary that, until then, had been all hers. But he left early, and she awoke alone, feeling contented and relaxed. It was still her home, her life, she who resided there, at least for now. He'd said nothing about Olympia.

After an exuberant Sunday three-hour ride on the Centennial Trail, Richard and Elaine went to her home and ate soup and bread to warm themselves. Richard was very quiet, but began to talk as soon as they pulled chairs close to the stove in order to eat and thaw out at the same time.

"Elaine, the Secretary of Corrections called me from Olympia last week. He had questions about the riot, your part in it and mine. I told him I would meet him for a drink, but I wasn't going to discuss his concerns on prison phone lines that could be tapped and traced. You remember we're old hunting buddies. We go back to when he was a lieutenant and I had just started teaching inside. I didn't think he wanted to catch up on deer season, but we agreed to meet."

"Interesting," Elaine muttered.

"He said he'd gotten his ass chewed out by some senators on the justice committee. Seems they'd gotten quite an earful about corruption and cover-up from some small dark-haired teacher the day before. They wanted him to convene an independent investigation, made up of citizens and staff who could be trusted, to get to the bottom of it and find the truth. He asked me to be on the committee. You can imagine how that thrilled me!"

"So, what did you tell him?"

"I told him no. That if I wanted to keep my job and my health, I wouldn't be involved. I was too close to the little dark-haired teacher, and wanted no part of any independent investigation she thought was such a good idea. What did you expect me to say?"

"That's about what I expected. Did you at least give him some recommendations?"

"I gave him the welding instructor and the auto shop teacher. And two citizens who can be counted on to do the right thing. You sure know how to stir up a hornet's nest, Elaine. Don't you think your lawyer can get Billy off and clear this mess up by himself?"

"Not with what he has been sending that he calls a case. Inmates' wives as witnesses and me? How far do you think that's going to get us against a S.W.A.T. team who will show up in uniform?"

"You have a point, but I still think you should have more faith in your friends." With that, he grabbed his hat and headed for the door. "Thanks for dinner."

"No, thank you. You have no idea how much these rides help me, how I look forward to them."

"Just the riding, huh? And here I thought it was the pleasure of my handsome face that made you rise and shine when you could be sleeping in like the rest of the lazy bums."

"Of course it's that too. You know how much you mean to me. It's just that right now when we have to be careful about what we say to each other, our friendship seems stressed or awkward somewhat."

"I understand. Well, it will all be over soon, unless they delay the trial, which I don't think they will."

"Good. Then we can go back to being more comfortable around each other. I hate the tension, but we both know it's there, and will be until this issue is resolved."

"I hope we can work on a relationship that's more than just comfortable, but let's not talk about that now. It can wait for a better day. I'll give you a call."

Elaine watched Richard walk down the porch. Was she leading him on? Was she leading Daniel on? What did she want from either? She loved them both, and together they actually created what seemed to her the perfect man, but she knew that kind of thinking was unfair and stupid. And then there was Billy.

She spent the rest of Sunday cleaning, washing, and doing the domestic chores that die hard when you've been doing them for others for thirty years. She felt better when the house was clean and decided to go grocery shopping before the day ended. Then she'd be all set for Monday, just another day now that she had no job to get up for, but still she liked the routine and was trying to keep one going in this, her new life.

Fred Meyer had everything in one place, which Elaine liked. She took off for Monroe without thinking she might run into people from the prison in their local one-stop store. After she got her cart and cleared the store scanner, she saw three of the S.W.A.T. team. They were in uniform and saw her before she could duck into the women's clothing section.

"Elaine, how are you? We've all been so worried about you," Lieutenant Percy said as he grabbed the front of her cart and the other two surrounded her.

She had mentally prepared for this moment, which she knew was probably going to happen after that day in the truck, but fantasizing and realizing the moment were two different things. These men were big and muscular. They had to be to do the duty. When not saving people they were allowed to work out and target shoot, activities built into every shift. They wore close-cropped haircuts and had more tattoos than the inmates, though theirs read differently. Typical inmates usually bore tattoos of gang signs, tear drops, roses, 'Dear mom' and the names of girls. These men had American flags and 'love it or leave it' branded on their huge biceps down to the wrists.

Violating D.O.C. policy, the three had their sleeves rolled up as far as they would go. Their physical presence was intimidating and she knew they were doing it on purpose. How she was, physically or mentally, was the least of their concern.

She'd decided that whenever she eventually confronted them, she would go for the gold and summon all the acting skills she'd acquired in college. She had her script memorized. She just wasn't sure she could pull it off without throwing up. But she knew she needed to create an Academy Award caliber performance so they would think she was in no one's court but theirs. She knew it was her best chance to help Billy and the lifers.

"You guys don't know how glad I am to run into you," she said, firmly holding her cart still. "I have wanted so long to thank you for saving my life. I had no way to reach you after I was fired so I haven't had the chance. Let me buy you something to eat or a drink, if your shift is over. Please?"

"We're still on duty," Percy said, pulling his arm away from her hand. "But we wanted to see you too, and find out what kind of shit you were telling the Captain about what went down the day of the riot. From what we hear, you've been talking trash, and worse, about us, and we sure as hell don't appreciate it after all we did for you!"

He had obviously rehearsed what he was going to say to her too. Now it came down to who was the better actor.

"Oh my God! I don't know who said what, but that's the furthest thing from the truth I've ever heard. At first I was shocked about Billy, but after it was explained, I realized it could have happened just the way you guys reported. I tried to tell someone, but they'd already pulled my badge and would not return my phone calls. What you say really upsets me," Elaine said, big tears welling up in her eyes, while she pinched herself hard on the arm.

"You trying to make us believe," one of the other bulls said, "that you didn't turn on us and say we committed the murders?"

"You guys have known me for twenty years. How could you think such a thing?"

"This came from the Captain, Elaine," the lieutenant offered. "She really worked us over after she talked with you. You saying Pepper's lying? That what you're saying?"

"Of course not! She and I were good friends. Still are, I hope, but she won't return my phone calls so I could never explain. I don't blame her, though. She misunderstood, is all. What can I do now? I'm looking for a job. That's my main concern. Can you believe they threw me out, after all the years I gave that damn place?"

"Well, that's pretty shitty. We were told you'd quit." Elaine knew her personnel files were confidential and couldn't be shown or discussed with these idiots, at least for the next month or so. So she didn't think they'd get the real scenario until the trial was in full swing, and what were they going to do to her then? She doubted they had the intention to physically harm her, but one never knew with these types. They loved power, control, and guns. They were heavy drinkers and hard on the women in their lives.

But she thought she bested them for now. They cared about their jobs, and felt bad for anyone, including her, they'd known for a long time, for losing one.

Gotcha, she thought victoriously. "I'm going to put in an application here. Do you think they're hiring?" she asked sweetly.

"We've got to go but let us know if we can help, Okay?"

"Thanks, guys. And I'm sorry about the misunderstanding. Please tell the rest of the team thanks for saving my life. I owe you guys big. But I'll be okay. Don't you worry about me."

They left and she went into a dressing room shaking with tension and fear. And with laughter. No longer hungry or in the mood for shopping, Elaine put the cart away and headed her car toward the Cascades to clear her head.

It was dusk, and she didn't want to go too far, but there was a small highway chapel she sometimes drove to between shifts to pray for patience and help when her job became too hard. It was just a small structure, barely high enough to stand up inside, but she loved it.

She parked off Highway 2 and went in—only to be disturbed, not comforted, by what she found. Her little sanctuary had been vandalized. There was graffiti all over the walls. The benches were knocked over and trash, fast food wrappers and bottles were everywhere.

Disgustedly Elaine turned to leave and only then saw a shadowy figure looming in the doorway. It was getting dark so she couldn't make out the face, but the person seemed somehow familiar. She knew it was a tall male, by the last bit of daylight shining through the open door.

Her acting skills wouldn't save her now.

Chapter 19

Elaine chastised herself for being so stupid to come to this desolate place without Yogi when she knew there were people out to harm her. Her purse was clutched in front of her. She quietly unzipped it, watching the still figure. She wrapped her fingers around her Mace and waited. She feared shooting it off in close quarters would disable her along with him.

She opted to make her move when he did, knowing any movement he made would momentarily distract him. Which was when she would push past him, spray, and run like hell to her car. She only hoped he was alone.

After what seemed like hours, the figure moved toward her and she rushed, hitting him as hard as she could in the groin with her purse as she rushed past the opening. As he turned to grab her, she shoved the spray in his face and pressed the lever. He choked, swore and stumbled backward long enough to let her make it to her car.

Elaine phoned the police while she drove to the police station in Monroe, where she had to wait for a black-and-white, as the station house had closed an hour prior. She told her story and rode back to the site with two cops. A lingering smell of Mace permeated the air, but there was no sign of anyone or another vehicle.

The officers took her statement, confiscated her spray with a warning it was illegal and that next time they would charge her. They promised they would dust for fingerprints next day but she knew they wouldn't. She could tell they saw her as a hysterical woman who was someplace she shouldn't have been, and got, or nearly so, what she deserved.

Great. Here she thought she'd convinced the guards at Fred Meyer she wasn't supporting Billy. One of them obviously followed her to scare her. Or if it was indeed a stranger, she was really too unlucky to leave the house anymore. She should just go back to the island, drink, and pop pills.

She knew it was someone who knew her. She knew it, and with that knowledge drove home; looking in the rearview mirror every mile and locking herself and Yogi in for a long night. She took the time, since she couldn't sleep, to compose an informal will. She placed it on the refrigerator where she knew it would be found.

The day before the trial Tony called out of the blue and said he wanted her to visit Billy.

And men think women change their minds a lot, Elaine mused as she showered and dressed. The new black dress fit perfectly. All the jogging she'd been doing to keep her and Yogi in shape was paying off. She completed the look with her wool coat, but removed her gold pin before the guards did it for her.

Billy was being housed in a cell close to the courtroom. After being ushered into a conference room, Elaine draped her coat over the back of the cold steel chair and sat down to wait. She heard the heavy metal doors slam open and shut. Three guards brought a shackled, cuffed, wasted-looking Billy into the room. A female guard helped him sit down and then stood a few feet behind. Obviously this level of security wouldn't allow them to be alone even for a minute.

Elaine reached over to pat Billy's cold, white hand, more to reassure herself he was still alive than anything else. The guard leaned forward, ordering Elaine to desist. Elaine pulled back because of the woman's nasty tone, but glared at the officer while she composed herself enough to look at Billy. He must have lost forty or fifty pounds. His orange jumpsuit hung so loosely, it fell off one shoulder even zipped completely to the top. His flaming red hair was pulled back in a dirty pony tail, and the dark circles under his dull blue eyes spoke of a loss of hope she was horrified to witness. His always fair skin had a transparent sheen.

"Billy, are you sick?" Elaine asked, at a loss of where to start the conversation.

"I'm fine. Just don't like the food and lack of fresh air, that's all. I'm fine, Elaine. That's not why I asked you to visit. I need to get a promise from you," Billy answered in a tone that precluded small talk.

"You know I'm here to help anyway I can. I haven't visited because Tony told me not to. You knew that, didn't you?" she asked, worried Tony had lied and because of that, Billy had given up on himself.

"Of course. It was partly my idea. You wouldn't be here now if I didn't need to see you face to face and get one little problem settled in my mind before the trial begins. You've done more for me than I thought anyone would, and I'm grateful. Tony is a great attorney and if anyone can get the truth out of these lying bastards, he will, but I don't hold my breath. And neither should you. That's what I want to talk to you about."

"Okay, sure. What is it?" Elaine asked, trying to come to grips with his disheveled appearance and sickly demeanor.

"I have great hopes Tony will win," Billy stated without conviction. "But if he doesn't, I want you to promise me you won't appeal. That you'll do nothing further to continue this travesty. Forget this cause. You have to promise you'll walk away. Go on with your life. Leave this alone if we don't win. I need you to promise me that!"

He stared at her urgently. Sweat beaded his forehead and he looked paler than when he'd first come in. "You have to promise me, Elaine. Don't retain Tony. Just drop it!"

"I most certainly won't," she shot back. "I can't believe you could think I would. We will win, but if by some chance we don't, I most certainly will appeal, and appeal and appeal until we get the truth out and you are freed, at least on this charge. I want you to get credit for saving our lives." Elaine responded with intensity.

"Listen carefully. That riot allowed me the opportunity to do the one good thing I've ever done in an otherwise worthless life. I'm proud of that and I want to keep it as an honorable action in my memory bank. What's going to go on in that courtroom will bring to the fore the murder of my victim.

"She is on my plate. I'm going to have to relive it in front of hundreds of people, who will then retry and convict me for it once again. I've tried for twenty years to accept and move beyond it, to turn that boy into someone who is more than that worthless piece of shit. Tomorrow I'll become a piece of garbage again. You can't understand, but trust me, I'm not particularly looking forward to it."

"Think of it this way, Elaine. Remember when you allowed the media to come into the prison one year to film graduation? And what did they do but shoot footage of the fools in the big yard instead of the graduates in cap and gown? They took the program, with our names and numbers on it, looked our information up in public documents and ran our mug shots on the evening news, with a description of our crimes next to the degrees we'd earned. Remember how badly you felt for setting us up?"

"Well, this trial is a setup! Why can't you get that through your head? They are going to drag out my victim's family, and any family who suffered a similar crime, so that maybe they can pin those crimes on me. I'm not going to be presented as Billy, the reformed criminal, excellent tutor and teaching assistant; the man who saved lives. I'm going to be hyped as Billy the Bully, #997543. You didn't know that was the handle the press gave me to sell newspapers, did you? So anyhow, that's why I need your promise, and I need it now."

"Or else what, Billy? That sounds like a threat to me," Elaine answered desperately, in a voice that didn't sound like her own.

"Or I'll plead guilty tomorrow and halt this phony trial before it starts. Tony knows that's my plan, and he can't stop me if I choose to do it."

"You wouldn't!"

"I would and I will. I need that promise, Elaine, or I'll simply plead out and go back to three hots and a cot, which frankly I miss, since they put me in this zoo."

"You know what you're asking? I'm just supposed to forget you and go do what?"

"Get a life, Elaine. If you didn't like your old one—and I don't think you were too happy—get a new one. Don't be a fool. You have all kinds of opportunities. The world is your playground. Go have some fun and forget this stupid system and my ridiculous case. They were never going to let me out anyway. And when everything dies down, they'll likely allow the other lifers to come back to their local prisons. Please just promise if we don't win, you will walk away. I need to hear it."

Elaine pushed back her chair and began to pace before once again being reprimanded by the custodial help. An officer started to approach her, so she threw herself back in her chair and placed her head in her hands. Close to tears, knowing neither of them could continue this particular conversation, not knowing where to go with any other, Elaine got up, glared down the officer, and said, "Fine, fine. I give you your stupid promise, but I'm going to promise you something in return, Billy. We're not going to lose."

"No system as broken as this one can stand up to the kind of close scrutiny we're putting it through. And there *are* good people out there who care about injustice, and those people are going to see the truth comes out in this trial. Hold onto that hope. Please, hold on a little while longer. And the media, and those who call themselves Christians but don't believe in forgiveness? Don't believe the whole world is like that, Billy. Okay? Can you do that for me, please? And I'll keep my word to you. I promise."

"You've got a deal. Now get out of here. I'd hate for you to

215

see a grown man cry," Billy said as he stared at the wall, away from her.

She knew he was close to breaking down, and he didn't want to lose it in front of her. With no other choice, she touched his clenched fists, looking above his head at the guard and daring him with her eyes to say something, anything. Then Elaine walked out without looking back. She didn't want Billy to look up and see the tears in her eyes too.

She was so angry, she went straight to Tony's office and barged in where he sat hunched over the table as always. He got up when he saw her and poured her a cup of coffee, placed it across from him, and sat back down. "I've been waiting for you," he said quietly.

She'd composed herself on the drive over so she no longer felt like crying, but the blood-red anger was eating away at her stomach and black coffee would only make it worse. She stared at the steaming cup in front of her. "Don't you keep anything stronger for times like this, when disgruntled clients show up to chew you out?" she asked.

"Sure," Tony said, going into the bedroom and coming back with a bottle of whiskey and one of Scotch. "For those late nights when I can't sleep or see which way to go with a case," he said, gesturing for her to pick a hand and thus a bottle.

She got up, took the whiskey, and dumped most of the coffee from her cup. Three quarters whiskey, one quarter coffee. That, she decided, sitting down, might take the edge off.

"I want to know what we have. I want to know how confident you are about winning. We will stay here all night if I don't get answers. I have played damsel in distress too long. I want answers, and the money I have been paying you says I will get them before we call it a night."

Tony didn't seem surprised by her attitude, except the shot about the money. Elaine really didn't care about offending him just then. Having seen the hopeless state Billy was in and having

216

had to give a promise that might kill her to keep, she was in no mood to consider Williams' feelings.

They spent the next six hours going over every aspect of the case, finally arriving at their favorite café around eleven p.m., to the greetings of the owner, who remarked he'd missed them and their money. By midnight Elaine finally felt she'd been brought up to speed. She excused herself to let poor Yogi out and catch some shuteye.

On the first day of the trial, feeling hopeless and helpless, she realized if there wasn't a break in this case, they were going to lose. She had to figure out a way not to let that happen, no matter what.

Tony had said she'd be called as a witness but not until later, so until then she could observe the proceedings. They were boring and technical. She stared at Billy's broad back as he stood next to Tony as they and the district attorney addressed the judge.

She hadn't heard from the Senator. She wasn't confident in the case Tony had built and she hadn't talked to Richard for days, so she'd no idea if he was helping them. Nothing seemed positive. Remembering what Billy had warned her about the media, she looked around for reporters and cameras. There weren't many. Of course they might be aware the first few days of trial would be boring and were staying away until they could grab the sensational stuff, true or not, that would sell news for their sponsors.

Judge Hinkell was a woman about Elaine's age. Elaine knew nothing about her, but she seemed to be aware of what was going on. Elaine had seen too many over-the-top TV dramas to even guess what a real judge was like. Tony said he'd worked with her before her and she was 'okay'. She didn't like to waste time, had no sense of humor, and everyone was to be prepared and serious in her courtroom. Elaine thought those were admirable qualities. However, the judge also had a reputation for being somewhat conservative, which worried her. But she'd keep an open mind, she decided, unless she saw unfairness occurring. Then she had no idea what she'd do, since preparing an appeal on any grounds was no longer an option. They would win now, or that was it. She still couldn't believe Billy had placed her in such a bind; but it was his life, and she'd respect his decisions.

"How do you plead?" the judge was asking as Elaine discontinued her daydreaming   .

"Not guilty, your Honor," Billy said.

"Fine. Then this trial is scheduled to begin tomorrow. Mr. Williams, are you prepared?"

"I am, your Honor."

"Mr. Bush, is the District Attorney's office ready to go to trial?"

"Yes, your Honor."

"Bail is not an issue here as you are already remanded from your other crime, so the accused is to be returned to his cell. Court will reconvene at nine a.m. sharp." The judge stood. Everyone rose as the bailiff instructed until the judge left. Elaine went up to talk to Tony and Billy, but they left with the guards before she had a chance to catch them.

It wasn't yet noon, and Elaine had no idea what to do with herself. She'd already run the dog. Unable to think of anything but Billy's trial, she decided to go to the library and look up what she could find on Jerry Bush, the district attorney trying Billy's case.

She found him cited in one of those vanity who's who publications people paid to put their names in. Not a good sign of character, she thought. She also found him recorded as a public official. He'd been Assistant District Attorney for only one year. He was sixty-two and from Texas. Dear God, she thought. The only advantage Billy would have with this guy was Billy was whiter than anyone she'd ever met.

But Tony was as black as any black person she'd ever met, so the two cancelled each other out. Bush's reputation was as a very conservative Bible-thumping redneck. Of course those words weren't used, but all you had to do was see where he had been raised and educated to have the hair on the back of your neck stand up. Billy Graham seemed liberal compared to what this guy brought to the table.

Elaine decided to look up the judge while she was there. She wasn't much happier once she'd read her prospective. Southern-born and raised; single career woman. Very involved with her Baptist church, and we weren't talking Black Baptist, Elaine thought. What was Everett's problem? The University of Washington, Central and Western couldn't produce enough decent legal professionals to fill their courthouses?

More depressed than ever, Elaine decided it was time to go home and call the Senator. An independent investigation might be the only card they could play as this trial proceeded. Pressure on local judges and lawyers who wanted political favors with those at the state level had been known to work before. It couldn't hurt. Nothing could, from what she saw. They were going to lose this case unless she somehow got the real murderers to do something stupid, like confess or kill her. She didn't care for the second option much at all.

The Senator, she was told, was out of the office for two weeks. Great, she thought. Now what? The only thing that came to mind was somehow provoke the S.W.A.T. team into confessing without meaning to. She'd seen stuff like that before on TV and in the movies. She'd wear a wire and go someplace where they hung out. Strike up a conversation and if they were drunk enough, one might slip up, and she'd have evidence on tape.

Several weeks passed before she seriously considered putting such a radical plan into action. The trial wasn't going well, but at least Senator Suvall was back and granted her another interview. He made the appointment for Everett because he had business there the next day. She hated missing any of the trial even if it was very cut and dried. She liked being there for Billy, though he never looked in her direction. And Tony never spoke to her or acknowledged she was involved. Once again they were definitely 'dissing' her, as her inmate students would say, but she no longer cared. If they thought it so important, she would let it proceed a while longer without intervening on their turf, as one of her gang bangers might say.

Richard had been canceling on riding without explanation. She felt lonely again and wondered how her wandering husband was getting along. He did call, but mostly they ended up playing phone tag with the answering machine. It certainly wasn't an enriching relationship. She knew she had other friends she could call, but it was exhausting to explain everything that was going on, so she hadn't done so nor returned their messages. The weather was gray and cold, not conducive for jogging, but she kept it up for Yogi's sake.

Pouring chill-to-the-bone rain was pelting down as she drove up to the Brewery to have lunch with Suvall. He did like his beer, she thought as she grabbed a hat and raced for the door. If she had to deal with the idiots Suvall did on a regular basis, she would have a definite drinking problem. She didn't need any more problems right now. Life was hard enough.

Today the media had shown up in force: TV, radio, and newspaper reporters from all over the state. There were cords everywhere, and pushing and shoving like she'd never seen and hoped never to again.

Billy looked handsome, if still too thin, in one of the suits Elaine bought for him. She could tell he was extremely uncomfortable. He kept pulling at the shirt collar with his hands. It was unfair he had to wear handcuffs. How would a jury presume him innocent with all the chains on him? But he was stoic. She knew today had been bad for him. The prosecutor was allowed to bring in witnesses who knew his victim. She didn't understand why his previous crime was being allowed; in cases she'd researched it wasn't.

That was one of the things she wanted to discuss with the senator. She studied her written list as she waited for him.

1. Had an independent committee been convened to look into the particulars and peculiarities of the riot?
2. Had he talked with Richard again, and was Richard helping?
3. If there was no committee, why not?
4. If there was a committee, who was on it?
5. When would they have findings?
6. Could he give her any new information?

Suvall was late, so Elaine spent the time replaying the day in court. Then she called her friend Connie who was always game for anything, and planned to met on Saturday night. Elaine was straight with her on the phone and explained she wanted to trick a confession out of some nasty characters, and there could be trouble. That wake up call didn't faze her good friend.

"What time do you want to pick me up? I have to work until six. But anytime after that is fine. What's the dress?"

"I'll be there by six or so. The dress is classy/sleazy. I'm finally going to take you to the guard hangout you always wanted to see. But first I'll buy you dinner anywhere you like, to make up for taking you there."

"Sounds like fun. I've been a good girl way too long. That may start defining who I am if I'm not careful. And you need to catch me up on your life. The address on your Christmas card was different. That's my flimsy excuse for not sending you one, but what's up?"

"Look, my date just arrived. I've got to go. I'll tell you everything Saturday night. Bye."

Elaine rose as the senator came in. "Sorry, Elaine. I try to get to places on time, but by the end of the day, it's hopeless."

"Not to worry. I understand how it must feel to be rich and famous."

"Very funny. Not famous, and certainly not wealthy. People just stop me because everyone wants me to do something for them."

"Like me, huh?"

"Sort of, but you I don't mind, because you never bring me stupid and petty. Trouble and problems, yes, but not stupid or petty."

"Sorry, I just don't seem to be getting help elsewhere."

"I'm starved," Suvall said, as a beer appeared in front of him. "Let's order and then we'll catch up."

Dinner was great, and the drinks satisfying. The news not so good, as she went down her list and listened to a litany of why nothing had been done. That awful word 'yet' peppered the monologue as he ate and talked at the same time, and not too prettily, she noticed.

"We did form a committee. Your friend Richard finally agreed to sit on it. No, we haven't met yet. We don't have an agenda for the first meeting yet. No, we haven't set a date yet."

She listened as patiently as she could, but was sure she and Connie had to implement Elaine's crazy plan on Saturday. By the time the committee met and did anything, if indeed they chose to do anything, Billy would be put away or have died of old age.

After asking her questions and making small talk until ten o'clock, Elaine excused herself. Suvall had already found another table and another beer before the check was paid and they said goodbye.

Chapter 20

The week of the trial so exhausted Elaine she slept most of Saturday. Even though it hadn't happened yet, one of these days the media was going to turn on her, and she was afraid of losing it. They were animals. No, not as good as any animal she'd ever met. Dogs, cats, horses, lions, tigers, bears, wolves, all had a wonderful code of ethics. These sub humans had none she could see. The papers were filled with half truths and innuendos she could scarcely match to the events she'd witnessed the same day. A few times she wondered if she'd been in the wrong courtroom, there was so little similarity between what she saw and what the hacks wrote about.

Television coverage was worse. Billy could sit perfectly still and attentive for eight long hours, but the pictures on TV and in the news papers would show the one moment he pushed back his long hair or yawned or stretched or looked away. Then cameras would click incessantly and the so-called journalists would describe him as arrogant or bored, with pictures on the 6:00, 10:00 and 11:00 news. And the pictures they chose made it look that way. Elaine knew she couldn't do anything to stop it, but she anguished all the same. She hoped Tony was keeping the coverage away from Billy, though that wouldn't stop the guards from spreading the bad press through the bars of his cage to grind him down further.

Digging through her closet for something suitably classy/ sleazy for the evening, Elaine debated on whether to take Yogi or not. It would be a long evening, but Connie liked animals, and Elaine knew the dog would want to come.

She decided yes, and after donning a faux-fur coat over a slinky red dress, accessorized with rhinestones, she piled Yogi into her car and set off for Seattle which Connie called home. Years before Connie and her husband had been friends of Elaine and Daniel, until Connie's spouse decided he preferred the cute young counselor at the school where he taught PE, and left.

Their children had been almost grown and Elaine knew Connie didn't really miss the jerk. In fact, they scoffed at how 'the fool' called Connie these days to complain about being too old to have new babies and a wife he was no longer interested in. He'd made noises about getting back together but Connie just laughed, saying it rejuvenated her resolve to never marry again, certainly not to that loser.

After the divorce, Connie did well in the field of real estate which before she'd dabbled in, because her man had 'wanted her home'. The money and awards stuck to Connie after she found her confidence. Top seller of the year, statewide. A beautiful statuesque blonde, she graced the cover of magazines and Sunday supplements on the real estate market.

Elaine was thrilled for her, but happy she hadn't changed inside. When Connie was a child, she'd been heavy; as a teenager, she'd been wild. When she married and became a wife and mother, she'd been made to feel like nothing at all. Now she was her own finished product. Elaine knew Connie didn't think herself pretty, but that made her more lovable.

Seattle was a long way from Monroe, but Connie was game, so they decided to make a night of it. If Connie ended up on Elaine's couch, it wouldn't be the first time nor hopefully the last. They weren't over the hill yet.

The wire Elaine taped to her body itched. She had draped a black silk scarf over the red dress and hoped the smallest recorder she'd ever seen in her life was well concealed. The tape could play for five hours; Elaine would activate it once they got to the White Stallion Tavern and Grill where the guards she was looking for would be.

This place, along with the weight room and shooting range, was their life. These officers had enough hours built up they didn't have to work odd shifts. They kept their Saturday nights free. The other officers were family and the Stallion their home. If she took the analogy far enough, they acted and lived much like the young inmate gang-bangers they considered themselves so superior to. This behavior was not true with all guards, but the S.W.A.T. team type certainly exhibited it.

Connie's new condominium was right above Pike Place Market. She lived on the top floor in a much bigger apartment than Elaine's entire house. Once Elaine's parking had been validated in the security garage under the building, she wondered again, considering her friend protected herself so well, why she would go slumming with her.

As the elevator took her up twenty floors, Elaine was just pleased Connie wanted to go. She was funny, smart and attractive. She was going to light up the Stallion and help Elaine buy her way into the officers' confidence.

Time to focus on her plan to help Billy. She couldn't depend on the system to do it, that she knew. Whatever the outcome, it had to be determined by what she did—or didn't do—if she wanted to sleep at night when this trial ended. No lawyers, no friends, no senators could get what she could, with a bit of luck and a lot of chutzpah.

Connie's place was amazing. The sky was dark and the skyline breathtaking. Cruise ships, tankers, ferries, fishing boats, all seemed parked just below the window. Then there was the wonderful Pike Place Arch welcoming people to one of the best known landmarks in the country. People were still out, though most of the shops that sold produce or flowers had closed for the day. The best pastas, freshest fish, finest wines could be found down there. As Connie handed her a red wine, Elaine marveled at the beauty of the Emerald City.

They chatted then continued talking as they walked to one of those wonderful restaurants down below, and enjoyed cracked crab and salad. It had been two years since the two had actually sat down for a meal. There had been hectic, unsatisfactory phone calls, funny cards, the occasional lengthy email, but face-to-face was so much better.

"Why have we waited so long to do this?" Connie inquired as the talk began to run down.

"I really miss seeing you. I don't know what happens. Life, I suppose."

"Let's make another date so we don't let so much time lapse."

"For sure. Now, do you still want to go with me? I will understand if you choose not to. It could be very dangerous. I told you what's happened to me so far. This is not a game. I have to do this, but you don't—and maybe shouldn't."

"Please, Elaine. You're not going alone. I've always wanted to see the Stallion, and I'm a big girl who can take care of myself. Come on, before you change your mind. We have a long drive and it's already nine o'clock."

"Okay, if you're sure, but when I say it's time to leave, you need to go."

"You got it. Maybe we can become Charlie's Angels."

"See? You're worrying me again. This is serious!"

Taking Elaine by the arm and swinging her along, Connie laughed. "Lighten up. I was just trying to see if I could push your buttons, and obviously I still can. I promise to be good and do exactly what you tell me."

"I hope so."

By then they had reached Elaine's car. Connie would follow her to Monroe so Elaine would not have to drive all the way back to Seattle. Yogi sniffed her, lost interest and was sound asleep by the time Elaine pulled into the tavern. She left the dog, knowing Yogi was good for at least two more hours, which was longer than

226

they planned to stay in this dive.

Elaine was right about Connie—she breezed through the door and all eyes turned. It was approaching ten o'clock and the place was packed. Music was blaring; sizzling steaks being served and the beer flowed. Elaine steered them across the room so everyone would know they were together, then found a table and stools. Predictably, complimentary beer was in front of them before they took off their coats. Elaine hated the taste of beer, but pretended to drink as Connie followed suit, just as she'd promised.

Elaine saw the prey she was looking for; they were definitely watching. She and Connie pretended to be involved in girl talk until the S.W.A.T. team lieutenant came over.

"Elaine. What in the world are you doing here, and who's your lovely friend?" he asked.

With a smile she hoped looked sincere, Elaine introduced Connie to the Lieutenant . "This is one of our most important officers in the prison. He actually saved my life during the riot. Remember I told you about the wonderful men who kept me from getting killed by those monsters?" She was laying it on thick, but these guys were fairly inebriated so she didn't think they'd catch the lack of subtlety. Several other S.W.A.T. team members walked over to preen and posture under her praise.

Connie hugged the one closest. "You guys really are heroes. I made Elaine bring me so I could thank you all in person. We love her so much and were so worried." Connie actually rubbed against the man. Elaine thought she would throw up as she watched Connie drag him to the dance floor. The others wandered off, while the lieutenant took Connie's vacated seat.

"Maybe I misjudged you, Elaine. I hear you and your husband separated. I always found you hot, though of course not when I thought you'd betrayed us. But I talked to Pepper, and she cleared things up for me."

Bless you, Captain Pepper, Elaine thought in silent prayer.

Maybe they were still friends. Elaine hoped so. She missed her. "What did she say to make you change your mind?" she asked.

"You probably won't like this, but she said you were basically a bleeding heart liberal who thought all cons had good in them. She thought it was hard for you to accept a criminal you'd worked with could be such a monster..."

So much for friendship, Elaine fumed to herself, but she smiled.

"She also said you were not yourself due to the trauma you'd suffered, and I should have understood that and not been so heavy handed. For that I'm sorry." His words were slurred as he ordered more drinks.

"That's okay," Elaine said, trying to stroke his inflated ego. "I was really confused for a long time. I was taking pills and drinking, which was one reason Daniel and I separated. He tried, but being a hostage really changes a person. I hope the bastards who did this all fry. I'm glad Damien is dead, but I feel terrible about Officer DeLory. I still don't understand why Billy killed him. I wish I could have killed Damien myself, I don't care who did it. They did me a huge favor."

It was the opening she needed, and good old Lieutenant Percy fell like a bear into the trap. "Look, Elaine. There's a lot more to the story than you know, but I didn't think I could trust you. I can, can't I? I mean, we go back a long way and I did save your life, so that makes us tight. Right?"

"Absolutely." She made herself lean toward him as she sipped her wine. "Honestly, you can tell me anything you think I have a right to know. It *was* my life on the line that day and I did get the others out. Didn't I?" This was said with a bit of coy whining, the kind this type of man loved.

"You did great. We were all impressed how you handled yourself the entire time. I tell you something, your friends owe you big time. But where are they when you need them? I guess it's just you and me, kid." He took her hand and began rubbing her palm. It made her want to jump out of her skin, but Elaine simply sat and composed her thoughts enough to go for the gold.

"Please, Lieutenant. You said you were going to tell me the whole story. Do you want another drink first? Mine's empty."

He got up, stumbled to the bar, and bought two more drinks for them. "You want to go outside?" he asked. "It's too hot and crowded in here to talk."

She didn't want to, but being so close to success made her bold. She smiled, put on her coat, and gestured to Connie to come get her after fifteen minutes. Connie was busy dancing with different men; she hoped she understood.

It was freezing outside, but the lieutenant didn't notice. His bloodstream was high octane by now anyway. She tried not to show how cold she felt, as he leaned over and whispered, "Billy didn't do it. We did."

Shocked and repulsed this evil man actually confessed, and concerned the tape recorder hadn't picked up what he said, she exclaimed, "I don't think I heard you. What did you just say?"

He was nuzzling her neck and she wanted to run, but she held firm while he repeated the words. "The S.W.A.T. team and I took out Damien, and DeLory too." This time it was said louder for effect. Elaine was definitely affected.

"Damien I get. He was worthless and you were angry, but why DeLory?"

"There's a whole lot more to this story, but I can tell you're cold. Why don't we jump in your car?" he laughed, his breath foul.

"First finish the story. Why? What's going on?"

"We were making a lot of money in there. That's what's going on. You think your rich husband could give you things? You won't believe what I have socked away, and if you are nice to me, I'll treat you real good."

"Money? How? With whom? None of this is making sense."

It was too much. She knew it as soon as his head rose

and his blood shot eyes bore into hers. This man might be an evil murderer, but he was no fool, and he was well trained in investigation. Giving them, not getting.

He became cold sober and it frightened her. She knew the fifteen minutes was up, and she prayed Connie would show soon. The lieutenant had become suspicious. He was no longer drunk or enamored of her charms. Quickly the suspicion turned to fury and she was on the receiving end.

"You little bitch. Look, I bought you drinks, told you stories I'll deny if you ever repeat them, and now I'd like a little payback for showing you a good time. Get in that car and let's get warm."

It wasn't a request. He had her by the arm and led to the car. Before she could react he grabbed her purse, pulled out her keys and opened the car door—just as Connie and some of the officers emerged from the bar.

Too late! Yogi leaped from the backseat and onto his neck. The lieutenant went down and Yogi with him. Elaine screamed. The sound her dog was making evoked the primitive wolf from centuries past. She wasn't pulling or biting on the man, simply holding him down by the jugular while menacingly growling.

Connie screamed and the men who'd come out with her pulled their guns. Elaine was terrified they would get a clear shot at her wonderful dog. Crouching beside Yogi, Elaine spoke gently. "Please, Yogi. Let go. Yogi, stop! Get off him, Yogi. Down."

Nothing did any good. She could not get the dog to release. Until a voice from the back of the crowd, she recognized as the prison dog handler, said, "Try saying yield."

She did, and like magic, Yogi let go, and came to sit at Elaine's feet, facing the armed men. "Thank you," was all she could whisper as she put Yogi back in the car. Elaine crawled into the driver's seat, keeping an eye on all the drawn weapons while Connie dove into the passenger seat. Elaine noted none of these men should have been carrying weapons off duty.

The two women were so shaken they decided to leave

Connie's car at the tavern for now. None of the men would know which was hers, but even if they did, Connie was too shocked to drive. Without speaking they drove to Elaine's house and went inside with Yogi. Connie kept eyeing the dog as though it would take her out next, but Yogi was completely back to her laconic self, and fell asleep by Elaine's chair, with Connie keeping one eye on her.

Elaine petted Yogi and crooned what a wonderful dog she was and how she was going to get her own T-bone steak as soon as Elaine could get to a store.

∞

In the gloom of early morning, she took Connie back to the Stallion. The women hugged and promised to call, but Elaine noticed there was no insistence in making a date for next time. She let it go, thinking it was only fair to give Connie time to put the night in perspective and see the humor in all that had happened.

As she watched Connie drive away, she again gloried in the spot where Yogi'd taken the lieutenant down. She half-expected to see blood, but Yogi hadn't even broken his skin. Elaine did have time to note as she pulled away, the only times in her life she'd been called a "bitch" were by an officer and a criminal. Interesting.

As she headed to Tony's with the tape, Elaine wondered if it would be admissible as evidence. She'd seen it happen on TV. She didn't know anything about entrapment laws, but Tony would. Hopefully she hadn't risked all that for nothing.

Chapter 21

Elaine waited not so patiently at Tony's door while Yogi sniffed her favorite bush. Cold and exhausted, Elaine was concerned Tony might not be as enamored of her escapade as she was.

"What the hell is going on?" Tony boomed as he opened the door wide enough to let her and 'the mutt' in. "Are you in trouble again? What'd you do now? I need what little sleep I can get these days."

"Oh, ye of little faith. I bring you a silver bullet that is going to make you rich and famous, and this is how you treat me?" Elaine joked.

"Right. I might as well give up my three hours of sleep. Put the coffee on while I get dressed for court."

It was almost five a.m., and Elaine knew he was at the court house each day by seven. She rummaged in the cupboard, trying to find something to make for breakfast, since he probably wouldn't have time to go to the café when he heard what she had for evidence. Finding Bisquick, eggs, milk and butter, she made pancakes. While they were frying, she set up the tape recorder.

Tony walked through the door, straightening his only tie as Elaine hit "Play" and the sound of her and the lieutenant's voices rang out loud and clear.

"What the hell—?" He stopped as he heard the voices and sat down to listen intently. When it was over, he simply said, "Play it again." She did but he wanted to hear it one more time. "You are one crazy lady, you know that?" Tony exclaimed. But he was smiling at her, which caused the tension between her shoulder blades to relax somewhat.

"Tell me the entire story. I need it all on tape." He brought out his full-sized recorder and copied the recording she'd made so they had a backup. They ate dry pancakes with coffee while Elaine recalled every moment of one of the best nights of her life.

"Will your friend Connie be a witness to all this?" Tony asked.

"I think so. She was scared, but once some time passes, I think she'll calm down and do it."

"You know those guys are going to lie through their teeth and give the lieutenant a stupid alibi."

"Some will, but I got the impression, since no one shot my dog or me 'accidentally,' they were just trying to save their leader and I was in the way. I bet a few in the crowd were not involved in what went on inside and might 'cowboy up' with the truth.

"Some are pretty good guys, and I don't think they like the way he was manhandling me. Most are heavy drinkers, but honorable with the ladies. There were about twenty people out there toward the end. We might be able to get a few to testify."

"Okay, Elaine. I'm going to tell you something Richard, the senator, and I have been working on that fits directly with the lieutenant's claim about making big money. But first I have to call the judge and tell her I have new information she needs to hear before court convenes today."

"So the tape *can* be used?"

"You bet it can. In this state, you're supposed to have permission, but I'll use it to compel witnesses who think they're gonna be under oath. I'll find some way to get this baby in. We should have a mistrial declared by this afternoon, but I've got to see the judge first."

Tony made his appointment for nine a.m. The judge's staff would clear the morning docket until the judge had talked to Tony and the district attorney about the new evidence. Tony decided it was too dangerous for Elaine to go anywhere, so she and Yogi hunkered down to wait until he'd met the judge.

"What we have found so far", Tony informed Elaine, "is that the riot was genuine, but the killings of Damien and certain guards, including DeLory, were carried out by officers because they could no longer be trusted with their parts in a drug/prostitution, racketeering ring being run from the inside by certain cartel kingpins doing time. It was facilitated on the outside by the officers from the S.W.A.T. team, and a few others." Elaine started to speak, but Tony held up a hand. "Don't interrupt please. I'll answer your questions when I'm done.

"This little enterprise—actually a *huge* one—had been going on for at least five years and was extremely sophisticated in nature and design. We've got our eyes on lieutenants, the captain, and probably twenty officers; the leaders were the twelve from the S.W.A.T. team. They were making the most money, as much as $80,000 a year apiece, and were smart enough not to spend much, thus not giving themselves away; but each one keeps a large bank account in other states we attained legal access to just yesterday. The proof each man has an account worth $450,000, unaccounted for, made them hot targets for the senator and me. Richard was the one feeding us information that led us in that direction initially. These creeps only make, with overtime, some $50,000 a year. We were going to call them to testify under oath starting next week. Now they can start explaining about undisclosed monies, but at their own trials, not Billy's"

"But—"

"Wait, I'm not done. This is how it worked. It was primo thinking, and the plan was really well executed. Of course, when you have crooked cops involved, it helps a lot.

"In this case, D.O.C. saw fit to allow three of the most powerful Colombian cartel leaders to do time for tax evasion together in the Reformatory because the federal prisons were overflowing. Smart, huh? Of course, with overcrowding you can't always separate everyone you want in different prisons, even state and federal. In any case, these three big-time players left their billion-dollar operations in the care of others to manage.

"They would not lose a dime of profits while incarcerated. In fact, their profits grow. And they called the shots from inside. Their family passed messages during visits, their phone calls carried coded messages. Spanish and gang slang were used to keep the businesses flush. Organized crime has nothing on these creeps. In fact, they learned a lot by studying Mafioso practices.

"The three king pins hadn't met each other on the outside and would never have been friends if they had. But on the inside, these types become brothers, and love to see if they can carry off bigger scams. It makes the days go by faster and keeps them street smart so they don't lose their touch for when they get out and go back out to their leadership roles. It was a lovely partnership, because each of the three brought a different talent, business-wise, to their prison playhouse. One's was prostitution. One's was bookmaking and one's was drugs. Together the three of them made one formidable, very awesome mastermind."

Tony found this statement quite humorous and chuckled while Elaine waited patiently for more information.

"Okay. These were the three wise guys, I'll call them. I don't think you need to know their names, Elaine. You would probably put yourself in more danger if you did. They got one of the S.W.A.T. team into a trick bag, which isn't unheard of. He brought one some dope. Then they began blackmailing him and threatening his family. He started working with them and got addicted to the absurd amount of easy money, first by being a mule and bringing in recreational drugs for the bosses."

"Here's where it gets amazing. It looks like from there, this endeavor turned into an undetected multinational criminal operation that could involve three countries, several states, and between staff and inmates, as many as fifty individuals. All the action was occurring out of the Reformatory, but between illegal gambling, prostitution and drug running the take may exceed

$50 million over five years. And that's just what these three and their co-conspirators made off it. Who knows what these men are really worth? We have no discovery yet concerning their outside businesses, but we are making a dent on breaking up their action with the inmates and staff."

"People are starting to turn on each other in order to avoid prosecution. We'll let the little fish off with loss of job or time in another institution, in order to get the real sharks. There's nothing like watching these 'brothers' sell each other out for a laugh. There is no such thing as loyalty among criminals. It's a joke. Once these guys start to sing, they'd give up their own mothers if they could. Add a respected Senator to throw at them, and it's really fun."

Tony stood up. "I've got to get to the judge with this tape, and I'm begging you to stay here until I get back. The downside to what you did is if these fools didn't want to hurt you before, they do now, and so do the wise guys. I don't know what to do once this tape's disclosed, but just stay put until I get back and we'll figure it out. Okay?"

"No problem. I really need some sleep. I promise you don't have to worry. This dog is amazing. And good luck."

Tony went to his bedroom and returned with a handgun. "It's loaded. Do you know how to use it?"

"Yes, I do. That was one thing my dad taught me. Now go."

He set the gun on the kitchen table and left. Elaine lay on the couch, her old army green coat draped over her, Yogi sleeping beside her. It seemed she'd been asleep only a few minutes when she felt Tony shaking her. She put her hands back over her head and tried to ignore him, but he wasn't having any of it.

"Elaine, wake up. We've got trouble. I called Richard and he's coming to get you. The judge didn't throw out the case. I'm worried she can't be trusted and may even, at this very moment, be talking to the wrong people. Elaine, get up."

What he was saying finally got through her exhausted mind,

and she sat up quickly, almost as though someone was already there who might hurt her. "What happened? You were so sure. Did you tell her everything?"

"No, thank God, just about the wire tape and how you uncovered some information that suggested the S.W.A.T. team was dirty. Look, I've got to get to Olympia and speak to the Senator in person. That judge is so conservative, I started getting the 'America and apple pie' speech about how she really believed that these 'wonderful officers' could do nothing wrong and she would not allow any secret tape recording done by some harlot into her courtroom. I decided to cut my losses and get the hell out.

"Court convenes tomorrow, ready or not. And *not* is the operative word. Unless someone above her intervenes, we will not get a fair trial for Billy, and you will be in deep shit, I kid you not. As soon as Richard gets here he is taking you to a safe place and you will stay there, or else I will not be responsible for the consequences."

Elaine had never seen Tony ruffled, much less seriously unglued. That, more than anything, scared her out of her wits.

"But this is wrong. I researched this judge. Yes, she's conservative, but the articles I read said she was also fair. How can she do this?"

"She's the Judge. She can pretty much do whatever she wants. And right now, she only wants to hear good things about her boys in blue. There has to be more to it, but until I find out what it is, you have to disappear. Can you, just this once, do what I ask?"

Elaine was properly terrified. It was one thing to go up against some idiotic criminal during a riot or an equally idiotic officer in a tavern, but to be thrown to the wolves by the judicial system she still had some faith in, was too much to accept and still continue to fight.

"Do all you can," she told him. "I'm out of here. I don't want to die for a system I can't beat. Billy's all but given me his blessing.

238

He knew, when I didn't, this system works for a chosen few, not the innocent or those working for them. I give up."

She put on her coat to wait quietly for Richard. There were no thoughts left. Her mind had finally become the blank everyone wanted it to be.

Richard showed up quickly, but as he and Tony talked, Elaine tuned out, petting Yogi and waiting to leave. In the truck she couldn't make conversation. Richard drove. Yogi sat between them. They were climbing the pass, Elaine noticed, but decided to go back to sleep. What difference did it make where they were going? She trusted Richard and didn't really care where she ended up.

Cashmere, a sweet little town past Leavenworth, was their first destination. Richard told her to stay in the truck while he stopped to buy rations. That was fine with her. They drove on until they were twenty or so miles further up in the hills, facing a small cabin on a river road. Elaine could hear the water rushing as she stepped out of the vehicle; it might be too cold to swim, but maybe it would feel good.

Elaine walked into the cabin behind Richard and Yogi, who was seriously checking things out. She sat at the small wooden table next to the window that looked down on the river. She liked it here, she decided. It was quiet, like the Caribbean island where Daniel had taken her. That reminded her. She began rummaging through the cupboards.

"What are you looking for?" Richard asked.

"I think a drink would be nice. Don't you?"

"Elaine, it's not even noon. Look, I know you're not too comfortable, but an old uncle I never knew just left me this place. Tony and I thought it would be the safest place to put you for a while."

"It's fine. I like the view," she said, as she sat down in the chair facing the river. There was snow still on the ground, but mostly it was covered with soggy leaves and bits and pieces of ice where the shade covered the dirt. But the river was wide and deep, and the water moved violently from the snow packs melting higher up as spring worked its way along the mountain ridges.

Elaine watched a chickadee jump from branch to branch of a low hung cedar, digging in the bark for food. Then she spotted a blue jay. Most who hiked or rode hated these birds because they were such thieves, but she liked them. Why not steal and cheat? That's how you got ahead in this world. Why hadn't she learned that? She thought she had now, but didn't care. A squirrel scurried along the ground, then stopped right under her window to dig under the wet leaves and pull out a nut he immediately ran off with. "Yes, run," she thought. "Run! Or someone might hurt or kill you just for your food. That's how the world is."

"Elaine," Richard announced, "I have to leave for a little while. I need the keys to your house so I can pick up some things for you and Yogi."

She dug in her purse and gave them to him, then turned back to her window.

Richard was concerned as he drove back down the pass into Everett to collect Elaine's things. Sure, he was unhappy about the judge and the trial, but what concerned him was Elaine. Tony had said she simply shut down after he told her about their latest setback, but Richard hadn't expected to see her so distant and remote. Sleeping all the way to the cabin, after Tony said she'd just woken up? Of course what had happened the night before must have been traumatic, and sleep was a good way for people to cope with trauma. But this? No, he didn't see it. He hoped by the time he got back she'd be her old self. She was right to be scared. What she'd done had been reckless and stupid, but that was the kind of activity he had come to expect from her. But this silence and passivity? This wasn't like her at all.

She was still sitting at the little window staring out at the pitch dark when Richard came back. He expected her to turn and greet him. Elaine always displayed the correct manners and protocol for any situation. Not today. She didn't look up or acknowledge him. Richard was relieved to see the dog at her feet, just as she'd been when he had left. The dog looked up, then put its head back on its paws, following Richard's movements with its eyes. Elaine did nothing.

He put away the things he brought for her, took out bowls for water and food to give the dog. He was beginning to feel fond of Yogi, after Tony told him about Elaine and the lieutenant. Richard knew Perry and what the outcome of pulling Elaine into the car would've been if the dog hadn't attacked. His own anger burned hot and righteous as he considered the scene, but he pushed it away.

After they'd eaten, he tried to discuss the events of the last two days, but Elaine was indifferent to him and any subject he broached. Giving up, he took her into the bedroom, showed her the personal items he'd brought to clean up and sleep in, and left her to it. He heard water running and the toilet flushing. After the noises stopped, he opened the door and looked in. She'd put on the sweatpants, what she might have slept in on a trail ride, and was asleep on the bed. He covered her, asked Yogi if she wanted to go out. Yogi made no move, so Richard used the bathroom himself and, mentally and physically exhausted, took the pillow and blanket he found in the hall closet and crashed on the couch.

Morning found him awakening to the smell of coffee; the bacon and eggs he'd bought were frying in a pan. Elaine was dressed and turned away from him as she fixed breakfast. He watched without speaking, then, when he saw the food was almost done, went to shower and dress.

They ate at the table near the window. Elaine let Yogi out, and they watched her track scents and water the big old cedar. Richard tried several different conversations that in days past would have elicited a barrage of ideas, questions and opinions from Elaine. But today, there were only one word answers or nothing at all.

He coaxed her out for a brisk walk. They ate twice more. He got her to play checkers he found in a cupboard, but soon tired of it, since he had to keep saying "Your move" until he wanted to choke her; which he knew wouldn't help her mood at all. Finally it was dark enough to hit the hay.

Elaine, who before would have done anything but turn in at seven, meekly went into the bathroom, came out in the same sweatpants and fell immediately to sleep as he got himself ready for another night on the couch. Before sleep took him, Richard decided the next day he was going to Ellensburg for more supplies. Elaine could come along or not.

She didn't. The last he saw of her, she was staring out the window at the melting snow, Yogi tucked neatly at her feet.

In Ellensburg he called both Daniel and Elaine's son. Daniel's call was expensive, he was in China. But Richard felt he had to inform him. He kept the message short and told him to call his son Rob if he wanted more details.

Then he explained to Rob the reasons why he thought they should let things be for a while. He'd known Elaine's son since he was small, which he felt gave him the right to give advice. Rob obviously agreed, as he thanked Richard and told him he would explain everything to his sister, who might not be so amenable to leaving her mother in a remote cabin in the woods. Richard bought enough supplies for two weeks, called his boss and claimed he needed extensive dental work and two weeks should do it.

Each day grew warmer. The sun gazed down brightly on the little cabin, but Elaine didn't seem to be changing back to her old self as quickly as Richard hoped. They cooked, took walks, played board games, even read some of the Zane Gray westerns he'd picked up. She just wasn't acting at all like Elaine. She bathed and cleaned up; but he did start to worry about her catching cold, as he had forgotten to bring a hairdryer and after she washed her long, thick hair, she would leave it dripping down her shoulders for hours.

This cabin was drafty and the only heat came from an old wood stove, so Richard kept the oven door open, stocked with kindling he'd prepared hours before. He told her to lean back as he took brush and comb to her hair, separating the strands until it dried and could be brushed smooth.

He looked forward to this part of the day more than he should; but rationalized if he didn't take advantage of the situation, brushing her hair was small payment for his time off work. His stress and money were literally going up the chimney of this old wood burner as he added more kindling he cut religiously from the trees outside.

The feeling of all that hair was sensual, ethereal, and nostalgic, all at once. Richard knew he cared about this fine woman, as a woman. He admired her as a person. He also knew that brushing her hair reminded him of his boyhood, when he would sit and watch his mother and sisters dry their hair the same way long ago. The feelings were bittersweet for him. They seemed to make no impression on Elaine, who sat letting him perform such an intimate act.

She tolerated his ministrations calmly, leaning her head back against his hand in a relaxed way and closing the blue-veined eyelids as he worked. She never spoke, and when he felt the silky threads cascade loosely through his fingers, he knew it was time to stop and did so. She then straightened her head, braided the strands at the nape of her neck with an elastic band he'd found in a kitchen drawer and moved back to her chair by the window, to read or simply watch the day unfold. Sometimes he asked her to cook, walk with him, play a game and then retire for another night, where she slept peacefully and he tossed and turned until dawn, at which time the ritual began again.

Richard's only companion was Yogi. Once the dog saw how

gently he treated her beloved mistress, she and Richard had formed an unspoken partnership. Each took turns staying alert to her needs. Yogi only went outside when she knew Richard was looking after Elaine, and when Richard left the cabin or napped on the bed in the afternoon Yogi stayed on guard. Richard petted her, talked to her, fed her. Yogi was starting to show signs of possessiveness toward him, which Richard encouraged and knew he'd miss when their sojourn in the wilderness ended.

It wouldn't be too long now. On a visit to town, Richard collected the newspapers, called Rob and Tony and found out he and Elaine were needed in Everett to testify at a hearing where eight officers, four staff members and the three wise guys would be indicted on charges of racketeering, murder, defrauding the government, tax evasion, and various other bathroom sinks. Billy's case had finally been thrown out once the Senator intervened and all the evidence presented.

Tony told him the dirty laundry would all be separated during that time. It was now a federal case—messy, but getting serious attention, which Tony attributed to Senator Suvall finally yelling and screaming for action, which happened after he'd heard Elaine's tape. There was a new judge presiding, one the senator said knew his shit. The media was going crazy now that words like cover-up, collusion, and other nefarious terms clogged the headlines.

Richard wasn't willing to bring Elaine back and put her in the middle of this fracas, not in her current state of mind, nor when it exposed her to more danger. He needed to talk to her son.

Rob reassured him that Daniel had contracted the best security company money could buy, the same one protected presidents. They were mentioned in that book Elaine recommended, *The Gift of Fear* by Gavin de Becker, a security expert. It helped women learn how to look for and protect themselves from predators. Richard had read parts of it during his prep periods at work because Elaine had gone on about how great it was.

Well, Richard decided, it must be a sign; he promised he'd

bring Elaine to her son's home the next day. Watching her that evening, he felt sad they just couldn't stay as they were. This old cowboy loved and needed the country life, and would have liked to share it with Elaine. But she wasn't the same Elaine he'd known, so he reconciled himself to telling her about the move scheduled for the next day. She seemed to hear him, because when he finished explaining, got up and went into the bedroom.

After a few minutes of petting Yogi, who seemed to sense something was up, he went to check on her. He found her leaning over the bed, her frail back to him, packing. Her son had asked a psychiatrist to meet them at the house. Richard couldn't help worrying how she was going to do, once he left her.

Once the lights were out, he sat on the couch with a snifter of brandy. He worried about how he was going to feel once she left. Well, the one thing you could always count on in life is things always change. He accepted that affirmation intellectually, but emotionally it wasn't going down so smooth.

The day of their return dawned glorious, with warm air smelling of Easter and renewal. Richard wasn't a religious man, but he considered himself spiritual. This morning the woods shone like a chapel and sounded like a rebirth. One could sense new little critters cuddled with their proud parents; the squirrels in the underbrush or holes in the trees; small helpless chicks waiting, eyes shut tightly, for their mom or dad to bring sustenance back to their warm, soft nest. Richard didn't want to leave, but Elaine was already seated in the truck with Yogi.

He would be back. He hoped like hell she would be with him.

Rob was as good as his word. He stood outside waiting as they pulled up. Richard noticed men parked in a car a few doors down from Rob's house, and had seen another following from a distance once they entered the town of Duvall.

Her son reached for Elaine and gently swung her down, while Richard calmed Yogi, who wasn't happy with the sudden moves.

245

"Rob, don't approach your mom quickly around the dog. I told you what happened to the lieutenant."

"Sorry, I forgot. Wow, that dog does look mad."

"Yeah, the fur standing up on her back should be your first clue. Step back from your mom while I introduce you. Okay?"

"Sounds good to me," Rob said, his hands in the air as he moved back several feet.

Richard called Yogi to heel. She did so and sat by his feet on command. "Now put your right hand out and let her smell you."

Rob did as he was told and the dog responded. Richard continued, "Pet her, now slowly take the suitcase and carry it in the house. Yogi, your mom, and I will follow. When we get inside, let Yogi scout around the place. Don't talk to her or touch her. You got that?"

"Yes, sir. No problem."

Richard hadn't noticed the big gray-haired man standing on the porch; but the man was watching them, particularly Elaine, as they climbed the steps and came in. He stepped out of the way, but followed while Rob made introductions. Richard didn't think he looked like a cop and was right, as the man turned out to be Dr. Henderson, the psychiatrist Rob promised to have ready.

Everyone shook hands and continued into the living room that overlooked the Puget Sound. Ferries passed back and forth between the small islands dotting the horizon. Elaine was immediately drawn to the big bay window. Richard grabbed a chair from the kitchen and set it so she could sit and gaze outside.

No one was sure what to say in front of her, so the doctor motioned them out to the kitchen where they took the remaining chairs around the table while Elaine looked out at her beloved nature as Yogi scouted and they talked in muted tones.

Richard didn't see any evidence of protection in the home, which bothered him until they heard a terrific growling and a man's voice saying calmly, "Come get this beast away from me before I shoot it."

"Damn!" Rob exclaimed, as they tore downstairs to the rec room where a very pale man in a black suit stood holding a small firearm on a crouching Yogi who had her hackles raised and teeth bared.

Richard pushed past Rob and placed himself between the dog and the man. "Put the gun away slowly."

"Hell, no! Get that beast to settle down first."

"Yogi, it's okay. Yogi, it's okay," Richard repeated calmly, moving slowly into the dog's field of vision. "He's okay, Yogi. He's okay. Calm down. Put the goddamn gun away now!"

Richard reached for Yogi and bent in front of her as the bodyguard finally complied. Yogi sat while Richard petted her neck and talked in a low soothing tone.

"Man, that was impressive," Rob said as he and the doctor sat heavily on the couch, completely exhausted by the scene.

They found Elaine just as they'd left her when they returned upstairs with the bodyguard and Yogi, who decided to sit at Elaine's feet for a while and watch her mistress. Richard felt Yogi giving him the eye, as though to say, "I thought I could trust you with her, but now I'm not so sure."

Oh well. All he had to do now was brief Rob and the guard; and then he was out of here. Elaine's safety was no longer his responsibility, and from the stiffness in his joints, maybe that was a good thing. He was too old for all this drama and such a serious responsibility. It was one thing to take care of each other on week long trail rides. But a woman this problematic needed professional help and family. Elaine had both now, so he could lay down the gauntlet and mosey down the highway of life.

Maybe he and Elaine would meet again. Maybe not. It was no longer in his hands, and the more he thought about it, the more relieved he felt.

Richard rose, grabbed his hat, shook hands with the men and went to give his farewell to Elaine and Yogi. Bending near her chair so he could pet Yogi at the same time, he twirled his sweaty old riding hat in his fingers.

"Well, Elaine, I've got to get back to my job before I don't have one. Your son and this man are going to be with you now. You talk to them, okay? And I'll see you two ladies real soon. Now I got to go."

Elaine looked up at him. He knew she saw him, but she only smiled and turned back to the window. Disappointed but not surprised, he stroked her beautiful hair as one might caress a beloved child, put on his hat, and walked out without a word.

Rob had known Richard since he was eight years old. He'd seen him pick his mom up for rides, and sometimes he'd help her put her tack and horse in the trailer and watch them ride away. Richard was a special man, a great friend, someone he knew he could trust. He started to go to thank him again, but Richard was pulling away by the time he reached the front door.

Never a fan of horses, Rob (like his dad), had never wanted to ride. His mom had pleaded with both children when they were young. In fact, the first horse they bought had been for his sister, but her interest quickly turned to boys; so Elaine worked the horse and began riding herself when she had time.

She'd never neglected any of them: She always had a meal on the table each night; made lunches and breakfasts each day; attended all their events. She was a disciplinarian who allowed noisy friends and parties; did all the laundry and kept their home clean and pretty. She also worked a forty-hour week without complaining.

So when the three of them finally got up on Sundays, his mom was often long gone, if the roads weren't too icy and she had someone to ride with, returning home for dinner with wonderful stories and rosy cheeks. Now she just sat there, and for the first time in his life Rob saw his mother as a frail fifty-year-old, who had wrinkles and age spots on her hands.

When had he quit noticing her as a real person? Maybe

children never did see their parents as human beings. He didn't fancy himself as a deep thinker. He was a good businessman, he knew that. And he cared about other people, but his friends and traveling and partying occupied most of his thoughts if he was honest.

Being around family was saved for holiday and birthdays, and his nephew and niece's events. He was a busy man who worked hard and liked his home, fun and the ladies. Trying to absolve himself of guilt for not having really been there for her, he walked over and took his mom's hand.

"You want to see your room, or do you want something to eat or drink, Mom?"

"Not right now, sweetheart. I love this view. I just want to sit for a while. Okay?"

"Of course. The doctor and I will be in the kitchen. You tell us when you're ready."

Giving Yogi a wide berth, Rob walked back to Dr. Henderson, who'd been silently watching this exchange. The bodyguard took the opportunity to leave by the back door, probably to inform the other team members about the vicious dog attack and how macho he'd been in handling it.

Rob went and sat down with the doctor, who seemed almost as taken with Elaine as she was by the ocean. Finally he told Rob to show Elaine her room and leave her there to rest. He wanted to see how she would handle herself placed in an unfamiliar setting alone. Rob did as the doctor requested and Elaine docilely followed him down the hallway to a nice guest room with a balcony facing the water. He told her where the bathroom was and what he'd done with the house since she'd been to visit the year before. He chatted about his work and she answered when asked a direct question, but didn't offer or encourage the give-and-take.

He went back to the kitchen, where the doctor asked him how she had reacted to her new surroundings. After twenty minutes, the doctor went down the hall and peered through the open door. Elaine had pulled the desk chair against the balcony doors, and was once again staring into the brilliant sunlight, as though she didn't have a care in the world.

Chapter 22

"I've seen enough for today," Dr. Henderson said as he got his jacket and walked to the door. "Let her watch the TV news tonight about the scandal with D.O.C.. Watch her while she watches. I'll be back at nine o'clock tomorrow. How many days did you take off work?"

"I can do most of my work from my office here, and when I have to go in, I thought I'd take her with me."

"That's a good plan. Hopefully we won't need it. I know Elaine from our parish. She's stable and what we're seeing isn't any psychotic split. She's simply mentally exhausted, somewhat like post-traumatic stress disorder. After the riot no one really helped her deal with the death fight she'd been engaged in. Then, she medicated herself on pills and booze, and jumped back into a too stressful environment.

"After that tape recording, once again at great peril, and it was rejected by authority figures, she simply withdrew for self preservation. We are going to move slowly, but push her to step back into life and win the battle she started. She needs to finish it, or she'll continue to withdraw until she develops a psychosis. That we don't want."

"I'm here to help," Rob said. "I know my dad is worried, but I think he feels if he returned, it'd only make things worse. And my sister cares too, but she has two kids who need her attention. My mom was always there for me. This is my turn to do for her."

"Okay, then. Have her watch the six o'clock news. Otherwise, just keep an eye on her until tomorrow. By then I'll have a concrete plan of action."

After the doctor left, Rob checked on Elaine one more time and then went about his day. His study was next to her bedroom so he could see her if she went out to the balcony which ran the length of the house, or she wandered down the hall. He booted up his computer and remembered his mom two hours later when he stood up to stretch. He dashed down the hall to her room and barged in.

Yogi raised her head and his mom smiled. Feeling terrible he'd been so immersed in his work he'd forgotten about his mom, he vowed not to work the rest of the day.

"Mom, you remember my trail down to the beach? Let's take Yogi for a walk. It's beautiful outside. Then we'll go out for an early meal, come back and watch TV. Sound good?"

"Sure. Just let me put my walking shoes on."

"Do we need a leash for Yogi?" he asked, as he put her sweater around her shoulders.

"No, I don't think so." Elaine said without conviction. Seeing how closely Yogi stayed beside her, Rob decided it wasn't necessary.

They crossed the one lane street and walked a quarter mile down an access trail, then descended old wooden steps into tall brush until they reached an overlook of railroad tracks and water lapping lazily on a small alcove beach. Holding her arm, Rob helped Elaine descend the steps and walk gingerly over the tracks. She sat on a beautiful piece of driftwood tree, one of many scattered along the five-mile stretch of waterfront. He sat down beside her with Yogi at their feet.

They stayed in companionable silence longer than was normal for Rob and his mother. Usually she'd barrage him with questions about work, his love life, even his eating habits. He never thought he'd miss the normal catch-up, but he did. She seemed terribly sad and horribly distant as though she really didn't care if he was there or not. He wanted his bothersome, nosy, caring mom back.

Finally, after Yogi had done her thing, they retraced their steps and got in his car for the ride to Edmonds to eat. Rob tried to put the dog in the house, but she insisted on pushing past him into the backseat. Giving into Cujo, Rob helped his mom into the passenger seat and went around to the driver's side. Elaine contentedly looked around, but dinner proved to be as lacking in conversation as the walk on the beach. Rob wondered if he should call his dad or sister, but decided to trust Dr. Henderson, and be patient.

It was approaching six p.m. when they returned to the house, and even though Elaine wanted to sit and watch the sunset, he steered her downstairs to the television. It didn't matter which channel he chose, if he turned to local stations or CNN—this story was big, all the stations were working it.

Elaine sat beside him as he switched the remote to the story billed as "Multimillion-Dollar Criminal Enterprise Making a Profit from Behind Prison Walls." Rob watched as Elaine watched and listened to several 'experts' discuss the case. They panned to the prison itself and a reporter standing in front of the stone walls. He saw her sit forward because she was having trouble hearing, so he turned up the volume.

"And here is the scene of the crime," the reporter was saying. "This is where a riot took place last year, when staff and inmates were killed. This is also the building where the biggest—and possibly the most lucrative—crime ring of the century ran for five years. Drug running, prostitution, illegal gambling. Amazing as it seems, all this and more was conducted by criminals behind bars for rehabilitation.

"Apparently society needs to find somewhere else to put people who break the law. Allegedly guards and staff were engaged in illegal activities netting millions of dollars, instead of providing the punishment taxpayers expect for their tax dollars. D.O.C. officials won't speak to us, but the shake-up inside this institution is so strong even the superintendent and captain were replaced. No word yet on whether they will face criminal charges for their culpability. Back to you—"

Elaine stood up as Rob looked for another channel. She began pacing. Yogi started to whine, and Rob found another channel covering the story. Elaine sat down and watched. One shot showed several guards in uniform being escorted off the prison grounds and placed in a white van. It was a long distance shot, but Elaine must have recognized them because she sucked in her breath and held it until the image receded.

He'd no idea how much stimulation his mom could handle, but after an hour of channel surfing, he switched to an old romantic movie he thought she would like. She watched the show until about nine, then started up the stairs. She went in the bathroom, came back out wearing her newly washed sweats and immediately got into bed in her assigned room. Rob kissed her, told her he loved her, and left the door open, Yogi at her feet.

Agitated, he grabbed a beer and called the doctor. It was too late to call his sister. The doctor assured him her reaction was a good sign. Not to worry, he'd see him in the morning. A light knock at the back door startled him and reminded him to let the bodyguard in. As he did, Yogi poked her head into the kitchen. She swiftly appraised the situation, found it to her liking, and retreated to Elaine's bedroom; but not before the bodyguard's hand moved closer to his revolver.

Rob decided he was bushed. He said good night to the bodyguard, whose name he thought was Allen, and crashed on his bed, fully clothed. Man, he thought, before sleep took him. All this responsibility stuff is rough.

Dr. Henderson found Elaine where he had left her; but, because he received a panicky progress report from Rob the night before, he hoped today to accomplish quite a bit. He carried a stack of newspapers he placed on the kitchen table while Rob and Yogi watched.

"How was her night?" he asked as he organized the papers

by date.

"Fine. When I woke up, she was dressed and sitting here. I started breakfast and she helped. She even cleaned up. Since then, she's just been sitting here looking outside. The dog went out for a minute, but came back in when she saw your car arrive."

A female bodyguard sat at the table drinking coffee. She didn't speak much. Rob had attempted to gain her interest for the last hour. Her curly brown hair was pulled up in a haphazard French roll, and her green-blue eyes set off the most exquisite features he'd ever seen. She was slender, but not fragile looking, with a shapely, feminine figure.

The severe black uniform couldn't disguise the turn of the ankle or slender muscle tone of her calf and thigh. She was also well educated. Rob researched the security company himself and knew only Quantico-trained graduates were considered for extensive training with this particular company. The salary for experienced guards was almost as much as he made, and that was saying something.

But he was getting nowhere. Quite an accomplished flirt, he had used almost everything in his bag of tricks. When the good doc walked in, he was ready to use his own mom as a pity ploy if he had to. Elaine wouldn't object. She'd approve because, when functioning normally, this was exactly the kind of woman she would have pushed at him—except for the gun holster pulling tight under her jacket.

Who cared if Amanda wouldn't talk to him? He still wanted to marry her. She made great coffee, the doctor pointed out, as he prepared to take charge of the day.

Rob sat down by Amanda and waited.

"Your mom, Rob, is suffering from post-traumatic stress disorder from the riot, when she was not properly debriefed, and instead became involved in a stressful investigation which led to extreme danger; none of which she was prepared to handle. Thinking the cause she was fighting for failed, she went into a denial state that led to the passivity we see now. The good news is I think this is quite temporary. She is strong mentally and physically, and should handle treatment well."

"But why would she withdraw like this? Rob asked worriedly. "She's always been able to handle everything and enjoy doing it."

"This isn't a matter of strong versus weak, Rob. This is a matter of preparation and training your mother never had. Take Amanda here. Unless you mind?"

"No, it's fine," she answered, with a smile for the good doctor Rob wished she'd given him.

"Amanda has been through a series of training designed to address all the ways to handle prolonged stress. She learned ways of coping, and more importantly, she was instructed on methods to avoid the stress when it becomes too much, or stop the stress altogether by turning the cause over to someone else. Your mother almost achieved this when she went to Europe. She essentially gave herself a time out. However, on returning and discovering the trial was not going how she'd hoped, she did the worst thing she could have done and physically confronted a very dangerous man she knew to be a murderer.

"She did this without any kind of backup or training necessary to pull off such a stunt without allowing it to affect her mental state. Amanda would have been smarter in that instance. She might still have gone to the tavern with the hidden tape recorder, but would have been mentally prepared to play out the scene without fear, and she would have had several trained officers with her for backup when guns were drawn; not some guard dog she'd never seen in action and a female friend screaming her head off. Does that help?"

Having forgotten the beautiful Amanda as he warmed to this explanation, Rob nodded.

"Amanda, can you add anything from a security point of view?"

"Just that I know this is hard to comprehend from a male point

256

of view, but I am amazed your mom didn't crash and burn before this. She's a remarkable woman. But without the proper training and mental defense techniques, what she put herself through was just too much." She said this looking at Rob, and he hoped she might have his children after all. He cleared his throat and turned back to the doctor reluctantly. "Let's get started then."

"Okay. I want to speak with Elaine. Please ask her to come in, and then you two make yourselves scarce for at least an hour."

Rob decided this was too good to be true. "Great. We'll go downstairs. Okay, Amanda?"

"Yes, I can hear you from down there, doc, but don't take Elaine outside. And call if you need anything. I want the dog to stay with Elaine."

"I don't think this dog would budge if you ordered her," Rob said, smiling as they rose and left.

Dr. Henderson walked to Elaine and asked if she'd sit with him in the kitchen. She agreed and once seated at the kitchen table, she stared at the newspapers spread out in front of her. He offered her coffee. She declined politely. Pouring a cup for himself, he sat down and pulled out a paper dated the day of the riot.

"Elaine, I want you to read this article to me," he said, pointing at the headline "Hostages killed during standoff in major Washington state prison." "Take your time, but please finish the whole thing."

She did as she was told in a monotone. He then had her read several follow-up stories that talked about 'taking back the institution,' how many killed, and one about 'Inmate being tried for murders of staff and inmates.'

"His name was Billy Robinson." Elaine froze and turned to the doctor. "This isn't right. He didn't kill anyone. He saved my life that day."

"I know, and someone should do something to help him, shouldn't they?"

"Yes. I think someone is, though. I think several people are."

"Who are they, Elaine? Do you know their names?"

"Yes, I think so. Tony Williams is the lawyer. And Richard works in the prison. I think one of the inmates' wives is helping. And a state senator."

Dr. Henderson knew about Tony, Richard, and the senator. He didn't know about any wife, but didn't think he needed to. "Is there anyone else helping, Elaine? Think carefully."

After a lengthy pause she finally said, "I think I was."

Thank God, the doctor said a silent prayer. "Yes, I think so, too, but can you tell me how you were helping? How were you trying to help this man who saved your life?"

"I'm really tired now, Doctor. I don't want to talk anymore. I'm going to lie down—"

Without emotion or farewell, she got up and went to her bedroom. Yogi trotted after her. Dr. Henderson sat for a while taking notes, and then checked on his patient before he went downstairs. She was asleep.

"She did great for a first session," he said. He looked into the two upturned faces and took a chair across from the couch where they sat watching a movie. Rob clicked off the TV and waited as he explained what he'd done, especially how she acknowledged her role in the events. He assured them tomorrow more of her contained memory of the event would surface and she'd accept her way back into her real life.

He didn't think this would take more than one week, and felt she would be strong enough to testify a week after that, if necessary.

The doctor left, and Amanda said she'd check on Elaine, as she'd be off duty for rest of the night. Rob wondered if he could get her assigned for twenty four hours straight, but thought better of it when they walked upstairs to check on his sleeping mom. Amanda purposely sat down by the big window in the living room and spoke into some kind of walkie-talkie on her collar while he stood and watched.

258

"Joe, I really don't like the client sitting for such long periods of time at this window. The sliding glass door in her room makes her an excellent target. You guys have a fix on this problem? Getting Elaine to avoid sitting at the window is a problem."

"We have it covered. Security now moves from line to line and has been given access to the empty house across the street. Plus we have a large boat with vision capabilities five hundred feet offshore. Problem resolved."

"Excellent. Two hours left." She shut off.

Rob went to the window and saw two men in hard hats standing on two power lines; in the horizon he spotted a private security yacht. His short stint in the Air Force had versed him on weaponry, espionage, and military thinking. It wasn't what he'd wanted long term, but it had supplied him some skills he wouldn't have acquired otherwise.

"I'm impressed," he said, thinking his dad's money was well spent on this outfit. Maybe he'd invest some money in their stock when he had a chance. It was bound to go up with all the need for security and the quality of their services.

"This is an excellent company. I like working for them because they don't skimp, which allows me to do my job better." Amanda walked into the kitchen; it was one she would have liked to cook in, if she were not on duty. "Do you like to cook?" she asked, having decided she liked him better once she saw how caring and gentle he was with his mother.

"Nope. My mom keeps enrolling me in cooking classes, but I never find the time. It could be fun, but for now I just eat a lot of pizza and Top Ramen. I'm ashamed to say, I eat out a lot, too, which isn't my kind of healthy lifestyle. Occasionally I can get someone to cook for me."

Amanda decided getting someone to cook for him was not a problem. He was easy on the eyes, for sure. About 5'11', with dark hair (could be a bit longer) and dark eyes with long lashes, he also had a hard body. He could be working for them, she surmised, but she'd figured out early he was a finance guy.

That was okay. Maybe someday she'd ask him what to do with her money. She had no head for business, but she made it easily enough. She knew she should plan ahead for when she retired or got hurt, whichever came first, but hadn't gotten around to it. Amanda chuckled at the standard professional joke.

"Do you cook?" he asked, hoping to keep the pleasant conversation going.

"With seven brothers and no sisters you'd better believe I cook. Mom made us all learn, but because I was the girl, the job mostly fell to me. My mom is an excellent cook, so whenever I remember my ingredients don't need to be for ten, I really enjoy it."

"How did you fall into this line of work?"

"Is that one of those 'for a girl' type questions?" she laughed.

"You've met my mother! Well, sort of. And No, it's not. I grew up with the highest regard, respect, even reverence for all the feminine gender can do, should do, and will do. Whether we cavemen like it or not. She made me."

Laughing, Amanda decided to be straight with Rob instead of responding with one of the cute lines she usually dropped on anyone crazy enough to ask her "why this job?"

"My dad's a detective with the Seattle police force. Two of my brothers are state troopers; one is a city cop. I have a brother who's a prosecuting attorney and one on the defense side. Not in the same jurisdictions, thank heaven. One brother is a priest and one a doctor. I'm not that good a Catholic and I hate the sight of blood, so some kind of investigative work was inevitable. As a little girl, I loved helping my dad solve cases. He never shielded me from the realities of life or tried to hide its ugly side. He always instilled hope and a strong sense of justice."

A Catholic *and* a social activist. His Mom had to get back in the game and meet this woman! Seven brothers and a father who packed a gun? Maybe he should quit thinking about having kids with this lady and get to know her as a person. Now that she'd opened up a bit, she seemed well worth the time and trouble.

"Look, I've got to get some work done in my study. Will you stop in and say goodbye before you leave?"

"I'm leaving now."

"You will be here tomorrow, won't you?"

"Yes, I'm assigned days for the duration of the assignment."

"Great! My mom has to meet you. You two will hit it off."

"I'm looking forward to it. And Rob, try not to worry. I've seen cases like hers before. She got in over her head. She'll bounce back just fine. I know Dr. Henderson from our parish. He's a good guy. If he says she'll be fine, you can take it to the bank."

She touched his shoulder, then left him standing in his kitchen alone.

By the end of the week, Elaine was almost back to her old self. Every day the good doc sat with her for hours while they read articles about the case. By Friday she quit sleeping in the afternoons and was initiating conversations herself. As Rob predicted, she was quite taken with Amanda and spent time asking questions about her career, which naturally fascinated Elaine, who might have been Amanda's colleague had she been born a generation later.

She was even talking about calling Richard to thank him for taking care of her and to see if he would go riding. "But why can't I go riding? I feel wonderful," Elaine complained to Rob and Amanda as they strolled along the shoreline one afternoon, after a scrumptious lunch the two had prepared.

"Because they can't protect you if you are up in the mountains on a horse, Mom." Rob answered in frustration.

"None of us know how to ride or have horses, Elaine," Amanda responded patiently.

"Well, I don't want to put Richard in danger, but this is aggravating. Let's at least take him out to dinner so I can thank him before too much time passes."

"That can be arranged," Amanda said, thinking how much fun it was to interact with the real Elaine. Her own mother, whom she loved dearly, was old school when it came to women and their roles in the world. She went to church every day and prayed to her patron saint that little Amanda Rose would find a good man and settle down. Amanda had gotten used to her thinking over the years; but it was stimulating to be around another woman who lived her own life but was still married, had children and even grandchildren to her credit.

They agreed to call Richard. Since he was a meat and potato guy, they took him to the Black Angus midway between their homes. Rob decided this was the perfect opportunity to ask Amanda to go as his date, since he knew she would be off duty.

"I can't fraternize with clients as long as the case is on-going and we are on the job; but if your mom invites me, I could give the night guy time off and join you as Elaine's bodyguard. There will be others around as well."

Elaine had been listening to the exchange and, though she was starting to chomp at the bit with this bodyguard arrangement, she approved the idea and the switch was made.

Richard was in the bar waiting, and after he hugged Elaine in a brotherly way, they decided to have a drink as they waited for a table. "Richard, I can't thank you enough, will never be able to, for all you did. Rob told me about it, but I still can't believe it. I have a vague recollection of a cabin, of walking and brushing my hair. I hope I wasn't too much trouble?"

"No more than you are on a week long trail ride—and I put up with you there, don't I?" He was glad they couldn't see him in the darkened room, since he knew the heat had climbed up his neck to his face when she mentioned the hair brushing. At least she hadn't remembered who had done the brushing.

Amanda and Rob laughed as Elaine defended her prowess against Richard's claim that she was a lot of trouble, which of course gave him the chance to tell stories about all the dumb things she'd ever done. They were still laughing long after dinner.

"Honest to God! My other riding partner John and I had to go through her pack, it was so darn heavy. She brought makeup, a mirror, and bottles of hand cream. We could barely lift it and put it on her horse."

"That was my very first trail ride in the high country. I didn't know." Elaine defended herself.

"She's gotten better as the years have progressed," Richard admitted as he took a bite of blood-red steak. "I'm actually proud to call her partner now." He lifted his glass as a toast to her and the others did the same. They hadn't explained Amanda's role, but Richard was sharp enough to figure out she was serving two masters, from the bulge under her jacket and the attention she was giving Rob.

After dinner everyone except Amanda drank brandy. They talked about the trial and Elaine's witness duty which was coming up. Richard couldn't get over the change in her. That must be one fine doctor, he thought. She was simply radiant. Her skin had a healthy color. Her eyes shone. She'd put on a little weight which she needed. As women aged, he decided, thinness was not attractive. He did not like women heavy, but a certain roundness to the figure enhanced the beauty of a mature woman.

He couldn't stop staring at her. He'd been terrified the next time he saw her, it would be in some fancy mental hospital. She was fine and he was pumped up to go riding; but Rob had privately asked him not to suggest it until it was safe. He would wait.

"We are going to meet with Tony on Monday and he will start preparing you," Rob was saying. "Dr. Henderson will be there also."

"Will someone please catch me up on where we are with the new trial? I'm curious." Elaine asked impatiently.

Rob looked at Richard, so he gave a brief summary, keeping the new events as non-threatening as possible, still careful of her fragility. "Tony is the lawyer. He should be doing this. But I'll put it in a nutshell for you: Billy was taken back to the reformatory to finish doing time on his original offense.

"The other inmates who helped us that day are still housed at other prisons for their own safety. They are being watched carefully so harassment has ceased. I know, because I act as liaison between the inmates and guards including Billy. I go in and talk with each man every week."

"That's wonderful," Elaine interjected. "I like that idea."

"Well, I'm not Mr. Popular since I turned snitch and decided to testify at Billy's trial, and I won't be in this one either. However, I can't hide in some hole. I think D.O.C. and the college thinks this is a good idea because it means they can keep an eye on me too."

"Whose idea was it?" Elaine asked. "It sounds way too smart to have come from D.O.C."

"It was Senator Suvall's." He continued, "Because the misuse of justice was flagrant, everything moved quickly. The indictments of the twelve officers were slam dunks. Currently they're all being charged with the murders of Damien and Officer DeLory; but Tony is confident as the evidence unfolds, including our testimony next week, the twelve defendants being tried together are going to start rolling over and squealing like stuck pigs to keep from being the one who bites the murder one rap. They will sing like canaries and squeak like rats to set up the other guy and plead out to lesser charges. That's the District Attorney's plan. He was so embarrassed about the public mess, he's going to try the case himself."

Elaine had to know more. "What about the wise guys who organized the drug running, illegal betting, and prostitution behind our own walls?"

"They've been sent to different institutions, obviously. They'll get more time and be sent out of state to the worst exchanges D.O.C. can make; but nothing much will really change. They didn't order the murders. Those were dreamed up by Lieutenant

Percy because Damien found out about the action and wanted in. The Godfathers didn't want him in because he was a moron and a loose cannon. We discovered that ourselves during the riot. The lieutenant saw an opportunity to take him out and make himself look good to the wise guys, so he took it. He simply took a shank off a rioting inmate during the chaos and used it.

"Poor Officer DeLory was just in the wrong place at the wrong time. He should've stayed at his post at Gate 7, the one we cleared through down by the big yard. He thought if he went up and helped the S.W.A.T. team, it would get him a promotion. Officers Jack and Bernie told him not to, but as you probably remember, he was the same guard who shot his own toe off during tower duty."

"That can't be true," Rob exclaimed. "Tell me you're joking."

"Nope. Really happened, a few years back. And the scary part is that D.O.C. is so desperate for prison guards, they didn't fire him. Instead they put him in a 'less vital' security post. That post was our last line of defense before the rioters got to the college staff. Smart, huh? I fought against his being our school officer but I lost.

"In any case, when DeLory left his post to further his career, he came upon Damien getting his throat cut in the administrative office, probably by the lieutenant, but it was hard for some of the witnesses to be sure because a group of blues was around Damien.

"He turned to run, was caught at the outside door by some of the S.W.A.T. team who saw him trying to flee. He was held there until the lieutenant got done with Damien and came for DeLory. They couldn't let him live. He would have squealed. He was weak. In their sick minds, that made it a justifiable killing."

Amanda sat mesmerized at the retelling. Rob felt horrified, thinking maybe his father was right to want his wife out of such a dangerous place. Richard looked down at his brandy as though the story was difficult to take even this long after the fact.

No one was watching Elaine. When Amanda saw her face, she immediately got up and took her arm. "That's enough. We need to be getting home. It's almost eleven, and I'm beat. Overtime pay or not, let's call it a day and turn in."

Rob paid the bill. Then he and Richard followed the women. They both worried again. Elaine's face had turned a pasty white and she wasn't speaking.

Chapter 23

Damn it, Rob thought. I should've had Dr. Henderson come with us. But he'd said no, that she was ready. Now look what we've done.

Richard was kicking himself for reciting the gruesome story. *What had he been thinking? What was his family thinking?* He thought she'd heard most of it and was prepared to repeat it in court in a few days. Now look at her.

He had contributed to her relapse. He would never forgive himself for this. Never.

Amanda took Elaine into the restroom as the two men feared the worst, each in his own hell, and waited. But when Elaine came back out, she smiled. Her color was good again, and she simply said, "Come on, you guys. Amanda's tired. These young'uns can't keep up with us anymore."

With that, she took Richard's arm, gave it a reassuring squeeze, and they walked back to his truck, leaving a relieved Richard with an open-ended date to go riding as soon as Amanda allowed.

Elaine patted her son's cheek with a gloved hand as he opened the car door and helped her inside. "I'm fine, Rob. I reacted to the horror, certainly, but it was also relief, to finally know the truth. It wasn't easy, but I needed to hear it. Can you understand?"

"I'm trying. But Dad really has a point about you not going back to work in *any* prison. What a terrible system. I never really understood. It needs to be completely overhauled and maybe you can do some good from the outside on that; but I agree with

Dad you should never go back inside. And I'm going to be upset if you do."

"I know you're worried now Rob, but I hope you support whatever I decide. You have to accept I need to do what I need to do. It's my life. I can't have you or Dad controlling it. That is one of our biggest problems. I love you both, but you only get one life. This isn't a dress rehearsal and I have to live every year, every month, every week, every day, every hour, and every minute to the fullest. I don't plan on going back in, if that helps right now, but don't give me ultimatums. They don't help."

Amanda knew enough to keep quiet on this one. First, it wasn't her place to interject. She liked these people, but barely knew them. Moreover, she could understand Rob's fear for his mom, but she wished he'd been more careful in his wording. His words smacked of a father talking to a child. She knew Rob would never have said those words to his father.

Oh well. She could see the two had a good communication line and they would work it out. Hey, it might make it easier for her and Rob, if it ever got that far.

Thursday came too quickly as far as Elaine was concerned. The closer the date drew, the more nervous she felt about testifying in front of correctional officers who stood accused of the murders of Damien and Officer DeLory. Tony had come over twice to brief her, so at least she knew to say 'I don't recall' and not 'I don't remember'. The rest of what he said she feared she'd never recall under pressure. Lieutenant Percy had frightened her more than she thought. Having to face him in the court room was going to be very hard. She'd gained a better appreciation for victims of rape and what their trauma was like, having to identify and face the men who assaulted them.

The day arrived. Rob and Amanda escorted her to the courthouse, where they met Dr. Henderson and Tony. The room was packed. Both she and Richard were testifying that week and the news people knew their testimony was key to blowing the trial wide open. Our discomfort makes great copy, Elaine thought sarcastically as Rob and Amanda pushed her through the obnoxious throng.

She paced outside the chambers until it was her time to testify. Richard was testifying at that moment and had been on the stand since Monday. Tony said he was doing a great job and she would too. There was nothing to fear. Just tell the truth.

"Please stop, Tony. You sound like a character from a B movie," she snapped nervously. "Sorry."

"It's okay. I've been talked to more harshly in my time."

Before long Richard emerged. He walked right past her and left. Tony explained Richard did that to *not* give the media more to print, which would certainly happen if he'd hugged her.

"What an ugly world we live in," Elaine said as she walked into the courtroom, with her entourage following close behind.

She was called to the stand immediately. "Please state....Do you swear...Hand on the Bible...Please take a seat." It went well. She did just as Tony said and kept her eyes only on the person asking questions. She told her version of the events of the riot. She answered pointed questions about Billy. Then they played the recording, and since it was getting late, court was adjourned for the night.

Exhausted, she sat through dinner at a restaurant Tony liked; while the rest of them, including Richard, hashed over the day's happenings. Rob owned a hot tub and Elaine pleaded with Amanda to let her get in when they got home. Amanda brought another bodyguard into the backyard where the hot tub was located. Rob joined her, and after a while the knots in her shoulders and back loosened. Bed sounded awfully good, and she was surprised to discover how soundly she'd sleep.

When this was over, she decided, she was buying herself a Jacuzzi. She'd earned it.

The following day she was kept on the stand the entire day. Strangely, she related all the events clearly and calmly. She was able to do so by keeping her focus on Tony, even during a nasty attempt by the defense attorneys to break her will. During lunch break, Tony brought food into the small conference room so they wouldn't have to face the masses. He complimented her on how well she was doing even though she couldn't remember what she'd said. Elaine wanted to help, but deep down she just wanted it all to be over. Her strength and motivation came from the mantra she kept telling herself: "You're helping Billy. You're helping Billy."

Just as Tony promised, they wrapped up by Friday, even after a grueling cross-examination by the nasty defense lawyers representing the twelve men. Attacks on her character, motives, and memory were rebutted well by the prosecutor. Friday night, Elaine went back to Rob's home, climbed into the hot tub and drank two glasses of wine . She finally started to unwind.

That evening, Richard and the doc visited. Her daughter and son-in-law brought the grandchildren over after Rob finally convinced the protective young mother no one was going to shoot them. The danger was over. Unless it was strictly vengeance—which everyone doubted would happen—neither Elaine nor Richard needed to worry. Their testimony was part of the legal record and to hurt them now would make things look even worse for the defendants. Besides Daniel, the only person who should have been there and wasn't, was Tony. He was still at the courthouse. Just as predicted, Elaine and Richard's testimony was strong and all twelve defendants begged to plead out. Tony was helping the district attorney's office sort the truth from the lies.

Finally, around eleven o'clock, Tony showed up wearing the first smile Elaine had ever seen on his handsome ebony face. The lieutenant was getting murder one. According to each of the other eleven accused, he'd done the actual cutting on both victims. The rest were pleading to murder two and would be incarcerated for ten to fifteen years; however they'd get even more time if the

DA wanted to yank them back on additional charges such as racketeering, prostitution and drug running. The very next day Lieutenant Percy stood and plead guilty to murder one.

"Couldn't happen to a nicer guy," Richard said.

"Or a more deserving one," Elaine added, as they raised their glasses in a toast to themselves, each other, and anything else they could think of. Even Amanda put back a few, since her security detail had been pulled. Earlier in the evening Elaine heard Amanda and her son making plans for the future, which they laughingly noted wouldn't have to be chaperoned by his mom.

She hoped it worked out for them. A better match of two people, one of whom she loved unconditionally and one she'd begun to care for a great deal, she couldn't imagine. But that was *their* lives. She'd start thinking about her own.

Before he left, Tony asked if Elaine wanted to attend the sentencing the next day. She said no. She'd moved past the trial. It was behind her and she was desperate to move on. Richard wanted to be present at court, but as he left, he promised to make a date to ride the very next week.

"Thank you, Richard. We need to talk about that time in the cabin. It's still somewhat of a blur—"

"We'll do that on our spring ride, I promise. And you are very welcome. The pleasure was all mine. And hey, congratulations! You nailed the bastards."

"We all did. And I learned a good lesson."

"What did you learn, partner? I'm very interested."

"I learned not to try and go it alone so much. It can be hazardous to my health. I also learned I don't have to."

"Good night, Elaine. You done good."

The doctor then left, and she was finally alone with Amanda and Rob. She found them downstairs watching a movie, sitting close to each other. Good for them, she thought as she said good night, realizing what she needed to say could wait. She fell asleep with beautiful dreams of riding through a meadow of flowers, with her dog running at the horse's hooves. She thought, as she dozed, maybe the world wasn't so ugly after all.

The next day Amanda was gone and Rob sat at the kitchen table with a hot cup of coffee and the newspaper. He tried to read her the headlines about the guilty pleas, but when he looked up and saw her suitcase and Yogi waiting beside it, he exclaimed, "Come on, Mom! You can't leave yet. We have to celebrate for a few days."

"This is probably going to sound strange, but I don't think there's that much to celebrate. I'm glad we caught the bad guys, but the whole experience wasn't fun. I want to put it behind me and I can't do it here, even though I love you very much."

He knew it was futile to argue. "So, where am I taking you? What are you doing next? And what do I tell Dad when I call to update him on your plans?"

"Take me back to my little house. I assume my car is there?"

"Mom, don't you want to go home?"

"Please, Rob, don't argue. You asked where I want to go, and I'm telling you."

"Okay, okay. I'll stop." He put his arm around her, picked up her suitcase and opened the front door. "In any case, I want you to know that, except for the danger, the growling dog, and the strangers wandering around my home, I really had a good time with you here. I liked having my little mommy around." He gave her shoulder a squeeze.

"I liked being here and I won't forget you came through for me. Big time. It's supposed to be the parent taking care of the child, but I suppose as we get older, the reverse happens."

"You'll never be old. Even Amanda is amazed at your vitality. But I would like you to live long enough to grow older, so try to stay out of trouble. And the next time you get in a jam, *if* you get in a jam, ask for help sooner. You know I will always be here for you."

Trying to keep tears at bay, Elaine said, "I know you will, son, and thank you for your support. It gives me strength."

"Well, you're an amazing woman. Amanda said so time and time again."

"Amanda this, Amanda that," Elaine teased as they drove toward the sanctuary she'd been missing. Rob took her suitcase into the little house and prepared to leave. "You'll have to keep me abreast of your progress. That is one awesome young lady, but I don't think you're going to have an easy time getting her attention away from her career."

"You know, Mom, I may be slow, but eventually I catch on. I want Amanda to do, be, go anywhere she wants. I will support her to the fullest while I live my life the same way. But I tell you, I hope we can live them side by side."

"I do too, son. Now you get out of here and catch up on that life of yours. I've kept you from it far too long. But thank you again. You're a wonderful son." She reached up on tiptoe and gave him a long kiss on the cheek. He smiled and waved as he walked away.

Elaine took off the battered old green coat and hung it lovingly on a hook in the hall. She walked Yogi to the back door, opened it and let her out. She stood watching her wonderful four-footed friend and realized soon she'd have to meet with the Senator and work to achieve early release for Billy and reduced time for the other men who had saved her life. She'd get them back to their old prisons. Then she'd concentrate on helping Billy and those like him—men who had done terrible things, but had paid for their crimes. They deserved a chance at a new beginning.

Elaine pondered for the thousandth time, what it would be like for a person released after twenty years of living, peeing, and washing in a steel-barred cage. What would it be like to come back into society? A society filled with decision making. How would a person decide what to eat or wear? Where to sleep? How to tell people you'd been convicted of murder? Or would you tell them at all? How would a person, who hadn't been on his own in two decades, deal with new technology or conflict? After using violence just to survive behind bars, would that person become violent when challenged in the outside world?

Elaine had no answers to these questions, but she wanted to find answers. She'd be part of the solution, not part of the problem. She vowed to start a nonprofit organization like Delancy Street. It would be devoted to transitioning ex-offenders into society and she'd name it the Jewel Foundation. It would be a wonderful use of Daniel's money.

Elaine went back inside to relax with Yogi, feeling a twinge of guilt about how cowardly she'd been with Rob. She should have told him about her newfound life and the way she intended to live. But there would be time. She'd have her extended family over for dinner. She'd tell them all together.

"Family," she'd say, holding up a glass of Chianti, "this is my new home. Welcome."

THE END

Acknowledgements

First, I must thank four men brave enough to allow me to delve into their personal lives; Ex-felons Rico, Willie, Vern and Brian. It took courage and humility to share painful memories and failures once released. Most felons prefer never to look back or speak up. I hope, while entertaining, I have done some justice to the complexity that dwells between appropriate punishment and rational rehabilitation methods.

Thank you Frances Dayee for mentoring this fictionalized approach to my research material and thinking there would be be people interested in reading about serious, hard core criminals as something other than 'bad'. Thank you Jessica Erler for thinking the writing had merit. The subject matter is tricky. There are monsters in prison, but many of this country's incarcerated are decent men and women who are functionally illiterate, drug abused and poor. You convinced me readers want to know that side of our prison system and that people do change. Brian, Willie, Vern and Rico are prime examples.

I will always be grateful for the assistance and care Department of Corrections' staff at the Monroe Correctional Complex took with me during my tenure behind the walls as an educator. I am a risk taker by nature and although those with the keys and guns always allowed me to do the educational work I was passionate about, they always 'had my back'. Line officers' jobs are dangerous and difficult. They deserve more credit and better pay.

My family is wonderful and I'm blessed with great friends. Except that I got to go home at night I've probably spent more time behind bars than most lifers. But the people who love me accept my dedication to correctional education, even if they might not understand it.

If not for Kristen Morris of Tigress Publishing my research, this novel, would still be notes, interview recordings, and pages of writing. She convinced me to allow her to take this story off my hands. I'm glad. Writing is one skill set. Publishing is entirely different and her brand of professionalism is much improved from what I had to deal with when publishing in the past. I like being inclusive, all writers should. After all writing is an extension of our souls.

Author Bio

Patricia Franklin-Therrell uses Patricia Cage as a pen name for her fictional writing. She left her childhood home in Nevada at 18 with $2,000 savings, a high school diploma and a burning desire to receive a doctorate by the age of fifty. She accomplished this personal goal working as an educator, writing and speaking in her field of correctional education. She worked for 40 years,while raising two children with her husband of 45 years.

A prison educator in Washington for two decades, Patricia served for ten of those years on a national board of Correctional Educators. She produced an independent award-winning film, "*Wha Ca Make It*" written, directed, produced, and performed with inmates. She published a well-used offender rehabilitation textbook entitled "*Honorable Relationships*" and wrote for the *Correctional Educational Journal.*

Her work, the film, the textbook, her national/international service, her dissertation, were all done to answer one question: Once a felon entered prison, and if he/she is to be one of the 87% who are released, how can society help that person not reoffend?'

After retirement, and surgery to fix a brain aneurism, Patricia delved intensely into finding the answer to that one question.

She spent five years researching the lives of four ex-felons she knew personally as they strived to become successful citizens. All four served straight life sentences. None have reoffended.

This novel is one of three Dr. Franklin wrote based on these four criminals' stories. Through fiction she endeavors to engage the reader in the struggles convicted criminals face before incarceration, during imprisonment and after release into a world that neither wants or understands them.

Patricia loves her family, her garden, her birds and dogs; singing, traveling, teaching and writing. She pens a column for her local newspaper, coordinates an ESL program, and serves on Everett and Seattle based social justice commissions.

Donate

A portion of the proceeds from this book
will go to
MATTHEW HOUSE.

Matthew House extends hospitality and needed services to friends and families of prisoners in the Washington State Department of Corrections. We invite you to join us in supporting them.

Matthew House is a 501c3 nonprofit organization.
All donations are tax deductable.
Please make checks payable to:

MATTHEW HOUSE
PO Box 201
Monroe Washington 98272

www.matthewhousemonroe.org